CHEERLEADERS

#32

TOGETHER AGAIN

JENNIFER SARASIN

SCHOLASTIC INC.
New York Toronto London Auckland Sydney

ISBN 0-590-40637-X

12 11 10 9 8 7 6 5 4 3 2 1   7 8 9/8 0 1 2/9

Printed in the U.S.A.   01

First Scholastic printing, August 1987

CHEERLEADERS

TOGETHER AGAIN

Scholastic Inc. New York 1987

CHEERLEADERS

CHAPTER

Sean Dubrow slipped into the driver's seat of his red Fiero and closed the door with a smart click. Then he pulled the shoulder harness across his chest.

"Okay, who'd rather go for a pizza?" he asked, looking back through the rearview mirror. "Speak now or forever hold your peace."

"Sean!" Olivia Evans laughed, tucking her bookbag under her feet. "Start the car and let's get going!"

"We agreed to go to the hospital, and we're going. You can have pizza later," Tara Armstrong told Sean firmly. She pulled the black angora beret off her lustrous red hair and shook out the strands, still damp from her shower. Cheerleading practice had been particularly rough, but she wasn't backing off. If the senior class blood drive was to mean anything, she would just have to donate a pint. And so would Sean.

"Hey, I'm cool," Sean protested.

"I never said you weren't." Tara smiled knowingly. "It's just that the sight of blood — particularly your own — gives you heart palpitations."

"Oh, yeah?" Sean grumbled something to himself, then put his key in the ignition.

"Yeah," Tara chided.

'Whereas *you* are Florence Nightingale, I suppose." He pulled out of his parking spot with a lurch.

"Will you two quit fighting?" Jessica Bennett, seated beside Olivia in the back, was just anxious to get going. "You know I don't like the idea of being near a hospital, let alone inside one. But I'm going, aren't I?" Jessica continued.

Ever since her father's death, hospitals had held a certain dread for her. And when Patrick Henley had been ill with pneumonia, it was all she could do to force herself to go visit him. But a blood drive was a worthwhile cause. Besides, Patrick was supposed to meet her there, along with the newlyweds, Mary Ellen and Pres Tilford.

"Peter and Hope are probably there already, Sean," Tara pointed out, as Sean drove slowly along the icy streets of Tarenton.

"What do you want me to do, cause an accident? It's slippery." Sean was driving *very* carefully, which wasn't like his usual slapdash manner. He wasn't a reckless driver, by any means, but he knew that his car had a certain amount of get up and go — which he generally used to the fullest.

Within five minutes, though, they were at the entrance to Haven Lake Medical Center. Although the parking lot wasn't jammed, there were a con-

2

siderable number of cars from Tarenton High.

"I guess everyone had the same idea," Olivia said, getting out and walking to the door with Jessica. "That'll mean a long line."

"Maybe they'll be all booked up and they won't need us," Sean said hopefully.

"Dear heart, there's always room for one more," Tara said with an evil snicker.

"What makes you so brave all of a sudden?" he demanded.

"I'm not. I just have a perverse desire to see you do something nice for somebody else." Tara smiled, tucking her arm through his and walking him briskly down the hall to the reception desk. The lobby, thankfully, didn't look much like a hospital lobby. It wasn't painted institutional green, but a bright yellow, and it was lined with lush, leafy plants.

"Oh, look! There they are!" Olivia ran down the hall, as she caught sight of the rest of the Tarenton High Cheerleading Squad. Hope Chang and Peter Rayman were both standing beside the water cooler at the end of the hall. Peter had a small bandage on his left arm.

"Wow! The guy really did it!" Sean exclaimed.

"No fuss, no muss." Peter grinned.

"I was too young," Hope grumbled. "You have to be eighteen to donate, or seventeen with a parent's permission slip."

"Oh, no." Olivia sighed. "My mother will never let me do it. She thinks I lose a pint every time I *blush*." Olivia had been very ill with a heart condition throughout her childhood, and had been in and out of hospitals for years. Although she was

3

now as healthy as the proverbial horse, her mother still insisted on treating her like a protected, fragile flower.

"You better sit this one out," Jessica nodded to her. "But you'll have all the more to give next year," she added kindly. She walked up to the front desk and nodded to the nurse in charge. "Hi," Jessica said. "We'd like to sign up."

"If we sign up, *then* can we leave?" Sean demanded.

The nurse said nothing, but handed him a clipboard. "Names and proof of age," she said curtly.

Sean, realizing that he was stuck, hastily scribbled his name and took a seat in the waiting line.

"Look, there's Mary Ellen." Jessica signed her name quickly and walked up to the front of the line where Mary Ellen Kirkwood Tilford sat, her unmistakable beautiful blonde head shining in the overhead lights. Jessica grinned as she approached the former cheerleading captain and gave her a quick hug. No one, seeing the girls together, would ever have suspected that they were anything but good friends. No one would have known the jealousy that used to rage in Jessica.

Even though Mary Ellen was a Tarenton graduate and was married to Pres — clearly no longer any kind of threat to Jessica's relationship with Patrick — Jessica used to feel funny about being with her. But over the past months, the girls had gotten pretty tight. Since Pres and Patrick were practically linked at the hip, it was sort of inevitable that Jessica and Mary Ellen would see a lot of each other. Luckily, they had really begun to enjoy one another's company.

"Am I glad to see you guys." Mary Ellen smiled at the group.

"Yeah," Sean pointed out. "Misery loves company."

"What?" Mary Ellen looked puzzled.

"Don't mind him," Tara said, giving him a disparaging look. "Sean is a little queasy about giving away his precious blood."

"Oh, I see." Mary Ellen laughed. "Here, squeeze in beside me."

"But that means we'll have to go in front of all these other kids," Sean pointed out.

"Perfectly all right," one husky football player Sean knew from trigonometry called out. Three boys immediately moved over to make room for the cheerleaders. Hope and Peter, who had decided to stick around and wait for their friends, took seats on the floor in front of Sean, Olivia, Tara, and Jessica.

"Where's Patrick?" Jessica asked Mary Ellen as casually as she could.

"Still hauling furniture. He got held up on a job, and said to say sorry."

Ever since Pres had gone to work for his father at Tarenton Fabricators and sold Patrick his share of their moving company, Patrick was managing the whole thing on his own, as well as running his daily garbage collection route, just as he always had. The guy was a workaholic, and there was nothing Jessica could do about it.

Mary Ellen saw the disappointed look on Jessica's face and shrugged. "He told Pres to tell you he'd have to meet you at your house later." She had to smile at Jessica's eagerness. She used to feel exactly the same when she thought of Patrick. How odd it was that now all she felt for him was close, warm friendship. It was Pres Tilford whose name, voice, and face set her heart racing. Pres, her husband. The concept was still rather unbelievable to her.

"Next!" the nurse called.

"Guess I'm up," Mary Ellen nodded.

"Sean, you go first," Tara urged him. "Jessica, Hope, and I have to tell Mary Ellen about the mascot — and darling Diana."

"Yeah, Sean, go get it over with," Olivia urged him.

"It doesn't hurt, really," Peter told him.

Hope gave Sean an encouraging pat. "Look at all the people who've survived it."

"It'll make you a bigger person." Mary Ellen giggled.

"Hey, I think I'm a great size right now," Sean said.

"Young man," the nurse thundered, "are you coming or not?"

Seeing that there was no way out, Sean held up his hands in mock surrender. "I have only one life to give for my country," he said just before the nurse stuck a thermometer in his mouth and led him around the sliding glass partition.

"So what's the news from Tarenton High?" Mary Ellen asked eagerly. She was beyond all this now, of course, a married woman, modeling at Marnie's in the mall, taking courses at the junior college, but sometimes she yearned for the old days. High school had been such a special time for her, and every once in a while she wished she were

6

captain of the cheerleading squad again, whipping the crowd to a frenzy at the games, being the center of attention, the darling of the whole school.

"Well, we've gotten ourselves in over our heads now," Jessica told her, "as if we didn't have enough to keep us busy. We only have six weeks until the play-offs."

"It's all her fault," Tara nodded, pointing at Hope. "She volunteered us."

"Don't pin it on me!" Hope said indignantly. "You said we had to do it. It was a noble cause, you told me." Her almond eyes flashed with annoyance as she nodded vehemently, her thick black hair swinging around her face.

Peter grinned and chucked Hope under the chin. "But you still were the one who dragged everybody kicking and screaming onto the committee."

"What committee?" Mary Ellen demanded.

"The one for the school mascot. Tarenton High is finally getting one," Tara explained. "Deep River brought this guy dressed up like a kangaroo to the last away game, with his little kid brother in his pouch, and they were the hit of the evening. Nobody even cared who scored the most baskets! Then, at the next game, Garrison High countered with a guy in an ape costume. He threw bananas into the stands all night. Then the rumor started going around that St. Cloud was coming up with something really fabulous — a big secret. So naturally, at the last senior assembly, the word went out. Tarenton *had* to have the mascot to end all mascots."

7

"Don't tell me. You're going to dress Sean up as a chicken." Mary Ellen smiled.

"No, much better than that!" Jessica laughed. "We're making a wolf. A giant, waterproof, papier-mâché wolf with a special battery-powered tail and eyes, that can come to all the basketball and football games and cheer *our* Wolves on."

"Brilliant!" Mary Ellen said.

"We thought so, but there's one problem," Olivia pointed out. "Diana Tucker volunteered to be head of the mascot committee, and all her friends voted her in."

"I said I couldn't figure out why we'd need a wolf when we had a jackal in our midst," Hope pointed out with a smirk.

Diana was not her favorite person. Actually, she was nobody's favorite. She was spiteful, conniving, and hated the cheerleaders individually and together — mostly because, despite her blonde good looks and long, graceful legs, there was not a chance in the world that she would ever be accepted on the squad even if there were openings. Team spirit was about as foreign a concept to Diana as fair play was. She was one bad customer, they all agreed.

"That's why Hope volunteered us, of course," Tara told Mary Ellen. "She wanted to make sure the job got done right. Frankly, I didn't see how Diana could be that much of a problem when it came to building a mascot. She'd never dream of doing anything that could ruin her manicure."

"But as supervisor, who knows what she'd be capable of, especially with that dumb boyfriend of hers, Beef Driscoll, doing her every bidding," Hope said.

"*Beef!*" Mary Ellen practically fell over.

"I don't even know his real name," Hope laughed. "He's just so huge and hulking, he's like a great big bull running down the football field."

"The best part is when Diana has something for him to do and yells, 'Where's the Beef?' Really cracks me up." Olivia smiled.

"How did you break the news to Ardith that you have a new extracurricular activity?" Mary Ellen wanted to know. Ardith Engborg, the cheerleaders' coach, demanded more than sweat and effort of her team. She wanted their whole-hearted, undivided attention.

"We told her it was for the good of the school. That helped," Hope said. "And besides, we're going to work in the morning before class and after practice in the evening to build this thing."

Tara was in the midst of describing Diana's despicable behavior at their first committee meeting that afternoon in the shop, when a very harried looking nurse came back around the partition. "You're next," she told Mary Ellen.

"You mean Sean's finished?" Tara grinned. "This I have to see."

They all followed the nurse around to the area where Sean was lying on a blue vinyl couch that tilted to keep his feet higher than his head. Beside him was Kate Harmon from St. Cloud. Kate, who did volunteer work at the community youth sports clinic with Sean, was an enigma to the other cheerleaders. Sean Dubrow had never gone for a girl with frizzy hair, freckles, and glasses before — particularly one as cool about him as Kate — but there was an odd attraction between the two. They were both holding their arms up in the air, and were laughing.

"Well," Tara said, looking at Sean's companion, "looks like it wasn't as bad as you expected it to be. Hi, Kate."

"Hello," Kate responded. "I don't want to give you the impression that I'm helping out *Tarenton's* blood drive, or anything, Tara. I just donate as often as I can."

"Is that amazing!" Sean chuckled. "She doesn't get recruited, she just comes down here on her own steam. But hey, it was a snap!" He turned to Kate. "I could do this every day. So, I'll give you a call tomorrow," he said, swinging his legs over the edge of the couch.

"You do that," she said, and a broad grin passed over her face.

Sean no sooner had stood up than all the blood drained from his face, and suddenly he was lying in a heap on the floor.

"Oh, no!" Tara, who had been about to drag him out to the parking lot and grill him about Kate, was immediately down on the floor kneeling beside him, stroking his face. "Sean! Speak to me!"

Kate was off her couch and on his other side, rubbing his cheek. "Sean, come on! Snap out of it. Take a deep breath. Somebody get him a paper bag to breathe into."

A nurse pushed her out of the way. "Thank you, young lady, but I think I can take care of this. I work here. Is it too much to ask if you'd both let me through?" She hauled him back onto his couch and pulled a brown paper bag out of the cabinet beside him.

The cheerleaders crowded around, asking questions, but the nurse waved her hands for silence. "It's quite common. Happens all the time. Just a drop in blood pressure."

Tara scowled at her angrily. "How could you bully that poor boy into doing something that might endanger his health? Sean! Oh, say something!"

He seemed to be coming around, but he still looked like he'd seen a ghost. The nurse held the paper bag over Sean's mouth and nose, encouraging him to take deep breaths.

"You have to get them to breathe into the bag. The carbon dioxide wakes them up," Kate explained.

Sean groaned, pushing the bag away. "You sure you still want to donate?" were the first words out of his mouth.

"Oh, honestly," Tara grunted, taking a place on the next vacant couch. "I've never seen such theatrics in my life."

"What that kid won't do for a laugh." Olivia grinned. "Well, folks, listen, I think I'll get a ride home with Hope and Peter. It's been swell."

Olivia was still chuckling to herself about Sean when she got back out to the waiting room. She was not prepared for the sight of a guy wearing a long red stocking cap sitting in one of the chairs. His head was studiously bent toward the notebook in his lap.

Olivia felt that flood of warmth that started in her toes and crept up along her spine right to the top of her head. This peculiar sensation always came over her whenever she saw David Douglas Duffy — '3-D' to his friends. For some reason, the reaction was stronger when she wasn't expecting to see him and he just showed up. Was this love? If not, it was very close to it.

"Well, what brought you here in the middle of a busy work day?" Olivia demanded, going over to hug the visitor.

Duffy looked up from his writing long enough to plant a kiss on Olivia's mouth. Then he went back to his writing.

"Don't I get a hello?" she asked petulantly, sitting beside him.

"In a minute. Don't go 'way." He leaned over for another kiss, then scribbled some more.

"This must be some story!" Olivia tried peering over his shoulder, but it did no good. She couldn't read his scrawl if her life depended on it.

"You bet it is!" He shook his head, marveling over the words that were fairly jumping out of his head onto the page. David was the sports reporter for the *Tarenton Lighter*, and his quick wit, easy smile, and infuriating persistence had won Olivia's heart — eventually.

"Are you here to donate blood?" Olivia asked, when he stopped writing and proceeded to sit back and read what he had written.

He slapped the piece of paper in front of him. "This is *my* lifeblood, girl. It comes out of me, drop by drop. Wait till you hear this. I rushed over from my interview, hoping to find you here so I could tell you about it."

"About what?" Jessica demanded. She and most of the rest of the group wandered back into the reception area together. Sean and Kate were nowhere to be seen. "Hi, Duffy. What's up?" she asked.

"Duffy's got a story." Olivia nodded. "It's so hot it's steaming up the pages of his notebook, but he refuses to tell me about it."

"C'mon, Duffy," Mary Ellen teased. "We won't go to some other paper and blow your exclusive."

"Okay, all right." He stuck his pencil behind his ear and proceeded to read:

" 'This reporter has a nose for the unusual, as many of his faithful fans are well aware. And his forays into the world of balls, hoops, and locker rooms sometimes open the door to some incredible news — not all of it sports-related. Imagine his surprise when interviewing Talbot Stevenson, a former Tarenton basketball coach, now retired and living in a remote cabin in the woods overlooking Grange Valley, to have learned that the coach had just sighted a real, live wolf the previous night when out walking his dog. It was reported that the dog could have made a dunk shot in the Tarenton basket without any problem. Watch out, Tarenton Wolves — you've got some stiff competition!' "

Duffy looked up at the group. "So what do you think?"

"You think it's for real?" Olivia asked skeptically.

"Couldn't it have been a big dog or something?" Peter asked.

"No way. The coach's Labrador isn't any scared rabbit," Duffy told them. "He wouldn't have taken a leap in the air like that if he'd smelled another dog."

"Well, I don't understand. What does this mean?" Mary Ellen wanted to know.

"Wolves aren't loners, which means if there's one, there's more," David said. "And even though you'd think Tarenton is too developed to attract a pack of wolves, anything's possible, I guess. We all better watch out, is what it means."

Sean and Kate came back around the partition, and Sean said, "I'm so glad I came. I must do this again, real soon."

"Listen, Mr. Wisecracks," Kate commented, taking his arm, "drink lots of fluids for the next forty-eight hours, take your vitamins, and get some rest tonight."

Tara started toward the exit door. "Well, I'm off. Want a lift, anybody? Sean, you probably shouldn't drive."

"I'll see to it he doesn't." Kate smiled, jingling the keys to Sean's Fiero.

"Oh, well, okay," Tara muttered. Then she turned back to the others. "Jessica, I'll give you a lift. Mary Ellen, are you coming?" she asked.

"That's okay. I'm waiting for Pres," Mary Ellen said, taking a seat.

"We'll wait with you." Olivia nodded. She shivered a little as she waved good-bye to her teammates and took Duffy's arm. *"Wolves!* That's pretty gruesome."

"Oh, we're not all that bad," Duffy responded with a sly smile. And then, he took Olivia in his arms and kissed her.

"David Duffy," she whispered when he finally let her up for air, "you're some animal."

"I know." He grinned. "Ain't it great?"

CHAPTER

The giant round clock above the admitting desk read seven o'clock. Mary Ellen was pacing the hall, her neat black pumps clicking up and down on the linoleum.

"Clever of Pres to wait until donation hours were over, wasn't it?" Duffy grinned. He scratched out a sentence on his pad, then quickly wrote another.

"I really hate being kept waiting." Mary Ellen frowned. "I can't count the number of times I've reminded him!"

"Just read another magazine," Olivia suggested helpfully. She herself had already been through every issue lying on the tables.

"But he knows his mother hates his being late even more than I do," Mary Ellen continued, making another pass along the corridor. "Especially on Friday nights when we're expected for dinner." Felicia Tilford was a stickler for good

16

manners, and that meant not being early (which was tacky), not being late (which was rude), but being right on time. And with Pres that was nearly impossible.

"I can't imagine what it must be like being married," Duffy muttered, shaking his head. "To have to live up to the expectations of two sets of parents instead of just one — whew!"

Another car pulled up at the entrance door and Mary Ellen ran to the window. "Well, finally," she said. The three of them grabbed their coats and ran outside to greet him.

Pres kept the Porsche running. There was an apologetic grin on his face when he pushed open the door on the passenger side. "Don't make faces. I'm not really late," he told her. "Dad won't even be home till eight, so we've got an hour. Who wants to go somewhere fun?"

"Olivia and I were going to grab a burger at Benny's," Duffy nodded.

"We'll follow you," Pres said, pulling Mary Ellen toward him, into the dark recesses of the Porsche.

Mary Ellen narrowed her lips at her incorrigible husband, then reached across the seat to envelope him in folds of red wool. Her new coat was oversized and had a terrific cowl neck from which her shining wheat-colored hair spilled like a profusion of gossamer silk.

"How can I be mad at you?" she whispered in his ear, kissing him again and again.

"Hey, this is nice." Pres's dark eyes peered at this lovely girl to whom he had the incredible good luck to be married. "Let's not go. Let's just stay here in the car and neck all night." He reached for her again, but she ducked under his arm.

"I'm hungry. And you know I can never eat all that creamy stuff your mother serves. C'mon — Benny's." She moved a foot away and he shrugged complacently.

"If you insist. But think of all those people surrounding us."

"Think of my growling stomach," she protested.

"Well, you have a point. But I'd still rather have you alone. Just you," he added simply.

She was thrilled at the fact that their relationship seemed to get better every day. Secretly, she had worried when he asked her to marry him that if she agreed, it might change things — for the worse. She was sure that they would spend so much time together they'd be bored, or their kisses would get stale and dull, or they'd have terrible fights about ridiculous things. There were so many stories of teenagers who had something great going, and then as soon as they got married, it all vanished. Somehow the responsibility of acting like grown-ups took the blush off the rose. It was too much, too soon.

But for Pres and Mary Ellen, nothing remotely like that had occurred. As she told her sister, Gemma, the only difference for them in being married was that they didn't have to say good-night at the front door.

"Have a good day?" he asked her, giving her hand a squeeze.

"Not bad. Mrs. Gunderson has some of the

18

most terrific spring things in. It's a pleasure just modeling them around the shop."

"Uh-oh." Her husband sighed in mock desperation. "I can just see the bills for the new wardrobe now. And *don't* tell me for the fiftieth time about your employee's discount."

"I'm not buying any new clothes this season," she said staunchly, looking straight ahead.

"Sure. And tomorrow you're flying to Outer Mongolia," Pres joked good-naturedly.

"No, really. Donating blood at the hospital today really made me think. By the way, we can stop in there tomorrow so you can give a pint."

"I have to work tomorrow. And don't change the subject."

"Don't you change it," she chided him. "It's important to look beyond yourself, Pres. Think about all the sick people who have to have operations and really need that blood. Your body keeps producing it, you know, so you get it all back within a few weeks. And what does it take to give a little something of yourself?"

"It's gross, that's all. Please don't talk about blood in front of my mother, okay?"

"Pres! You're not listening to me."

"Yes, I am. You think if you give up buying new clothes it'll somehow, someday, help somebody less fortunate than you. But sweetie, you look terrific in clothes, so why shouldn't you have them? And we contribute to charities and drives and so on. It's not as if we don't care."

Mary Ellen took a breath. "You don't understand. You've always been rich. It's easy for you.

But I'm not used to having everything I want. And I don't much like the thought that I can buy my way out of every commitment. There are some things, like sickness and health, that just make you think."

"You can think about them all you like." He smiled as he pulled into Benny's parking lot. "But you will never keep me from wanting you to look fabulous. Not that you need clothes to look fabulous," he added in a soft undertone.

She leaned over and kissed his ear.

The restaurant was filled with kids from Tarenton, Garrison, St. Cloud, and some of the other local schools. Duffy and Olivia had already taken a booth in the back, and Pres and Mary Ellen pushed through the crowds to join them.

"Great. Wonderful." Pres pushed a lock of dark blond hair off his forehead. "Always love to eat in the middle of a demolition site."

Mary Ellen giggled. "I love it here. Lots of energy. Lots of spirit. Pres, did you hear there's a wolf in town?" she demanded as the waitress brought them menus.

Pres looked at her as though she had a very important screw loose. He leaned over and nibbled her ear. "I love you, sweetie. Even if your brain has melted."

"She's right, Pres," Olivia said excitedly. "Duffy told us."

Duffy confirmed the statement. "You believe what you read in the *Lighter*, don't you? Well, today you have it from the horse's mouth. A genuine, honest-to-Pete wolf-sighting."

"There haven't been any wolves in these parts since the turn of the century," Pres said, but he was very interested.

"Well, kids, you know how it is." Duffy grinned, spearing a pickle from the bowl on the table. "The clock is turning back. The polar ice cap is melting. First wolves, then, before you know it, the woods'll be filled with dinosaurs."

The food arrived and Mary Ellen dove into her hamburger the instant it was set before her. She didn't mind seeing Pres's parents once a week, but there was something about eating amidst all that fine china and antique silver that made the food sort of tasteless. And she really couldn't stand it when Felicia Tilford rang the little crystal bell to call the maid, in between courses. It made her think about her own parents, sitting down to a meal of spaghetti and meat sauce. And their china came from the supermarket; the flatware from a discount store. Mary Ellen had always hated the poverty and lack of elegance of her own household — but the ostentatiousness of the Tilfords did make her wonder if there wasn't a middle ground somewhere.

Like Benny's. The food was good, the conversation great, and it made Mary Ellen feel like a part of things, like she was one of the Tarenton cheerleaders once again.

"This mascot you're working on sounds like it's going to be fabulous," Mary Ellen said, after they had filled Pres in on the details. "I can't wait to see the progress."

"It better be." Olivia sighed. "I hear St. Cloud is working up something extraordinary, and we

21

have to beat them. If you can help, it'll move along a lot faster," she suggested. "And having you around might just put Diana in her place. She can't stand being outranked by anyone blonder, prettier, or smarter."

"You win in three categories," Duffy pointed out.

"Mary Ellen, if you can take time from modeling and your college courses — not to mention fixing up your new house, will you come over?"

"Well, I — " she began.

"Say," Duffy broke in, "I've been meaning to ask you guys. How are things in your little house?" He slathered his burger with ketchup and relish. "You find the kitchen yet?"

"Actually," she said pointedly, "Pres does more cooking than I do."

Pres leaped at her throat in mock fury. "Don't spread that rumor around — especially when there's a reporter present." He was secretly proud of the fact that they shared everything in their new life, including the housework. With a loan from the Tilfords for a down payment, they had bought the apartment that Pres had rented just before he proposed. It was a wonderful space in a one-hundred-year-old carriage house just six houses south of the Tilford mansion on Fable Point. The kitchen window boasted a view of the lake, and the stone fireplace in the living room was flanked with grand windows. Mary Ellen could never get over the fact that this was her own place, to do with as she pleased. "Luckily, neither of us is that fussy about the way things look," Mary Ellen admitted. "Unlike some people I could mention.

Oh, Pres, it's past eight! Your parents!"

"Don't bother — we'll get the check," Olivia offered. "Just promise to stop by and help with the mascot tomorrow afternoon after practice, okay?"

"It's a deal," Mary Ellen agreed as she grabbed her coat and her husband's arm. They made it out the door and into the parking lot in record time, and were at the door of Pres's parents' house on Narrow Brook Lake in an astounding five minutes.

The conversation over the Tilfords' dinner table ranged from clothes, to decorating the new house, to why Mary Ellen and Pres didn't seem very hungry. After coffee and dessert, they sat in the beautifully decorated buff and blue living room and dutifully admired the Tilfords' latest acquisition — an abstract painting by a new, hot New York painter. And then Pres said it was getting late and they would really have to run and thanks for the great meal and they'd see them next Friday. And with that, the two young people escaped into the night.

"I'm sorry I have to drag you to these obligatory dinners." Pres sighed, as he turned the key in the ignition.

"Oh, they're not so bad. Sometimes I really like talking to your parents," Mary Ellen admitted, cuddling closer to Pres in the car.

"Don't be polite," Pres told her firmly. "They're boring, period. I tried to get you some better in-laws, you know, but this was the only pair available at the time."

"Silly!" She stuck her elbow in his ribs. "Speaking of which, can we stop off at my folks' house for a second? Mrs. Gunderson gave me some clothes I wanted to portion out between my mom and Gemma. They're here in my model's bag."

"Sure, sweets. But do you mind if I just drop you off and pick you up in an hour? I promised Patrick I'd go over his books with him after dinner. The poor boy just can't manage that business without me."

"I get it." Mary Ellen smiled knowingly. "You've had enough parents for one evening."

"Something like that," Pres admitted. "Is it okay?"

"Everything you do is okay with me." Mary Ellen touched his cheek lovingly as he turned to her. They had stopped for a red light in the middle of town, the dividing line between the very rich section and the rest of Tarenton, and the street lights illuminated the couple's faces. "You're terrific," she whispered, bestowing a soft kiss on his ear.

He would have responded in kind, but the light changed again, and there was a car right behind him. "Then you're not too sorry you left New York and came home and ended up marrying me?" he teased.

"Never!"

"But your modeling career might have really taken off," he went on. "Another month, and you might have been on top."

"And I might have been really depressed, desperately waiting tables to earn a few nickels, living in that awful apartment with two girls I hardly knew!" Mary Ellen shuddered, remembering those difficult times in the big city.

"And what about cheerleading? And the old gang? Don't tell me you don't miss that part of your life?" he pressed her.

"Well, maybe a little. But I get vicarious thrills by going to games and watching Olivia and Jessica and Tara and the others. I don't feel so awful anymore when I see them performing, and I'm just sitting in the stands."

"What? You mean you've lost your ambition?" he teased.

"No. Just redirected it. I'm past being a cheerleader. I'm past being a struggling young model in New York. Let's face it, Tarenton is my home. Everything I know and love is here. Including one Preston Tilford III."

Pres turned into her parents' driveway and turned off the engine. He took her in his arms and kissed her, his mouth covering hers with sheer pleasure and delight. They stayed that way for a long time, until the porch light snapped on and Mrs. Kirkwood appeared in the doorway in fuzzy slippers and a huge blue chenille robe.

"Who is that? Mary Ellen, is that you?" Mrs. Kirkwood called into the night.

"Come back for me soon," Mary Ellen whispered, hugging Pres around the neck. "I miss you every instant you aren't around."

"That goes double for me." Pres nodded, getting out and opening the car door on her side. As she slipped away from him, he grabbed her fingers and brought them to his lips. "I'm going to make you very happy for the rest of your life. I hope you're prepared to handle that," he said.

"I think I could get used to it." She grinned,

grabbed her giant model's bag filled with makeup and clothes, and got out of the car, giving her mother a hasty wave. Then she watched as Pres backed out of the driveway and down the block toward the intersection.

It was true. Being with him had made her more accepting of herself. In the old days, when she was captain of the cheerleaders, she would have considered anything less than international superstardom a terrible comedown. Now, she thought, life was exciting being married to Pres, going to college, and working at Marnie's. Maybe she had grown up. Or maybe she was just wonderfully, totally in love.

"Hi, Mom. Got something for you," she called as she ran up the driveway. "Hi, Gemma," she called to her little sister, who had run out to meet her at the door.

Gemma, at fourteen, was in awe of everything Mary Ellen did. She was not as tall, not as beautiful, not as outgoing as her older sister, but she had a spark of self-sufficiency that Mary Ellen really envied. She knew Gemma would go far.

"Ooh, you look gorgeous! As usual." Gemma sighed. "C'mon into the kitchen and have some tea, and you can tell me every tiny detail about what you had to eat for dinner at the Tilfords'. And don't leave out the salt and pepper!"

Mary Ellen grinned, following her sister down the cramped hallway with its awful flowered wallpaper. It was just the opposite of the Tilfords' elegant home, and Mary Ellen used to hate being inside it. Somehow, now, because she had a place of her own, it was easier for her to take.

"Did you hear about the wolf?" Gemma demanded as she set the kettle on the stove.

"Isn't it incredible? Was it on the news?" Mary Ellen wanted to know.

"The anchorman said there were two sightings over near Grange Hills. Isn't that where Pres and Patrick like to go rock climbing?" Gemma shook her head. "You better make sure they don't go anywhere near there." She shuddered.

Mary Ellen laughed. "I'll do what I can, but you know Pres does whatever he wants, whenever he wants."

Gemma sighed and put a tea bag in each cup. "You want dessert?"

"No, you bottomless pit!" Mary Ellen laughed.

Suddenly Mary Ellen stopped joking and went over to her sister, taking her firmly by the shoulders. "Do you have something you want to talk about?" she asked softly.

"No," Gemma said briskly. "It was just about the usual. You know."

The usual, in the Kirkwood household, was money. There was never enough of it around. And despite both parents working and Gemma's part-time job after school, the issue of whether Gemma could buy something new to wear was always a hot one.

"Hey, I brought you some stuff," Mary Ellen said, unzipping her model's bag. "Just a few hand-me-downs from Marnie's."

"Ooh, Melon! You're great!" Gemma shrieked at the top of her lungs, digging into the bag.

"Here! A navy pleated skirt that might fit. And

I thought of you the second I saw this sweater. Go ahead — try it on!"

The kitchen quickly turned into a fashion showroom, with the two girls pulling things on and taking them off again. By the time Mr. and Mrs. Kirkwood came in to see what was going on, every item had been tried, singly and in combination.

"Pretty noisy in here," Mr. Kirkwood commented, smiling at his daughters indulgently. "Where's that husband of yours, Mary Ellen?"

For the first time since she'd arrived, Mary Ellen glanced up at the kitchen clock. More than an hour had gone by. That was odd. Pres wasn't that eager to do Patrick's books — particularly when he had to work the next day.

"I'll give the Henleys a call, see what's keeping him." Mary Ellen nodded.

But when she dialed the number, and Patrick answered, the first thing he wanted to know was where her dumb husband was. He'd been waiting for Pres for over an hour.

Mary Ellen collapsed in a chair.

CHAPTER

Pres drove more slowly than usual down the streets of Tarenton. Just like his good buddy, Sean Dubrow, Pres considered cars to be a vital part of his life. He liked looking at cars, driving cars, tinkering with cars. But unlike Sean, Pres had a wife. A gorgeous girl who was everything he'd ever dreamed of. And the neat thing was, whenever he got in his car to go home now, it was going home to *her*.

Maybe it was too perfect. Maybe things weren't supposed to be this good, and something, some bolt of lightning or trick of fate, would come along and mess it up suddenly and completely. Maybe not, though. His life was finally settling down, chilling out, getting good.

He grinned as he pushed the Porsche harder, gunning it along the silent road. There were a few simple things that made him happy: Mary Ellen, some easy times with the cheerleaders, respect for the job he had just started doing, and every once in a blue moon, an adventure. That stuff about the wolf was really unbelievable! He couldn't actually believe it when he heard Duffy say it, but there'd been a report on the radio just a few minutes ago. When he got over to Patrick's, they'd plan a trip up to the hills for the weekend. It would be okay to be away from home for a few days — Mary Ellen always understood when he wanted some time alone. Anyhow, this was too good to miss.

Wolves weren't natural enemies of humans. He'd seen a great movie once about this guy who went off and lived in the wilderness all by himself, and spent a whole season with a pack of wolves. After a while, they accepted him, became buddies, almost. Not that Pres wanted to drop out or do anything weird. He just wanted to see a wolf up close — stare into its eyes.

Patrick would understand. Like Pres, he was a guy who needed the intensity of once-in-a-lifetime experiences to temper the everyday routine. And they were both people who liked a challenge. If you could look into the eye of the storm and survive it, you were all right.

He took the curve onto the steel-deck bridge a little too quickly, and the Porsche swung sharply to the right. Pres corrected it just as another set of headlights came rushing up to him. The night, so totally dark, was suddenly blinding. He squinted ahead, blaring his horn and turning the wheel as hard as he ever had.

The approaching car seemed to jump off the road, then careened back toward him like a cannonball shot at short range. Pres was aware of a line of cars behind him, all stopping short. Then, the impact of metal on metal. He felt the world upside down, his head resting right on the roof of the car. There was a ripping sound, glass shattering, a feeling of something wet rolling down his face. He didn't even have time to scream.

Sean leaned his head back against the passenger seat and stared dreamily at his chauffeur. She was busy maneuvering his car past the mall, and she neglected to slow down for the cars zooming out down the access road. She jerked to a halt just in time.

"You have a masterful touch, Kate," Sean teased her.

"Oh, shut up. This is tough! Nobody watches when they come out of the mall."

"Stop jiggling the steering wheel. It'll drive itself."

"You have no business telling me what to do. You're weak from loss of blood." She smiled, and stole a glance at him as the car rolled back onto the asphalt road.

"All right, I'll be quiet. Home, driver!" He sighed and folded his arms, enjoying the fact that Kate had cared enough to take him home to her house and feed him dinner. After a couple of hours by a warm fire, eating a bowl of microwaved popcorn and watching a great movie with his arm around Kate's shoulder, Sean was almost too comfortable to move. But in her practical manner, Kate had insisted that blood loss required extra sleep. As soon as the credits rolled, Kate unwedged herself from Sean's embrace and grabbed her own car keys.

"Say, I almost forgot to tell you," Kate began, "I've got a secret."

"Oh, yeah? Wanna tell me about it?" He reached over and playfully tugged at one of her curls.

"No way, José! But I'll give you a hint. I'm head of my mascot committee."

"You're kidding. St. Cloud's supposed to be cooking up a doozy."

"Yup." She nodded as they got onto the boulevard and started toward Sean's house. "We sure are. Gonna beat the Tarenton mascot by a mile."

"Oh, now just a second, lady," Sean protested. "What gave you the impression that St. Cloud could do anything better than Tarenton?" He was egging her on, trying to get her to let out just a hint of what their mascot was. But she was onto his tricks.

"Sean Dubrow, you have a vastly inflated opinion of many things, including yourself, which means that your comedown, when it arrives, will be particularly hard. I'm so glad I'll be there to see it." She smiled like the cat who has just finished a particularly delicious bowl of cream.

"Hey, Katie, you're never going to be able to convince me of the brilliance of your mascot if I don't know what it is."

"Very smart. No," she sang gleefully, "I think I'll just let you sit and stew."

"I just thought that any girl who would be nice enough to scrape me up off the hospital room floor might consider being straight with her boy-friend, that's all."

"Boyfriend!" Kate said. "Who said anything about — "

"Hey, slow down!" Sean sat up straight, peering down the road. "What's that?" he demanded. They could hear, quite distinctly, the whine of a police siren.

They were on the other side of the lake now, and as they drew closer, they could make out the spinning lights of an ambulance.

"This looks bad. Go past it. No, slow down!" Sean put his hand on hers on the steering wheel.

"Do you want to cause another accident?" she asked him sharply. But she pulled into the slow lane, and as the cars in front of her inched along, she craned her neck out the window, trying to see what had happened.

"Pull into a driveway. I have this feeling. Oh, Kate!" Sean gasped as they peeled off past the wreckage.

"What? What did you see?"

"It's Pres's Porsche. I'd know it anywhere."

She jerked the car to a halt on the edge of the next driveway and pulled the door open. Sean was already running back toward the scene of the accident.

"Get back. What are you kids doing?" A tall policeman had set up a cordon over the bridge, and he wasn't letting anyone past. But they could see two ambulance workers right behind him. The men were lifting a stretcher very gently into the back of their vehicle.

"Oh, no. No, I can't believe it." Sean could taste fear in his mouth, and he ducked under the cop's arm, making a dash for the ambulance. All he saw, before they closed the door in his face, was a strange, twisted form covered with a blanket. He would never forget the sight of that shock of dark blond hair, streaked with red, lying limply on a flat white sheet.

"Is it him?" Kate called over the cop's shoulder.

"Who's in that ambulance?" Sean demanded. "Who was killed?"

"He's not dead, kid," one of the workers said, "although I bet when he wakes up, he'll wish he were." The man shook his head and snapped the lock on the back door. "His license says Preston Tilford III. Hey, that's the kid whose father runs Tarenton Fabricators, right?"

Sean bit down hard on his lip. The pain made him sense every nerve in his body throbbing. Kate was beside him in a second, and she didn't have to ask. She knew by the look on his face exactly what he knew.

"We'll go to the hospital. We'll call everybody. Sean, are you okay?" She grabbed him and hugged him hard, and the touch of her hands rallied his spirits slightly. He nodded, walked beside her to the car.

"He's not dead," she repeated softly.

"Yeah, right, fine. That's the important thing." He helped her into the passenger seat and pressed the door closed, leaning on it for a second. Pres was a friend. More than that, he was everything Sean had always wanted to be. But tonight, he wouldn't have traded places with him for a hundred million bucks.

The state trooper's car pulled up at the Kirkwoods' house while Mary Ellen was still on the phone with Patrick. One look at the man's face, and Mrs. Kirkwood knew that something terrible had happened.

"Mrs. Preston Tilford?" the officer said, stepping inside.

Mary Ellen stared at the man. She still wasn't used to being called Mrs. Tilford. That was Pres's mother's name.

"Your husband's been in an accident, down by the bridge on 206. Not his fault. The other guy's responsible. But he's hurt pretty bad. I'll get you over to the hospital."

Gemma burst into tears and Mary Ellen patted her hand as she got up and went with the trooper. Suddenly, it was very important that she think clearly, that she do things right. "I'll take my father's car and go over to the Tilfords' to pick them up," she offered, although she didn't feel capable of driving to the corner, let alone all the way across town.

"No need for that. We've got a car over there already," the trooper told her.

"Go along, dear. We'll follow you," Mary Ellen's father said.

All the way over to the hospital, Mary Ellen had this peculiar sensation that she had known even before she called Patrick and found out Pres wasn't there, even before the policeman rang the doorbell. It was the strangest feeling, sitting there in the squad car, but she could see the other car hitting him broadside, *see* Pres in that heap of mangled metal, see the Porsche being tossed off the bridge and into the ravine below like a child's toy, flung into the air.

She knew, too, even as they arrived at the emergency room entrance and she raced into the waiting room, that he was going to be all right. Very hurt, hanging on by a thread, but conscious, and all right.

"Mrs. Tilford?" A kind voice beside her made her jump.

"Yes?" Her blue eyes, shining with tears, took in a young doctor in a white coat.

"You can see him now. But not for very long. He's extremely weak, and we've got him on some pretty powerful medication."

"Thank you."

The doctor touched her hand. "Are you going to be able to take this? It's a little difficult — "

"Yes, thank you," she said staunchly, trying to keep her knees from shaking. "I can manage." She started down the corridor with the doctor, the same corridor she had paced hours ago when she was waiting for her incorrigible husband, who was always late, to come and pick her up.

Pres was in a private room, lying in a pristine white bed, nearly invisible for all the machines and tubes and bandages on him. His face was completely swathed in white gauze, and both his legs and arms were in plaster casts. If it weren't for the tiny mole on the little finger of his left hand, Mary Ellen would never have known that it was Pres.

She steadied herself at the door. She couldn't fall apart, not now. She had to be brave and strong — for him. "Sweetie, it's me. I'm here."

She saw his parched lips move and she rushed to him, not wanting to have him exert himself. "You don't have to talk. Just be still."

"Mmm. Honey. Bad. I'm so dumb."

"No! It wasn't you. The policeman told me. The other guy was responsible. And he wasn't even hurt." She felt the anger surge in her again, just the way it had when the state trooper first told her. Some awful, terrible driver who just wasn't looking had walked away from that bridge, and Pres was lying here in a mass of bandages.

"We should never be separated," she whispered to him. "If I'd been with you — "

"Uh-uh. No way. Then both of us here. Not too romantic." It was all he could do to get the words out.

"Oh, I love you so much!" She sobbed, finally letting the rush of tears claim her. She was so grateful it hadn't been worse, but so miserable to see him in crumbled pieces.

"Love ya, sweetie. Gotta sleep."

"I know. You rest and get well, okay? Your parents and I will be here the second you wake up." She touched his forehead, or the place where it usually was. All she felt was tape and gauze, but she knew exactly what was underneath the bandage. She remembered, just last night, sitting on their couch together, his head on her shoulder, as she stroked that forehead gently and they talked about the day. It had been so wonderful. And she had taken it for granted.

She walked back down the corridor to find the Tilfords, and was stunned to see a familiar face at the end of the hall. Patrick Henley rushed toward her, taking her hands in his.

"Are you all right?" It was all she could do to keep from screaming. Patrick, so good, so kind, always there when you needed him. Patrick, the one whom everybody in town had suspected she'd marry. Patrick, Pres's best friend. His kind, rugged face was creased with concern — for her.

"Yes, yes, I think so. Oh, Patrick, I just saw him and he's such a mess. There's no part of him that isn't all wrapped up, and he can hardly talk, and I'm so worried, and I should have been with him, and — " She rushed on, all her words and thoughts hurtling out into space.

"Whoa! Wait. Mary Ellen, don't do this to yourself. Pres was on his way over to see me, to do me a favor. That's all. You aren't supposed to be with him every hour of every day, you know. You're married to him, not attached to him at the hip."

Guilt was a very powerful feeling, and Mary Ellen had never experienced it as keenly as she did that very minute. When she was captain of the cheerleaders, she had been responsible for getting her group to the top. That meant caring, really caring, about five people other than herself. But letting them down would have meant only a poor performance at a game. It would never have hurt anybody.

"I'm part of his life. I'm his best friend. I'm

supposed to *be* there when he needs me, not trying on clothes with my kid sister!" She let down all her defenses and wept in his arms, and only when she had calmed down a little bit did he even bother to try and console her.

"He needs you now, more than he ever has in his life, and you're right here. From the looks of it, you're not going anywhere. Now you can eat yourself up alive with 'should haves' and 'why didn't I's', but believe me, Mary Ellen, that's not going to do anybody a bit of good. Pres Tilford isn't the kind of guy who needs a weepy wife smothering him with pity. He needs your love and your support, and most of all, your strength."

All tears spent, she looked up into his eyes and nodded. "You're right. Let's go back. He's all alone in that room."

Patrick walked with her to the door and peered in. The machines buzzed softly, but above that mechanical noise, they could hear the easy breathing of a person asleep. He looked so peaceful, so still, that the two of them just stood there a moment, studying him. Pres was always on the go, the most physical person either of them had ever known. Even in his sleep, he was usually restless. But tonight, it was different. Everything was.

"Let's get a cup of coffee at the cafeteria and come back," Patrick suggested.

Mary Ellen nodded in agreement, and together they went down the hall. She felt the distance from Pres tug at her heart, and the coffee tasted bitter to her, mixed with all her doubts and fears.

"Has — has anyone said anything about how

bad it is?" Patrick asked when they wandered back to Pres's room half an hour later. "Maybe we should try to find out."

She gave him a pained look. "I don't think I want to know."

"Hey, he may be breakdancing in a week, Mary Ellen," Patrick suggested with a half-hearted laugh. "You never know anything until you ask a few questions of the people in charge. We could be getting all bent out of shape for nothing."

She smiled a little, for the first time in two hours. "What would I do without you?" she sighed, linking her arm through his. "You're the most level-headed person I know. And a true friend." They walked, not quite jauntily, but with a definite briskness to their pace, back to the nurse's station.

"There — that's one of the doctors. I saw him before. Let's ask him," Mary Ellen said.

The man had his back to the two of them, and he was leaning over toward one of the nurses, deep in conversation, so he didn't see Patrick and Mary Ellen approach.

"Well, I tell you," the doctor was saying, "you see everything in this business, so it shouldn't surprise me. But a kid like that, still in his teens, it's criminal. If that boy ever walks again, it'll be a miracle."

Mary Ellen lost her footing and stumbled. She wasn't aware of Patrick coaxing her to come and sit down beside him. She didn't see the doctor turn to her and shake his head apologetically. She was devastated by what she had just heard, by the words that had just changed her life irrevocably.

CHAPTER

Olivia took a running leap off the minitramp and hurled herself into the air, opening her legs in a perfect split. Plastering a smile on her face, she started the group off, screaming the cheer at the top of her lungs:

> "Tarenton Wolves, just watch 'em glow!
> Place that shot and go, team, go!
> Get another basket, score another one,
> Show the other side just how it's done!"

She leaped at Peter, doing an aerial over Hope. She caught Jessica's eye in midflight, and together they yelled,

> "We're the guys with spunk!
> We know how to dunk!
>
> Wolves are on the warpath,
> Gettin' hotter, yes!

We can do it better,
We can do it BEST!"

Tara and Sean wound up the cheer with double cartwheels around Olivia and Hope, who were up in the air doing perky jumps for all they were worth, lifting their arms as though they were sure they could touch the roof of the gym.

"Okay." Ardith Engborg, their tiny blonde coach, snapped off the tape deck. "It's working better, but I know you've got more in you."

"Mrs. Engborg, we can't just now," Tara complained, wiping the sweat off the back of her neck. She picked up her soaking mane of red hair and fanned herself with it. "We simply have to get out of here and over to the hospital."

"I know you told us to do it for Pres," Olivia said softly, sinking down on a crash mat and curling her legs under her, "but don't you see it's impossible?"

"We haven't heard from Mary Ellen yet," Jessica reminded her. "She must be going out of her mind. She's probably been there all night, with just a cup of coffee to keep her going."

"I called right after French class," Hope said softly, "and they said only the immediate family could go in to see him. But we have to be there for him anyway, Mrs. Engborg. Please, can't we be excused? It's totally useless to keep going like this, feeling the way we do."

"We've got to *know* something," Peter said. "It's so frustrating just sitting around."

Only Sean was silent. He hated to admit being scared, but this experience was unlike anything he'd ever been through before. Patrick had told them about Pres's condition, and the thought of his friend not being able to move cut through him like a knife. He wasn't good with pain or weakness, particularly in people he saw as above it all.

"I want you to do it again," Mrs. Engborg insisted. "You have a game next Friday night, and as I recall, you've already asked for some extra time off to work on that mascot. None of you are superkids, you know. You can't just pull it out of your hats at the last minute. If you're cutting down on practice time until that wolf is built, you're going to have to work extra hard when you *are* practicing. And you'll have to make time to see Pres . . . whenever. I'm not being cruel, just realistic. Okay. Again."

She turned the music back on and they got into position, because that was what they knew they had to do. And this time, they all screamed the cheer louder, screamed with power and determination and anger — at what had happened to a boy they all had thought was invincible, untouchable.

They were working so hard, they didn't see the door to the gym open. A slight figure slipped in unnoticed and climbed to the top of the bleachers. She was haggard, and there were deep circles under her cornflower-blue eyes. She didn't want to be here, but the doctor had insisted that she go out for a while. So the logical place to come was back where she belonged. Back home, to Tarenton High's gym, where she and Pres had been so happy and carefree.

She watched Olivia's masterful forward roll

turn into a split, and she swallowed hard. These cheerleaders were her friends, and yet they were free and easy and able to take life as it came. They were still kids, living at home, doing as they pleased, with the world spread out before them. Not like her.

Hope, so graceful and talented. She could be a violinist, or with her brilliant grades, she could probably go on and run a corporation someday. Peter was so steadfast, a real winner, a genuine good guy. Sean . . . well, it was hardest to look at Sean, because he reminded her so much of Pres. Laughing, flirting, sure of himself, too concerned with the moment to ever consider the future. And then there was Jessica — so earnest and vibrant, such a terrific gymnast, too. Mary Ellen was glad that Patrick had her by his side. They were a great couple. And Tara, with her great looks and that special smile that turned heads wherever she went. Of course, finally, there was Olivia. She had been with Mary Ellen and Pres from the start. And she knew them better than anybody.

All of them, leaping and running, grinning through the cheers. They just looked so . . . well . . . so young. Mary Ellen felt about a thousand years old. Suddenly she was furious, angry that she couldn't be one of them. After all, she was just a kid, too. She was too inexperienced to be saddled with the responsibility of a paralyzed husband.

What a horrible way to feel, she chastized herself. And then she took a breath and sat up a little straighter and concentrated on watching the cheer. It was very, very expert. Perfect, in fact.

"I like that! I like it a lot!" Ardith Engborg cheered, raising a fist in the air in mock salute. "Let's see what our visitor thought of it." She turned to the girl sitting up above them. "How about it, Mary Ellen?"

The six cheerleaders were off the floor and climbing the bleachers in an instant. They were practically on top of Mary Ellen, pummeling her with questions, demanding to know how Pres was, trying to find out how and why the accident had occurred and what the prognosis was. They were so wonderful, so clearly worried about her and Pres, that she had to forget her troubles for a second and smile. With people like this supporting her, she could walk through a wall of fire and come out unscathed.

She raised her hands for silence. "He's conscious and his spirits seem okay, but it's hard for him to feel any of his aches and pains yet because the doctors have kept him really immobile. But they're planning to run some tests on him later this week, when he's ready to take it, and then . . . we'll know more," she finished hopefully.

She couldn't repeat the awful words she'd heard the doctor say the previous night. After all, he didn't know anything — it was just a guess on his part. And recoveries that nobody expected *did* happen all the time. She knew Pres. He wasn't the kind of guy who was going to lie back and not fight.

"What did they do to the clown who was driving the other car?" Peter wanted to know.

"A complaint has been issued against him. I know he's going to lose his license for a good,

45

long time," Mary Ellen said in a tight voice.

"That's not enough!" Hope exclaimed. "They should slap him in jail and throw away the key."

"When can we see Pres?" Jessica demanded.

"Soon. I'm sure he'll want to have as much company as possible." Mary Ellen smiled.

"Hey, we'll be there with bells on." Sean grinned. "We'll turn that old hospital into a real party, day and night. We'll put in a standing order for pizzas, and the whole squad will be there every day as soon as practice is over."

"Yeah." Olivia nodded. "And Duffy is going to write daily reports on Pres's progress for the paper, just like sports coverage. That means Pres *has* to turn up a winner!"

They were all too busy telling Mary Ellen exactly what their plans were to hear the door open and close again. But when the clicking of impatient high heels caught Coach Engborg's attention, they all turned around.

"Excuse me," an annoyed voice said.

"Excuse *me*." Ardith Engborg walked over to the impeccably groomed girl who had just walked in. "But there are no high heels in this gym, at any time."

A frosty glaze covered Diana Tucker's face. She positively loathed being told what to do and what not to do. "I'm only here for a second. I won't hurt your precious little gym floor."

"I don't like your tone of voice," Mrs. Engborg said softly. The cheerleaders knew all too well the danger inherent in that hushed tone. It was always worse to have Mrs. Engborg whisper than yell at you. But Diana seemed impervious.

46

"Well, I'm terribly sorry about that," Diana said, sounding not in the least sorry. "I just came to find out where the rest of my mascot committee was hiding."

"We know we're supposed to be starting to construct the wolf today, but something came up that's more important," Tara informed her.

"Oh?" Diana scanned the room and focused on Mary Ellen. Her face, generally wearing a smug, self-satisfied smile, suddenly changed to a mask of pure pity. "Oh, my goodness! I must say I'm surprised to see you here, Mary Ellen."

"How did *she* find out?" Sean muttered to Jessica.

"It's all over school by now. And you know if there's any dirt to dig, Diana's right in there with a shovel," Jessica responded, moving protectively closer to Mary Ellen.

"I — I'm taking a break," Mary Ellen said, looking Diana right in the eye.

"It's just *awful*! The absolute worst!" Diana said. "I can't tell you how sorry I am to hear about your poor husband. Imagine being married to somebody who's going to be confined to a wheelchair for the rest of his life. But he always was a crazy driver, wasn't he?" she finished.

Nobody could believe that Diana had the insensitivity to say that.

"I don't know what you're talking about. He's going to be fine," Mary Ellen insisted, with no expression in her voice. But the others could see that if this went on any longer, she was sure to burst out crying.

"Listen, we're calling it quits for the day to get

over to the hospital," Peter said quickly, taking Mary Ellen by the arm and steering her toward the gym door. "Olivia, why don't you, Jessica, and Hope come with us in my car?"

"Sean and I will follow you," Tara said.

"Fine," Olivia said, turning her back on Diana. "Coach, it's okay if we cut out a little early, isn't it?"

"Of course." The coach started picking up her tapes. "We'll pick up where we left off tomorrow."

"See you," Jessica said, following the others.

"Yeah, right," Sean nodded. He walked across the gym to get his practice bag, and swung it over his shoulder, nearly hitting Diana's arm.

"But Beef and I are waiting in the shop," Diana protested. "We have all the sketches ready and he's already putting up the wire frame."

"Guess you better get busy on that wolf yourself, Diana," Sean suggested, "seeing as how Kate Harmon is cooking up something really terrific for St. Cloud. And I have it on the best of authority." Then he looked down at her feet. "And say, how about those high heels?"

She sniffed and then, because Ardith Engborg was still watching her, she very slowly bent down and eased her shoes off. In stockinged feet, she walked gingerly across the polished floor, stopping at the door to put her heels on again. She watched the cheerleaders escort Mary Ellen down the hall, and waited until she couldn't see them anymore.

Oh, who needs them? Diana thought. I can build that whole wolf by myself. Then something else came to her mind, and she smiled slyly. Or I can see that it doesn't get built. I can do that, too.

She had a plan now, a very simple plot. It wouldn't be at all hard to put into action.

It was crowded in the halls of Haven Lake Medical Center's eighth floor, where Pres had been moved. The cheerleaders got off the elevator and ran right into Patrick, who had already been there for half an hour.

"Mary Ellen, I just saw Pres's mom. She says he's awake, so you can talk to him."

Mary Ellen's eyes looked like those of a deer caught in the headlights of an approaching car. "I'll see you guys later," she promised. "Please don't leave. Maybe you can go in for a second if he's not too tired."

They watched her walk down the hall, pause for a second at Pres's door, and then walk inside.

"Have you heard anything?" Jessica asked Patrick.

"No. Everyone's very hush-hush. I don't like the feel of it, though."

"What do you mean?" Tara asked.

"There are too many doctors in there, which says to me that it's worse than just a few broken bones." Patrick sighed and took a seat in one of the orange plastic waiting room chairs.

"Mary Ellen looked so shaken when Diana talked about Pres's being in a wheelchair," Jessica said. "I just wonder if Mary Ellen knows something she isn't telling us."

"Listen, it's dumb to second-guess these people," Sean told her, starting to pace. "Let's just take a wait-and-see attitude."

Hope grimaced and sank down into a chair.

"As a doctor's daughter, I can tell you that's all we can do. And all Pres can do, too."

Another set of doctors marched steadfastly down the hall and disappeared into Pres's room. The group sat back to wait.

Mary Ellen drew up a chair by her husband's bedside. His eyes, puffy and with black and blue splotches around them, flickered open.

"Well, well. So how do I look?" he asked.

Mary Ellen calmed the fear inside her and smiled. "Kind of like a raccoon who's had a bad day. How do you feel?" she asked.

"Hmm, now that's a very interesting question. It's sort of weird, but you know, I don't feel so bad. Maybe this whole thing is just an optical illusion. I'm really doing a cartwheel right beside you at the moment."

She was in the middle of a weak laugh when the door opened and two doctors walked in. She remembered she had seen both of these men the previous night.

"Mrs. Tilford?"

"Yes," she responded.

"I'm Dr. Davies, the neurologist, and this is my colleague, Dr. Adelman. He's an osteopath."

"Okay." Pres chuckled. "That's nerves and bones, right?"

"You've got it, young man," Dr. Adelman said.

"I'd come over and shake your hand," Pres said, grinning, "but I'm a little hung up here."

"I'm delighted to see your progress, Pres," Dr. Davies said. "Why, last night, we were really worried about you."

"Oh, he's tough," Mary Ellen said. "That's one of the things I love about him," she added in a whisper, so that only Pres could hear.

"Well, now, we thought we'd like to discuss . . . the future," Dr. Davies went on.

"Sounds good to me," Pres said. "Like, you mean, when I get out of here and when I can start jogging again."

Dr. Adelman did not smile. "Not exactly."

Mary Ellen stood up, gripping the side of Pres's bed. "Just what do you mean?"

"Perhaps you'd like to step outside, Mary Ellen, if I may call you Mary Ellen," the doctor said softly, "and we'll have a little conversation — "

"No way!" Pres practically yelled. "If you've got something to say to her about my condition, you say it to my face. I'm not an idiot, you know."

"We just wanted to make the whole process easier for — for both of you," Dr. Davies said.

Mary Ellen glanced down and saw her hands shaking on the metal frame of the bed. She tried to control them, but they seemed to have a life of their own. And her stomach seemed to be tied in a succession of knots. "Just say it. Whatever it is, it's better that we know."

Dr. Davies sat down on the side of Pres's bed and licked his lips. His balding head shone in the overhead lights. "I'm going to try a little test now, if I may, Pres." He produced a straight pin from the inside of his lapel and he moved down to the end of the bed. He lifted the sheet, exposing Pres's feet.

"You just tell the doctor when you feel a pin-prick, okay?" Dr. Adelman said.

Mary Ellen watched as the doctor made a pass near the ball of Pres's right foot.

"Yeah. There. I felt something," Pres said confidently.

"I didn't do anything yet," the doctor said. Then he turned back. Mary Ellen saw him prick the big toe, then the heel.

Pres had his eyes closed, concentrating. He said nothing.

Dr. Davies moved the pin to the left foot. He touched it gently to the ball, then to the heel. When Pres was still silent, he put pressure on the pin, pressing it against the skin.

"Okay, you can get started," Pres muttered.

Mary Ellen felt the knots tighten. "He's already finished, Pres," she said quietly.

Dr. Adelman shook his head. "Now I don't want you to get the impression that this is permanent. When you've healed a little more, you'll have physical therapy, of course. We don't really know how badly you've damaged your spinal column, Pres, and that's the key thing here. You'll have to wear a neckbrace for a while, and we want the bones to set properly. After that, it's anybody's guess."

"About whether I'm a cripple, you mean," Pres said in a flat voice.

"About whether you'll walk, yes," Dr. Davies nodded. "But it's very premature to even consider that."

Mary Ellen's eyes were hot with unshed tears. She couldn't, she wouldn't believe that this was happening to them. She refused to give up hope — she knew that Pres would be all right. It was just a matter of time.

Pres cleared his throat and started to speak. At first, his voice was low and unrushed, but soon it was edged with fury. "You know, you guys are really something. You come in here like you own the place, and you start making stupid judgments about what I can and can't do. Just because I don't jump when you stick a pin in me doesn't mean a thing, okay? You listen to me," he went on, his tone growing in intensity, "if I want to walk again, I'll walk! And I don't give two cents for your opinion."

The doctors looked at one another, then started for the door. "I'm glad to hear you say that, Pres. It's going to take that kind of will and persistence to make progress. We'll leave you two alone now," Dr. Adelman said. "I'm sure you have a great deal to think about." And as smoothly and quickly as they had entered the room, they now vanished.

"Darling — " Mary Ellen began.

"What incredible nerve! Where do those guys get off saying stuff like that?" Pres demanded angrily.

Mary Ellen was stunned — by the doctors' awful uncertainty and by Pres's reaction. "Listen, I don't want to believe — "

"Then don't!" Pres yelled. "Sorry," he said immediately afterward. "I've really had it. You mind getting lost for a while, Mary Ellen? I could use a little time alone."

"But we have to talk," Mary Ellen protested.

"Sure. But it'll wait. We've got all the time in

the world to talk," Pres said. His voice echoed around the sterile room.

When he turned his head away from her, she knew she had no other choice but to leave him alone. All she wanted to do was take him in her arms and hug him hard, assure him that he was going to get well, but she sensed his deeper need to just be alone with this terrible news and absorb it all by himself.

"I'll be right outside," she told him. "I'll be back."

He settled down into the pillows as she closed the door behind her. There was no sense in getting all riled up about this. None at all. And then, he realized with great relief, for the first time since the accident, he felt pain. Not in his legs, but in his heart and in his mind.

That was a start, at least.

CHAPTER

"Now, as you can see, the tail will be here, activated by a battery pack that will also control the eyes." Diana used a yardstick as a pointer, walking around the spare wire frame of the wolf as she indicated its various parts. The wolf was in a crouching position, one front paw lifted as if to spring. From top to tail it measured nine feet. It would really be spectacular when it was finished, but it was going to take a *lot* of work.

Hope, Jessica, Peter, and Olivia were sitting around in a circle with the other kids on the committee: three guys who were former boyfriends of Diana, and two girls none of them knew very well.

"The battery's going to be on a timer, so the tail will wag and the eyes will roll every ten seconds. Show them, Beef." Diana gave the floor to her latest prize, Beef Driscoll. Beef was a junior, a gigantic boy who was completely infatuated with Diana. The funny part was seeing this 6'4", 220-pound hulk acting like an adoring puppy around the tall, blonde girl who couldn't have cared less about him.

"This is a great idea, Diana," Jessica said, walking around the frame of the wolf, "if it works." She was completely skeptical. She'd seen Diana in action on the homecoming dance committee, and the girl was all talk and no action. She loved to put grand schemes into motion and then just walk away.

"Maybe we should concentrate on the waterproof aspects of this wolf, Diana," Olivia suggested. "Like the paint, for example. Who's buying it and what colors are we getting? We should get the basics out of the way before we go on to fancy battery packs."

"You know, Olivia," Diana said, smiling and looking superior, "your problem is that you can't see the big picture for the little details. Beef has already ordered the paint *and* the undercoating. Of course, we have about two weeks of padding and papier-mâché work first, before we move on to the next stage. And I've called in Tommy Bridgeman to do the electrical work."

"Oh, well, then we're in good hands," Peter said. Tommy was Tarenton High's scientific genius. There was nothing he couldn't fix, make run, or construct from scratch.

"So the only question is who does the nitty-gritty stuff. Okay." Diana grabbed her clipboard and started reading. "Now, Olivia, you and Hope will mix the base; Peter, you and Tara — where is Tara, anyway?"

"At the hospital," Jessica said promptly.

Diana put her hands on her hips. "Oh, what *is* this? You people committed yourself to this work, and now you're shirking your responsibilities. I should have known better than to let cheerleaders have anything to do with something as important as the school mascot. All right, just forget it. You can tell Tara she's off the committee. I'll get some-one else."

"Just a minute, Diana." Olivia got up and walked over to her. "We're in the middle of a crisis with a good friend of ours, so we're taking turns over there with Pres. And we're going to keep on doing that, whether you like it or not. We'll get the mascot built — don't you worry about it."

Diana shook her head, then handed her clip-board to Beef. "What am I going to do with these people?" she said to him.

"That's a good question, Diana," Beef said, speaking for the first time that afternoon. He had a slow, deep voice that made him sound like he was underwater. "Actually, I don't know," he finished, after wracking his brain for a brief second.

"Oh, never mind. You boys, Jimmy and Mike, and you, Alison and Gracie," she said, speaking to her other committee members, "you're my back-bone. I'm relying on you," she said. "Beef, let's get started. Get that cotton batting over here and start tearing it into clumps. We have to shape it around the frame and then mold it on with tape. The papier-mâché goes over that. Understand? Well, what are you waiting for?"

Diana's friends jumped up and went to work

immediately. The cheerleaders got to their feet and looked at one another.

"How are we going to take her, day after day?" Peter grumbled.

"Just think of the end result," Hope encouraged him.

"This had better be good," Olivia said. "Sean told me that Kate is positively delirious about St. Cloud's mascot."

"Has he found out what it is yet?" Jessica asked.

"No, but he's working on her." Olivia giggled, taking a huge roll of the cotton batting off a high shelf and tearing it open.

"How's this, Diana?" Alison asked after about half an hour of working with Jessica to stuff the batting around the wolf's right leg. Diana, true to form, had been thumbing through a fashion magazine while the others worked.

"Oh, it's just *fabulous*, Ally!" she exclaimed as she slid down from her perch on the steps that led to the shop door. "Keep it up! Um, Jessica, did you ever take an art course or anything? Or maybe biology? I mean, the basic shape of an animal's leg isn't that hard to remember. It bends at the joint in front, you know."

Jessica just stared at her and continued what she was doing, exactly as she was doing it.

"Did you hear me?" Diana asked.

"Yes, quite clearly." Jessica smiled.

"I'm really glad Sean and Tara aren't here," Hope whispered to Peter. "The fur would be flying — and I'm not talking wolf fur."

Alison shrugged nervously at Diana. "You

know, Jessica was the one who showed me how to do this, Diana. She was really very helpful."

"Helpful and talented are two very different things, aren't they, Ally?" Diana sighed in dismay. "Too bad some of the people who go out for sports and cheerleading and things like that have such one-track minds they can't even master something as simple as basic sculpture."

Jessica, who had been doing a slow burn, finally got up, shoving a wad of cotton at the committee chairman. "Gee, Diana," she said with as much control as she could muster, "since you know so much about wolf anatomies, why don't you do it? I'm sure you could show us all a thing or two."

All the other kids stopped work and waited while Diana, angry but determined not to show it, started slapping cotton around the wolf's middle. But as nobody would come and assist her, she had to stand there, holding the stuff on all by herself.

"Does anyone have tape? Beef, where's the tape?"

"Coming, Diana!" The poor boy, stumbling over rolls of wire and cans of paint, ran to her with a huge roll of tape.

"Now start there. No, you idiot! Here, where my hand is," Diana directed him.

Beef then proceeded to put a large piece of tape right on top of her index finger. When she yelled, he immediately pulled it off, ripping three carefully applied coats of Passion Pink nail polish along with it.

"Oh, you are so incredibly dumb!" she shrieked, jumping away from the wolf as if it had bitten her. "Look what you've done!"

Beef tenderly took her hand in his. "It's not bad," he said. "It looks kind of interesting this way."

Olivia wandered away from what she was doing to check on her fellow squad members. "Only half an hour to go," she whispered to Jessica, looking at the clock above them. "Then we can take off for the hospital."

"Poor Diana's the one who needs a trip to the hospital," Jessica told her. "I think the shock of losing her nail polish was too much for her."

"Peter Rayman!" Diana raced over to him. "What are you doing?"

"I just thought — "

"Well, don't! Thinking is *my* job," she told him in an authoritative manner. "You aren't supposed to do anything on the head of the wolf until" — she consulted her clipboard — "until the end of this week."

"But there wasn't anybody working up there, and it just seemed to me — " Peter, ever the diplomat, always tactful, was having a hard time keeping his temper.

"I am the chairman of this committee, if you recall, and that means I am the one in charge of the division of labor. And if you think that I would entrust as important an element as the wolf's head to a cheerleader, you are severely mistaken." She moved away to praise the rear leg, which Gracie and Mike had just finished taping.

The next fifteen minutes were tense and quiet, until finally, when the clock read six-thirty, the cheerleaders excused themselves and started for the shop door.

"And which one of your delightful presences will be missing tomorrow?" Diana asked pointedly. "I assume one of you will be on hospital duty with Pres Tilford."

As a group, the four cheerleaders quickly turned and walked out the door.

Pres's room looked like a flower shop. All his friends had sent something, and of course his mother had placed a standing order with the florist for a fresh bouquet by his bedside daily. The nurses were informed that they could take the previous day's flowers to their station. Pres's Uncle James, the artist, had sent a giant seven-foot cactus with a note stipulating that it was not to be overwatered, on pain of the plant's death.

When Patrick walked into Pres's room that afternoon, though, he was carrying a stack of tapes. He had stayed up late the night before taping all of Pres's favorite albums.

"Hey, this place looks like — "

"Don't say it," Pres cautioned him. "I think enough is enough. Boy, am I glad you didn't bring another living thing in here."

Patrick moved to the side of the bed, hesitating as he looked at the impressive set of machines and dials and the traction apparatus. "Can I sit down?"

"Wish you would. Everybody else pulls up a chair, like they think if they jar my body one more millimeter by plopping down on the bed, it'll break me in two." He chuckled a little. "They might be right, come to think of it."

"Hey, you! No talk like that." Patrick had been

wracking his brain all day for positive things to say to his friend. He had a few ready quips, but it was going to be tough, especially after the phone conversation he'd had with Mary Ellen that day. The doctors had nothing but dire predictions, and she was getting worried about them leaking to Pres.

"I don't want to get his spirits down in any way," she'd told Patrick that morning. "If he's left to his own devices, he'll get sick and tired of being an invalid and just throw off the covers one day and jump out of bed. But if he listens to the doctors, who knows what effect it might have."

Patrick had promised to be as cheery and light-hearted as he could. But looking at Pres, his head still swathed in bandages, his face bruised and battered, it was all he could do to keep from crying.

"So, what's new in town?" Pres asked.

"Well, there's a dynamite detour going from Carter Road that's rerouting traffic down to Route 531, and I hear they're thinking about putting an extension on the playing field at the high school," Patrick began very seriously. "Oh, yeah, and the absolute key topic of conversation is one Preston Tilford III, and how he's doing and when he's due out of the hospital."

"Nice," Pres murmured. He turned his face away slightly, so that he didn't have to look into Patrick's eyes.

"You know, you ought to be used to this kind of thing. As I recall, you had a lot of aches and pains when you were cheering for Tarenton, buddy. And remember our days on the moving van express? How about the job we did for the Thompsons when they relocated to the top of that hill over in Deep River? They must have put rocks in all their dressers, and anchors on the dining room table. You told me when we were done with that move that you were certain you weren't going to be able to lift one foot in front of the other the next morning. But guess what? You did."

"Right." Pres cleared his throat, then reached for the automatic TV control. "It was nice of you to come over, but I guess you probably have to meet Jessica now, right? You don't have to stay — Mary Ellen will be here soon."

"I don't *have* to stay. I *want* to stay." Patrick didn't like Pres's tone of voice.

"Well, maybe I'm just not in the mood for company." He turned on the set. A soap opera flickered onto the screen.

Patrick reached up and turned off the set. "Don't be like that, Pres. I know you're a mess now, but you'll get better."

"Who says?"

"Oh, come on!" Suddenly, Patrick was mad. "You want sympathy? If you do, I'm not your man. If you think I came here to tell you how sorry I am for you, then you have another thing coming. Look, you drew a real bad card, I'll admit that, but it could have been worse. You should thank your lucky stars."

"Oh, I certainly thank them. It's just wonderful being here, laid up like this."

"You know," Patrick said, increasingly frustrated and furious that he was not communicating, "if there's one thing I hate, it's a cynic. That's the easy way out. Okay, have it your way. Don't try at all. Just lie there." And then, even though he wanted to hug Pres and tell him he really cared, he started for the door.

"This is the end of the line for me," Pres said softly. "I'm not being cynical. I'm looking at things clearly."

Patrick whirled around. "What are you talking about?"

"Look, you know me, man. You know what makes me tick. I'm a physical person — activity is my reason for being. I can't sit still a minute. At least, I couldn't until last night. Think about it, Patrick. Why else would I have gone into business with you to move furniture after graduating and leaving the cheerleading squad? I had to be on the go. I had to be walking, lifting, pulling. Even now, working for my dad, I never sit still in the office. I run from one part of the factory to another. That's me in a nutshell."

Pres threw off the hospital sheet, revealing the plaster casts that covered his legs from the balls of his feet to above his hips. "It's the reason Mary Ellen married me, man. Because I am — was strong and healthy and a terrific physical specimen." He stopped and looked down at his useless legs. It was as if they didn't belong to him at all.

"She married you because she loves you, whether you can run around or not. You're a real dope if you think all she cares about are your dumb muscles."

Pres slowly shook his head from side to side.

64

"I'm not sure about that. But I do know one thing. Something very big has changed. I can never bring back the Pres that was before the accident."

"But if you try real hard," Patrick persisted, "maybe you'll come up with an even better Pres."

For the first time, Pres managed a smile. "All I know is that I'm going to be on my back for a long time, whether I like it or not. So I might as well get used to it."

Patrick was about to tell him it would be a criminal offense to want to get used to anything that awful, when there was a knock on the door of Pres's room.

"Come in!" Pres ordered, glad to be relieved of this heavy conversation. He couldn't take any more of Patrick's well-meaning but impossible help.

Tara and Sean stuck their heads in. "We heard you were holding court here, and we wondered if we could get a royal audience." Tara grinned.

"Hey, Pres!" Sean declared, pulling a chair close to the bed and swinging a leg over it. "Am I glad to see it's only a few broken bones. Somebody told me you needed a toe transplant. Boy, I was really worried there for a minute."

Their jokes were forced, but they had made a pact before they came in to be as ridiculous and off-the-wall as they could. And by the time the rest of the squad arrived twenty minutes later, Sean and Tara had managed to get Pres and Patrick to be just about as silly as they were.

"Hey, what is this?" Jessica asked in astonishment, coming in and looking at the four of them. "I thought it was a sick room."

"No such luck," Pres announced. "I have declared myself officially well. Tell *that* to the doctors."

"In that case, let us regale you with tales of how horrible Diana was today," Hope suggested.

"You'll be fortunate enough to have one of us playing hooky from mascot duty every day," Peter told him. "Whichever one is closest to punching Diana in the nose gets the time off."

They were all too busy trying to entertain Pres to realize that there was something different about his mood. The cheerleaders had all been casual friends of his; they couldn't be expected to see the subtle difference in him. But Patrick was determined now to shake him out of it. Only by getting Pres back on his feet emotionally would they ever be able to get him back on his feet — literally.

It was almost seven-thirty when Mary Ellen walked into the room. She seemed flushed, almost elated. There was a brightness in her blue eyes and a lilt to her walk that had been totally missing since the accident.

"Hi, everybody! Hi, sweetie." She walked over to Pres and bent over to give him a kiss. "I met somebody really wonderful today."

"Oh, really?" Pres nodded. "Who?"

"She's your new cheerleader. Among other things." Mary Ellen laughed and went to the door to open it. "May I introduce Connie Lapino, your physical therapist."

A small, wiry woman who looked no older than any of them in the room, with close-cropped dark hair and snapping black eyes, walked into the

66

room. She was wearing jeans and a leotard, as if, in fact, she'd just come from cheerleading practice. "Hi, Pres," she said matter-of-factly.

"How're you doin'?" he responded.

"Well, you guys probably need some time alone," Olivia said immediately. "We'll be back tomorrow." She well knew what hospital routine consisted of, having been through it all in her early years. How many doctors had examined her, and how many nurses had egged her on and encouraged her?

The cheerleaders said their good-byes and filed out. Patrick was the last to go. "Remember what I said, okay?" he counseled Pres.

"It's engraved on my brain, good buddy," Pres nodded gamely, so that Patrick couldn't tell whether Pres was putting him on. With a sigh, Patrick, too, walked out of the room, leaving Mary Ellen and Connie alone with the patient.

"So you're *another* doctor," Pres said skeptically.

"Not an MD, no. But I have a lot of experience with spinal injuries. I think I can help you."

"Interesting," Pres said noncommittally.

"Pres, be patient, okay?" Mary Ellen warned him.

"Hey, that's all I can be. A patient," he quipped sardonically.

Connie paid no attention to this. "Now I've examined your chart and your current X rays," she said, "so I guess I should examine you to determine your course of therapy. It's much too soon yet, of course, and we won't get into the difficult stuff until a few weeks from now, but I always feel it's good to go over what's on your mind before we go out onto the floor. Like with cheerleading. You used to cheer, your wife tells me."

"Yeah, but that was another lifetime ago."

Connie smiled. "Well, we'll see if we can't include that activity in your *next* life, too. I used to be a cheerleader myself, so I know the drills. Once I'm done with you, you'll be flying, not just walking."

Mary Ellen saw the thunderclouds race across Pres's brow. He had had one pep talk too many today.

"All right, lady, you can just forget it for now," he growled. "I've been poked and prodded and looked at like I'm some kind of rare buffalo at a county fair. I've had it!"

"I hear you," she said simply, backing off. "I don't think we have to do much more than talk for right now, Pres. But I want you to get ready to work. Because unless you cooperate, you're not going to crawl, let alone walk." And with that, Connie brusquely turned on her heel and left the young couple together.

"Oh, she's a real prize!" Pres exclaimed.

"You didn't give her a chance," Mary Ellen told him. She was angry at his rude behavior, and yet she couldn't yell at him — not in the condition he was in. But she had to agree that Connie's bedside manner was not the greatest. That was weird, too, because she'd had the most wonderful talk with the therapist that afternoon, learning all about the special things that could be done for people who'd had multiple injuries. She had really seen a light at the end of the tunnel for the first time after their discussion. But Pres had just snuffed it out.

"Give her a chance," Pres repeated softly. Maybe I will. We'll have to see." Then he got out his portable tape deck and stuck in one of the rock tapes Patrick had brought that afternoon. He played it loud — loud enough to drown out the nagging voices that echoed in his head, telling him he'd never walk again.

CHAPTER

6

Kate Harmon sat in the bleachers, trying to concentrate on the action. It was an incredible basketball game, as a matter of fact: Tarenton was topping Deep River, 32–30, at the end of the first half, but she just couldn't get into it. Even watching Sean race along the floor with the cheerleaders, hurtling himself in the air, tucking his legs for a forward roll, looking up every once in a while to give her a pleased wink, she *still* couldn't make herself pay attention.

The problem was keeping a secret, of course. She had always been terrible at secrets. Well, Sean called her a loudmouth, and he wasn't half wrong. It wasn't that she was a gossip or anything, but she didn't see any reason to keep opinions to herself. The thing was, with Sean unofficially on the Tarenton High mascot committee, there was no way *he* could keep a secret about the St. Cloud mascot if she told him.

70

She liked Sean a lot — perhaps almost as much as he liked her. He was fun to be with, easy to get to know, and he was crazy about her. That was the nicest part. He was such a great-looking guy, too — as a matter of fact, he was the most attractive boy she'd ever dated. Face it, she didn't have the great figure and face of a Tara or a Jessica, and she certainly wasn't a delicate sprite like Hope or Olivia. She was just an ordinary-looking person — handsome, her mother called her. She personally thought that term should be reserved for boys and horses, but she knew her mother meant well, so she never corrected her.

Kate watched the Tarenton center loop the ball in the air and place it neatly through the hoop. His opposite number on the Deep River team snatched the ball, dribbling it down the length of the court. He passed to one of his teammates, but a Tarenton guard was too fast for them. He had it back down the court in a second, quickly passing it to the center, who easily scored another two points.

"Give it all you got!
Tarenton is hot!"

Olivia jumped up on the sidelines to lead the squad in a cheer. Sean quickly boosted her onto his shoulders, and Peter did the same with Jessica, while Tara and Hope picked up their megaphones and blasted the cheer to the stands:

"It's nothing new,
We're always true!
We've got the team,

71

That will come through!

The red and white,
Has zing and bite!
We can't go wrong,
We're always right!

YAY, Tarenton!
YAY, team!"

Kate applauded and cheered along with the
rest of the people in her section, but if you'd asked
her to describe the play she'd just seen, she would
have been at a total loss. She was just imagining
the Rivals Game, as it had been named, between
Tarenton and St. Cloud six weeks from that day,
when the two teams agreed they would unveil
their mascots. They would be right in the thick of
play-offs, so both teams would know if they had
a shot at the championship by that time. The
Rivals Game was going to be a *really* big deal
this year. If only it were sooner! Six weeks seemed
such a long time away.

Kate knew, of course, that the Tarenton High
mascot would be a wolf. She didn't know the
details, had no idea what it would really look like,
but everyone acknowledged that the Wolves had
selected one of their own to represent them on the
court. David Duffy had even hinted that much in
a recent column of his in the *Lighter*.

Kate's brilliant innovation for St. Cloud was a
huge, threatening gray storm cloud, vaguely
formed in the shape of a man, with metallic
lightning bolt arms and a fierce expression on its

face. The cloud would be wearing high-top sneakers and holding a basketball on the end of one lightning bolt, and would be perched right over the St. Cloud basket throughout each game. During the football season, he'd wear a helmet and knee guard.

It was all too much. She was spending an awful lot of time with Tarenton High cheerleaders lately — when she wasn't building the mascot — and although she considered some of them her friends, she couldn't very well spill the beans to the enemy. And even if she could trust them, which she undoubtedly couldn't, what would happen if the news leaked to Diana Tucker? Disaster, utter and complete. No, it was too risky. She had to consider the ultimate sacrifice: not seeing Sean until this whole thing was over.

The game was just getting hot and heavy. One of the Tarenton guards dropped the ball, leaving it free for a Deep River forward. The ball seemed to zoom back and forth between the baskets for a while, with each side scoring each time. Then, suddenly, Tarenton lost their edge when the referee called a foul on one of their guards. Deep River started scoring when the ball got into play again, and Tarenton couldn't stop them.

Kate saw the cheerleaders go into a huddle, and then the six of them sprang up for a quick "Pride" cheer, immediately followed by "Growl, Wolves, Growl." It seemed to do some good, because the next time Kate looked up, the Tarenton center got three baskets in a row, evening the score. Tarenton tightened their defense and prevented Deep River from getting off good shots as the clock started to run down. Suddenly, the Tarenton team was alive with energy, as determined to win as they had ever been, scoring hook shots, alley-oops, and reverse lay-ups faster than Kate could count them. When the final buzzer sounded, the score was 60–54 — a Tarenton victory.

She hurried down from the stands and raced over to give Sean a huge hug.

"Whew, are you wet!" she exclaimed.

"Well, what do you think I've been doing out there, sipping a soda? The result of physical exercise, my dear girl, is perspiration." Then he gave her a sweaty kiss and she laughed.

"Will you two stop jabbering and get ready for the victory party?" Jessica demanded, scouring the stands for a sign of Patrick.

"Oh, I saw him a while ago," Kate informed her, not even having to ask whom she was searching for. "He just wanted to stop at the hospital a minute, then he'll be back to pick you up."

"I'll get changed then. Tara, you coming?" Jessica asked.

Tara was clinging to the arm of the Tarenton forward, Ray Elliott, whom she dated on occasion. It wasn't that she really liked him that much, it was just that she couldn't bear to appear at a party alone. She thought, suddenly, of Nick Stewart, the teacher she'd gone out with for a while — before she knew he was a teacher and he knew she was a student. Now *there* was a man to walk into a party with, but completely wrong for her — she was well aware that she'd been far over her head. Still, he was a nice memory.

"I'm coming as soon as this extraordinary ball

player will let go of me," Tara said at last, giving Ray a sly look. "Meet you in the parking lot, okay?" she told him, running off to join Jessica, Olivia, and Hope.

Sean told Kate he'd see her at the car in ten minutes, and she wandered out into the hallway outside the gym with some of the other kids who were on their way to the victory party. She walked down to the water fountain, killing time, then strolled over to the glass case in the center of the hall, where Tarenton's trophies were proudly displayed.

Kate heard voices behind her and turned around to see Diana Tucker and Beef Driscoll strolling toward her, arm in arm. It was too late to cut out for the parking lot — she had no choice but to talk to them. What she really would have liked was to say casually, Why don't you two go jump in the lake? but Kate knew better. She'd settle for hello.

"Well, if it isn't the girl from St. Cloud," Diana said, disengaging herself from Beef. She walked down the hall and stood over Kate.

Kate hated looking up to anyone, so she pointedly stared at Beef's shoulder. "Wonderful game tonight, guys," she said. "That jump shot from midcourt that Joe made was just terrific."

"Yeah," Beef nodded, trying to button up the vest that was two sizes too small for him. Beef wasn't used to wearing anything but sweats, but Diana insisted that he dress for games, so he was forced to borrow his younger brother's clothes.

"Oh, what do you care how well we do?" Diana

asked Kate. "What difference could it possibly make to you?"

"Why, my dear, all the difference! If Tarenton loses, then St. Cloud won't get to beat you in the play-offs. And our new mascot will be so lonely without the big, bad wolf to keep him company."

"You think you know so much," Diana said, looking not at all worried. "Well, you might be surprised. We have our spies, too," she shrugged. " 'Bye now, dear. Better watch out for Sean at the party. You know the boy has a roving eye."

"And you ought to have a couple of black ones," Kate muttered to herself as she watched Diana move away.

She was so annoyed by the time she got to the parking lot, she didn't even want to go to the party. Sean's headlights caught her on the steps of the high school, having an imaginary conversation with some clearly awful person.

"Hello? Am I missing something, or have you started getting chummy with invisible people?" Sean asked out the window.

"Oh, it's you!" she barked at him, pulling her coat around her tightly. Had Diana made that up about her spies, or was there some truth in it?

"Would you like a ride, or are you walking the five miles to the party?" he questioned, when she didn't make a move to get into the car.

"I'm not going. I'd be out of place," she exclaimed, walking to the far end of the steps, away from Sean.

"Kate, we've been through this a hundred times," he moaned in exasperation, getting out of the driver's seat and going over to her. "You know all my friends think you're great. And just because you're concocting some super-duper mascot and refuse to even give me a hint about it — "

"It's not that. It's just. . . ." She scooted under his arm as he reached for her, and marched to the other end of the steps. "I'm not Tarenton. It wasn't my victory tonight. It's — it's not a good idea for me to be seen with you," she blurted out.

He stalked her across the steps and wouldn't let her get past him this time. "You are so dumb sometimes, you know that?" he demanded, taking her by both arms. "In the first place, I like being seen with you. For some crazy reason I can't explain, it makes me feel good. And in the second place, we always share things, victories, defeats, bad stuff and good. Oh, Katie." He sighed, embracing her and burying his face in her short, curly hair. "I wouldn't have a good time without you."

"But I hate keeping secrets from you," she exploded.

He knew he had her. "Then don't," he said simply.

She pushed away from him, ramming her fists against his chest. "You see! This is exactly the kind of thing I'm talking about. You get all soft and mushy and nice, and then I feel I have to tell you. And I can't. Sean, it's no good. I'll see you in six weeks — if you're still interested," she added, because she knew full well that Sean Dubrow was not the kind of guy who would go dateless for any period of time.

"You get in that car this minute," he told her forcefully, grabbing her hand just as she was about to slip away into the night. "The engine's running and I'm wasting good gas," he finished as he gently shoved her into the passenger seat. Quickly, before she could escape, he ran around to his side of the car and jumped in, gunning the motor and taking off into the night.

Kate sat back and leaned her head on the headrest. "Well, just this once more," she said softly. Then she looked at him closely, almost trying to see through to the inside of his brain. He couldn't be a spy for Diana. It was impossible.

It took two weeks for the wolf to take very basic shape. Even with twelve full- and part-time workers, it was a big job. There was the padding and wrapping to be done; the strategic placement of limbs and features; the all-important hatch for the battery pack, located in the animal's stomach; and then the papier-mâché.

There was a big setback when Olivia discovered that the head was not balanced properly and had to come off. She and Hope figured out a way to do the head and ears separately and then attach them later, but it took a week to convince Diana. She finally had to agree to their plan when Beef ruined the original head by jamming it down into the neck. There was simply no choice but to start from scratch with the head. Then, when Peter explained that the tail would also work better if it was a separate element, it was back to the drawing board once again.

"Ugh, this stuff is never going to come out from under my fingernails," Tara complained as she mixed yet another barrel of flour and water.

"My fingers have a permanent impression of this paw in them," Sean groaned.

Diana was always checking up on them. She was constantly hovering over the cheerleaders' shoulders — but she left her own friends completely alone to do whatever they wanted.

"Well, the tail finally has some definition," Hope declared, holding it up for all to see.

Peter came over and shook his head in amazement. "You've done a great job. It looks real — except that there's no wolf attached to it."

"And it's impervious to rain, sleet, snow, *and* Beef," Hope reminded him. She had figured out a way to attach pieces of a synthetic wig she'd bought in a five-and-dime store onto the dry papier-mâché. The end piece hung loose like a real wolf's tail, and the center was hollowed out to accommodate the connections from the battery pack.

"Call the boss over and let her see it," Olivia suggested. "It's not finished until she says it is, unfortunately."

"I'll get her." Peter, who was the only one of the cheerleaders still able to speak civilly to the committee chairman, brought her back for the official inspection.

"Why, that's very nice, Hope," Diana said in a patronizing tone after examining the tail carefully. "You've certainly put a lot of effort into this."

Hope didn't trust Diana's praise for a second. "Well, it's good of you to say so." She nodded. "Because I couldn't do it again."

"Oh, I'm sure you could if you had to. All right, class dismissed for the day." Diana smiled, giving the tail one last appraising look before walking away.

"You know, even when she says nice things, they sound awful," Olivia commented.

"Better stick the tail in a bag and seal it tight," Jessica suggested. "So Beef can't get his hands on it."

"Was that hands, or *paws*?" Sean asked.

"All right, you guys, enough with the cracks." Olivia grinned, giving the work a once-over. "I'm going to see Pres. Anyone else coming?"

"Definitely," Tara agreed.

"Give him my love," Jessica said. "I promised my mom I'd make it an early one tonight." Although she was telling the truth, the others understood about Jessica and hospitals.

They said they'd see her tomorrow, and switched off the main lights in the shop. Diana and her friends were already halfway down the hall. The rest of the lights in the high school were out; the janitor was just cleaning up, dragging a mop along the basement corridor. The cheer-leaders nodded to him and started down to the parking lot.

"Is this ever going to get done?" Tara asked. "The Rivals Game is only four weeks away, and we haven't even started the detail work."

"We'll make it," Peter told her.

"How's Kate doing?" Olivia asked Sean curiously.

"Hmm, just fine." Sean nodded noncommittally. Things weren't fine, and it was probably stupid of him to lie, but he didn't want to sound like a complainer. He couldn't seem to stop himself from pressuring Kate for information, and she was acting very suspicious, like she thought he knew something — or somebody he *knew* knew something — and he was just trying to get her to confirm it. This was no way to run a relationship.

"Meet you at Pres's room if we get separated," Tara said, climbing into Peter's car with Hope.

"I'm coming with you, Sean," Olivia said.

The two cars set off into the night. They were several blocks away from the high school when a beat-up pickup truck pulled into the Tarenton High parking lot. And then, a few minutes later, a light went on in the shop — and, just as quickly, went out again.

The cheerleaders were surprised to find Diana waiting for them in the doorway of the shop the following afternoon. It was unusual for her to be early. She generally showed up after everyone had started a particular chore and there was nothing left for her to do.

"Okay, who's playing a joke?" she asked in a bored tone. "Where is it?"

"Where's what, Diana?" Jessica demanded.

"The tail. The wolf's tail, of course."

Hope gasped and ran to the shelf where she had carefully placed the precious piece of work the previous evening. Nothing.

The cheerleaders searched the shop thoroughly, even went through the trash to see whether the janitor might have thrown it out by accident. Nothing.

Diana was right. The tail was gone.

CHAPTER

7

Tara, seated in a chair opposite Pres's bed, stretched out her legs and rested them on the metal frame. She took an emery board from her purse and started to file her nails.

"So that was that. Hope worked like a maniac to finish that wolf tail, and for what? Diana's theory is that the kids who had shop the next morning misplaced the stupid tail. Can you believe it?"

"Frankly, no," Pres said.

"Me, neither." She held up one rounded pinkie and examined it for perfection of form, then started on the opposite one. "And I don't buy the business about the janitor not knowing what it was and throwing it in the dumpster. That's another of Diana's bright conclusions." She put the nail file away and glanced over at Pres's hands, lying on the white sheet. "You could use a manicure," she said.

"Over my dead body!" he exclaimed. "You're not going to paint my nails purple just because I'm a helpless captive in this bed." He hurriedly stuffed his hands under the sheet.

"I'm not talking nail polish, silly. I mean a manicure. Lots of men have them — my father has one every other week. Oh, please let me! You'll love it! It's so relaxing," she said. She jumped up and ran to the bathroom, returning a minute later with a bowl full of hot, sudsy water. "Now you soak." She wheeled over the tray and adjusted it to the height of the bed, then pulled Pres's hands out from under the sheets and stuck them in the water.

Pres grimaced, but there was nothing he could do now. He didn't know what he was in for, but he figured it couldn't be *that* bad if Tara's father went in for it. "So what happens with the mascot now?" Pres asked. It was great having Tara make a fuss over him. He really could get into this, he decided.

"Now Hope has to start all over again with a brand new tail. As if we didn't have enough to do! Boy, what rotten luck. Your hands are a mess," she said, examining them. "You need me."

She produced a manicure kit from the depths of her purse and proceeded to push back his softened cuticles with an orange stick. "And speaking of luck," she continued, "I read your horoscope in the paper this morning."

He tried to pull his hand away, but she retaliated with a jab of the stick in his palm. "It said you should never resist a woman who wields a weapon," she teased, working away at his index finger. "No, what it really said was that Geminis always snap back at this time of year. You're in for a streak of good luck."

"Great!" He gave a weak laugh. "I sure could use some."

"How long are you going to be in traction, anyway?" she asked him, skillfully paring away his cuticles with a nipper. "It looks painful."

"Nowhere near as painful as what you're doing to my hands. Watch it, Tara! You almost drew blood!"

"You're going to be gorgeous, dahling," she told him in a fake European accent. "So when do they let you out of this rig?"

"The nurse says I'll be unstrung for a while starting on Thursday. Then, if all goes well, they'll unhoist me completely next Monday."

"We'll have a celebration," Tara declared, finishing up one hand and starting the next. "Pizza, Cokes, the works! Oh, I almost forgot. I . . . uh . . . have something for you."

She got up and retrieved her practice bag. Fishing around in the depths of it, she finally discovered what she was looking for: a baggie full of brownies. They were a little the worse for wear, having been carried around with her books all day, but they smelled heavenly when she took off the twistie and offered him one.

"Tara! Far out! I love brownies," Pres exclaimed, diving in with his soapy right hand.

"I baked them myself," she said with a self-satisfied smile.

"You're kidding! I didn't know you cooked,"

Pres said, eagerly biting into the rich chocolate confection.

"I don't," she told him emphatically. "This was an experiment."

She watched his face turn from pleased to confused. "They're . . . ah . . . real interesting. Not too sweet."

"Oh?" She fished a brownie from the bag and bit into it. "Oh, no!" she exclaimed, striking her forehead with her open palm. "How could I have been so stupid? I left out the sugar."

"But I really appreciate this, Tara," Pres assured her. "First you take care of my hands, then my rumbling stomach." He quickly gulped down the end of the brownie. It tasted awful, but he felt he had to be polite.

"I can't believe I did something that dumb," she moaned, grabbing the baggie back from him.

"Don't worry about it. What you lack in culinary ability, you make up for with all that nail equipment. You know, you give a mean manicure," he said, wiggling his fingers in the air. "I mean, I wouldn't even confess to letting you do this to me, but it does look terrific." He reached for another brownie.

"Pres, don't eat any more. They're too disgusting."

"No, really, I kind of like 'em this way. Don't want to put on a lot of pounds while I'm just lying 'round in bed not exercising, right? So brownies without sugar are the solution."

He was touched by the thought that this girl would have gone out of her way to do two such nice things for him. When he'd first met Tara, he took her for a pampered, spoiled kid who wouldn't walk when she could ride, or wear anything that wasn't stylish, impressive, and expensive. But whether it was the positive effects of cheerleading or something else, she had changed substantially since he'd first met her. This Tara actually cared about other people — and Pres liked the change.

"You give those back to me. I'll feed them to the dog." She giggled.

"No way. These are *my* brownies and I'll stand by them to the death," Pres said stoically.

They were both laughing over this when there was a knock on the door and Olivia stuck her head in. "Hi, guys. What's up?"

"It's feeding time at the zoo." Pres chuckled. "Here, have one of these yummy brownies Tara made me."

Olivia looked at him. "Tara, in the kitchen? Cooking? You're pulling both my legs and arms."

"Don't you dare eat that," Tara yelped, snatching the baggie away, before Olivia could touch it. "I'm removing these from the premises before they do any severe damage to life, limb, or property. See you tomorrow, Pres." She smiled, giving his hand a gentle pat. "Say, they do look good," she said, grinning. "Take care."

When she'd closed the door behind her, Olivia sat down on the side of the bed. "She didn't really make brownies, did she?" she asked.

"Honest and true," Pres said. "They were sort of unusual. . . . Well, maybe she can use a couple of them for the wolf's eyes."

"Oh, I get it." Olivia nodded wisely. "So, how's physical therapy going?" she demanded, quickly changing the subject.

Pres rolled his head from side to side to relax the tension between his shoulder blades. "I don't know. I haven't gone yet."

"Well, but Connie's told you all the stuff you're going to do, right?"

"Ah, actually . . . no. She came to see me a couple of times, but I was sleeping." He cleared his throat and reached for a magazine on his bedside table, but Olivia whipped it away from him.

"Why are you avoiding this subject?" she asked him suspiciously.

"What do you mean? I'm not avoiding anything."

"Look, this isn't a vacation," she said sternly. "You're here to work."

Suddenly, Pres's eyes flashed. "I'm here to get well! And what business is it of yours, if you don't mind my asking?"

It was Olivia's turn to be angry. "Don't you yell at me. I have every right to tell you how to recuperate, because I know from firsthand experience. I spent years in hospital beds — and not because it was any fun."

"You were a kid — "

"And I knew what was at stake. Do you?"

He was slapped in the face by her question. He had already asked it of himself. And yes, he realized exactly what was at stake.

"The longer you resist, Pres, the longer it's going to take. After you fall off, you have to get back up on that horse again fast, otherwise you miss your chance. And as a dear friend of yours — " she paused for breath in her tirade " — I feel obliged to tell you that you are doing yourself no good at all by sitting around on your duff."

"Olivia," Pres started slowly, as though he were explaining a very difficult concept to a child, "you have to understand that I was in a major car crash a few weeks ago. I'm in no condition to go running around like a nut."

Olivia's answer was to stand up, move the chair out of her way, and reach up with flattened palms. She leaned backward, slowly arching into a wheel. Then, effortlessly, she did a back walk-over, ending right beside his bed. "When I was lying in bed, that was my goal — to be able to do *that*. I wasn't strong enough for a long time. I fell again and again. I had to work on my arms, my legs, my back. Mostly, I had to work on my spirit. But I cared enough to give the very best, Pres. I hope you do, too."

With that, she snatched up her practice bag and her parka and marched out of the room, her spine tight and rigid, her mouth set in a grim line.

Mary Ellen and David Duffy were sitting in the reception room, waiting for her. They had been laughing about something, but when they saw Olivia's expression, they both sobered up immediately.

"What's wrong?" Mary Ellen jumped to her feet, all the color suddenly draining from her face. "Is something wrong with Pres?"

"Nothing that he can't cure," Olivia said enigmatically.

"What happened between you two?" Duffy wanted to know.

"Oh, he's no worse than yesterday," Olivia assured her friend. "But he's no better, either."

"Well, he did just survive two tons of metal crashing down on his body. What do you expect?" Mary Ellen demanded. She shook her head at Olivia.

"I'd expect that at the very least, he'd *want* to get well. But he doesn't."

"Well, I never heard anything so ridiculous in my entire life," Mary Ellen retorted. She turned her back on Olivia and started down the hall toward Pres's room.

"I'm not talking about what happened to him physically," Olivia said to Duffy when Mary Ellen was out of earshot.

"Then what?" he asked.

Olivia plunked herself down in one of the plastic seats and stared off into space. "That guy used to be a fireball — you couldn't stop him. He was so determined, so sure he could conquer the world. But now he won't do a thing. He won't even try! He acts like he's in that bed for good. I don't know what's happened to him."

"You're expecting an awful lot from a guy who could have been wiped out in that accident," Duffy pointed out. "I mean, Olivia, he's lucky he made it. Give him time. He'll come around."

"You don't understand," she said in a feverish tone. "I've been there, I know. You don't get up and walk if you don't want to. And he doesn't."

"You're full of donkey dust, that's what you are." Duffy smiled, taking her by the arm. "Too much mascot-building. C'mon, let me buy you a Coke and calm you down."

Olivia went, but not without a backward glance at Pres's room. She was going to keep hammering at him until he was so furious with her, he would get up and walk. It had to work — eventually.

Mary Ellen ran into Pres's room, nearly frantic. "What is it, Pres? Why was Olivia so upset?"

"Hi, Mary Ellen! Oh, *her* — well, you know. . . ." Pres looked up from his magazine. "She means well, but she's all wet. She thinks everybody functions like her, like a machine. Don't get me wrong — I've always admired her, but sometimes she's too much. She never gives another guy a break. So, tell me all about modeling and school." He leaned back on the pillows, settling in.

"When she came out, I had this feeling. . . ." Mary Ellen's eyes scoured his face as she leaned over to kiss him. "Oh, Pres, I wish you'd get well soon."

"Yeah, me, too, sweetie," he shrugged. "But it's not going to happen tomorrow, from what the doctors tell me. We have to have patience. Well, I'm waiting. Give me all the good news that's fit to print — and some that isn't." It felt good to be entertained, to be cared about and taken care of by this lovely girl.

"Okay, well . . . the store got in a new shipment of sweaters from England. Mrs. Gunderson thinks they're going to sell really well, and. . . ." Her voice trailed off lamely. "Pres, you can't really want to hear about this."

He reached up and touched her soft golden hair. "I'm interested in you, period. And that means what you do."

"But we have more important things to go over, like what we're going to do to make the house more comfortable for you to live in when you get home. I was thinking of calling a carpenter and having him put up a ramp next to the front steps for the wheelchair."

This was the first time she had broached the subject of what would happen after the hospital. The doctors had told her that they wanted to release Pres as soon as he was out of traction, that it would be better for him to come to the hospital every day for physical therapy, but to live at home.

"Oh, well, yeah, sure . . . if you like. But my mom kind of thought that when I first got out I should stay with them."

"Oh, Pres, no — "

"But you've got a busy life now, Mary Ellen. And Mom's there alone all day with the maid, and they were thinking about hiring a private nurse — " He stopped when he saw that she wasn't taking this very well.

"Sweetie, it's only for a while. She wants to baby me a little. And right now, that sounds good to me. You know what my problem always was? I was just too wrapped up in tomorrow, in shooting down all my ducks before I'd even lined them up in a row. Maybe this accident will turn out to be all for the best," he said as though he really meant it. "It'll give me time to just lie back and take stock. So, I'll stay with Mom till I get the hang of things. It'll be easier on you that way."

"I don't want it easier!" she exclaimed. "I'm your wife and I want you with me."

"Okay, all right, don't get all hot under the collar," Pres said. "You can do the ramp if you think it's a good idea. How about this? I'll hang around my mom's until I can't stand it anymore, and then you can whisk me away on your white horse."

"Don't joke about this, Pres. I'm serious." Suddenly, Olivia's words came back to her. *He doesn't want to get well.* It was a peculiar thought, but it sort of made sense. He'd avoided seeing the physical therapist or returning any of her phone calls. Then, this business about Mary Ellen coming to get him on a white horse, like she was some knight in shining armor who could save him. From what? From himself, perhaps?

"I'm serious, too," he said, taking her hands in his. "And I'm also really beat. Amazing how lying around makes you so tired. Go on home, sweetie. I'll give it all some thought and we'll hash it out tomorrow."

"Okay," she agreed. But as she kissed him good night and softly closed the door behind her, she felt that tension in her stomach again. If he didn't want help, and he wouldn't help himself, she was going to have to do something drastic. She walked out of the hospital, and the feeling of sadness that enveloped her was almost overwhelming.

Pres lay back against the covers and closed his eyes as soon as she had gone. All this company was getting to him. Except for Mary Ellen, of course, he'd have to ask that his pals rotate. It was just too hard keeping up a front for this many people.

"May I come in?" asked a voice at the door.

His eyes shot open, then closed when he saw who it was. "Not now. I'm resting."

"You're rested enough," Connie Lapino said curtly. "Let's talk." When he averted his eyes, she went on. "It couldn't hurt. At least I can describe the course of therapy and you could hear me out, see how it sounds to you."

"Yeah, maybe." He smiled.

"No, not maybe. Really." She moved around his room like a butterfly, darting here and there, shutting the door, touching a vase of flowers, repositioning a pillow beside him. "How have you been doing, Pres? Please answer the question truthfully — don't talk nice to make me feel better."

He was immediately put off guard. "Why should I want to make *you* feel better?"

"Because then I'll go away and leave you alone." She walked over to the traction apparatus and reached up toward his leg. He flinched as though she had yanked at it. "Cool down, boy. I'm not in the business of creating pain. I try to take it away."

"You're pressuring me," he said nervously.

"Sure I am. I've tried waiting for you to come around to my way of thinking, but it hasn't worked. So I'm going for the hard-line technique.

I promise, you don't have to do anything you don't want to do. Why do you mistrust me so, Pres?" she asked, suddenly seeing the panic in his eyes.

"I'm not ready for physical therapy," he said defensively.

"And you don't think you'll be ready a week from now, or a month from now, either. You know, you're not the first kid I've seen in this situation — scared stiff."

"I am not!" he barked. But he pushed back his pillow protectively, shying away as she walked toward him and began to unhook his legs from the apparatus above his bed.

"You're going to feel a little pressure now. All right, gently," she said, placing one leg at a time down on the bed. She stood back. "How's that?" she asked.

He let his breath out slowly. "Okay . . . I guess."

"May I continue? I just want to see what the limitations of movement are." She didn't go toward him until he nodded his assent. Then she took his right leg in its cast along her arm and rotated it in a small semi-circle, and put it down again. When he didn't object, she did the same with the left.

"Well?" he demanded.

"Well, it's fortunate that all your bones didn't fracture into tiny pieces. The breaks you did have are clean and neat, and your knees are worthy of a linebacker. You couldn't put any weight on anything right now, of course, but I predict that your breaks should be completely mended in another couple of weeks or so."

"Hey, neat!" His face brightened considerably. "So I'm going to be fine, then. I can walk and run just like I always did."

"Oh, I didn't say anything about walking." She crossed her arms on her chest and stared hard at him. "We still don't know the extent of your spinal injury, Pres. And it's difficult to determine that until the course of therapy begins. What we have to do is keep you moving."

"They've been moving me a lot," Pres insisted. "They come in and turn me like a pig on a spit every few hours, so I won't get bedsores."

"But, as an athlete, you must realize that we're not just worried about your skin, Pres. Other areas of your body degenerate if you don't work on them. And you haven't been. Your joints and tendons, particularly your muscles, are in pretty weak shape now. So I want to start you on the easy stuff, even with the casts still on. It's important that when your bones are healed, your muscles will be in shape to support them. After that, it all depends on you." She picked up his right leg and put it back in traction.

"Okay, so what do I have to do?" he asked as though he didn't really care.

"Everything. Some of it mental, a lot of it physical."

"No problem," he said casually. "Ask my coach. She'll tell you I'm not a shirker." He wasn't sure that he really liked Connie, but he saw her now as a means to an end.

"Well, it's good to hear that. But I have to tell you that for a very long time, you won't see a bit of progress at all. And then, just when you see a breakthrough, you'll slip backward. You'll feel defeated and depressed. Are you able to take that, and keep going? That's what I have to know before we get started."

He felt a surge of intense longing to get up off the bed and walk out of the room, just to prove to her that he could do it. He clenched his fists and raised his head up off the pillow for a minute, feeling his neck muscles strain. Then, exhausted, he let his head flop back. "Just leave me alone, will you?" He turned his head away from her.

"Of course." She nodded. "I'll get your answer some other time."

When he turned back, she was gone. He tried again to lift his torso as far as it would go, but it was impossible.

CHAPTER

8

Patrick shifted his weight again, leaning against the side of the phone booth. He grimaced at Jessica as he talked to the person on the other end of the line. "Hey, man, I have to get that car back this week. Not next week. It's really important."

He listened while the mechanic made his excuses yet another time, and then cut in, "That's my buddy's car — the guy who was in the accident, remember? I told him the Porsche would be in top shape, ready to go, when he got out of the hospital. And I told you the same thing when I had the wreck towed over. You made me a promise, man. I'm holding you to it. Mr. Tilford is going to be real upset when he finds out you've broken your promise."

There was a long pause, and then a sigh. The mechanic knew he was beat.

"You will?" Patrick smiled at Jessica and stood

up straight. "That's fantastic. Hey, thanks again." He replaced the receiver and gave Jessica the thumbs-up sign.

"Well, I did it." He grinned, leading her back toward his moving van.

"No, the Tilford name did it," she corrected him. "But who cares so long as it's done?"

Patrick helped her up into the van and ran around to the driver's side. He'd been the one to suggest to the cheerleaders that what Pres needed was the reassurance of seeing the car in one piece again. "If that heap of nuts and bolts can make it, then so can he," he'd explained to Mary Ellen. Her personal feeling was that she never wanted to see the thing again in her life, but she realized that Patrick knew what he was talking about. There were times when she thought that her husband loved the car more than his wife.

"When's he due to arrive at the ancestral mansion?" Jessica asked, as they drove off down the street toward Hope's house.

"Tomorrow noon. We'll pick up the kids and be there in time to greet him." He looked across at her flushed cheeks and bright eyes. "Say, good lookin', don't be mad at yourself. You really didn't do anything wrong."

"But I didn't visit him in the hospital since the day after he was admitted," Jessica muttered. "He probably thinks I'm a creep."

"He understands how you feel about hospitals," Patrick countered. "You're the only one honest enough to admit it."

"Don't cover up for me." She sighed.

His response was to take her heart-shaped face

in his hands and caress it softly. "I can if I want to. You know, Jessica, there are other ways of being a good friend. And you seem to know all of them." Then he kissed her softly on the lips, his dark hair lightly brushing her forehead.

She threw her arms around his neck and pulled him closer. "You're very good to me." She sighed. "Even when I don't deserve it."

"I can't help it. I'm crazy about you. Anyhow, to return to the subject, just for a second," he said, smiling as he reluctantly drew away from her and put his key in the ignition, "Pres told me yesterday that if he'd had any more regular visitors to deal with, he would have gone bananas."

Jessica nodded, seeming to accept his statement — and the convenient excuse it offered for her behavior. That night, as she did her prebed exercises, stretching and bending, she realized it wasn't going to be easy for her to look Pres Tilford in the eye tomorrow and tell him how great he was doing.

The rest of the cheerleaders and Kate and Duffy were sitting on Hope's porch when the van drove up. Sean had a bunch of helium balloons, Tara was carrying a giant chocolate cake (bought, not homemade), Kate had an inflatable six-foot alligator (deflated), Olivia and Duffy had a dozen yellow roses, Peter had a stack of records, and Hope had a collection of the latest magazines. Only Patrick's moving van would have fit all the stuff they were carting around.

"The brigade is ready, I see." Jessica grinned as Patrick helped load the back of the truck.

"We're prepared, like boy scouts, to give Pres the encouragement of a lifetime." Sean nodded. "Months of experience as cheerleaders are finally paying off."

"Yeah, you better ask Ardith Engborg about that," Kate smirked.

They all piled into the van and Patrick pulled out, driving toward Pres's parents' home. He took the road around the lake slowly, then continued on out to Fable Point.

The house looked quiet, deserted. But in another moment, the group heard the thrum of a motor coming up around the point, and soon they saw the nose of a black minivan pulling up the drive.

The cheerleaders surrounded the car, making way for the chauffeur who opened the back and pulled out a ramp. Mr. and Mrs. Tilford emerged from the car.

A white-uniformed nurse came next, an older woman with an officious manner who ordered everyone out of her way. "All right, Steve, wheel him down." The chauffeur went back into the car and the cheerleaders could see him maneuvering Pres's wheelchair onto the ramp. He worked some mechanism on the side of the van that lowered the ramp down to street level, and Pres emerged, smiling, into the sunlight.

"Hey, good buddy," Sean exclaimed, rushing over to pump his friend's hand. "Nice to have you back."

"Pres, how are you feeling?" Jessica said shyly.

"You look really fine," Tara said, chuckling,

"for someone who hasn't seen the light of day in weeks."

"Oh, Pres, it's only a matter of a little more time now," Hope told him. "I spoke to my father about it, and his colleagues at the medical center say you're going to do just fine after you get into therapy."

"Which is supposed to be this week, I hear." Olivia nodded.

Mary Ellen suddenly emerged from the van and took her place by Pres's wheelchair. She turned him away from the cheerleaders with a warning look at Olivia. "We have everything ready for you, darling," she told Pres. "You should see the spread your mother put out. I told her we weren't an army, just a bunch of kids, but she said it was the same thing."

Pres hung onto her hand, drinking in the sight of his friends and the house and the sky and trees. "It's all great, folks. This is too much. You don't know how happy I am to get out of that place."

"Wait, wait just a sec!" Patrick said, as he heard another engine coming up the road. "We have another surprise in store for you."

A green and yellow tow truck came into view, chugging up toward the Tilford house. Pres's eyes grew wide, then wider as he saw what was attached to the back of the truck. "No, man, I don't believe it." He looked like he'd seen a ghost.

Mary Ellen held his hand tighter as the mechanic got out of the truck and unhitched the shiny red Porsche from the rig. There wasn't a scratch on it.

"Got a message to deliver this to the Tilford

residence," the man said. "Who gets the bill? It's a whopper."

Mr. Tilford, who had been standing by watching the proceedings, hurriedly came up to the man and took the piece of paper he handed him. Without even glancing at it, he shoved it into his pocket, then disappeared, shaking his head, inside the house.

"Oh, boy. Oh, wow." Pres breathlessly wheeled his chair toward the car. He ran his hands over the bumper, then moved around so that he could open the door on the driver's side and examine the dashboard. When he turned back around to his friends, there were tears in his eyes.

"So, when are you taking one of us for a drive around the lake?" Tara asked, wondering if it was okay to joke about something like that.

Pres licked his lips and closed his eyes. "Hey, well, I don't know." He reached in and pulled the key out of the ignition, rubbing it between his palms as though he thought a genie might spring out and offer him three wishes. "Sweetie," he said softly to Mary Ellen, "here, you take her home to our house and put her in the garage, okay?"

Mary Ellen just stared at him. "You don't mean it."

"Sure. Go on. Take her now. Please." It was as if it was too painful for him to have the car around where he might catch sight of it if he glanced out the window.

"But Pres. . . ." She glanced over at Patrick. He knew that Pres never let anyone get behind the wheel of his car without a long, involved discussion. Mary Ellen had teased him countless times about having it written into her marriage contract that she got to drive the car at least once without having to ask permission in the next twenty years or before it had to be put out to pasture, whichever came first. Pres had never thought her suggestion was very funny.

"It's okay, honey. I trust you," Pres said quietly. He pressed the key into her hand. "Hurry back, okay?" Then he wheeled himself away toward the house and allowed the chauffeur and the private nurse to help him inside. He didn't even hear Mary Ellen start up the engine, listen to it hum, and then tool off down the road.

Sean kicked a pebble in the road, then started toward the house behind Kate and Olivia. This was a terrible turn of events. He had always looked up to Pres, tried to emulate him, felt that he could do no wrong. He'd been such a great cheerleader, and when Sean had started with the squad in the fall, it was the image of Pres he always had in front of him as he himself performed. He was trying, consciously, to be just as terrific an athlete as his predecessor had been. The greatest compliment he ever received was when some girl told him she'd mistaken him for Pres out there on the court.

Before Pres got married, Sean had kept tabs on the hearts his friend had broken — or, at least, had wounded slightly. Sean had dated a couple of girls after they'd broken up with his friend, and he knew that the memory of Pres Tilford died hard. The guy was such a knockout, in more ways than one. He was sexy, he was smart, he was funny, and he knew what he wanted out of life.

The business about the car, though, set Sean back on his heels. If Pres could just allow Mary Ellen to take over in what had been one of *the* most important areas of his life, then he wasn't functioning on all cylinders. This wasn't the person Sean had looked up to. As a matter of fact, it was hard to see that he had anything in common with Pres at all right now. It made him nervous just seeing the guy's year-round tan faded to a pasty white after weeks in bed. And it certainly gave him the willies to see Pres hand over the keys to that Porsche to Mary Ellen.

"Come on in, children," Mrs. Tilford was saying when he reached the front door of the house. "Preston should rest, of course. It's taken so much out of him, traveling from the hospital. But you're all welcome to come on into the dining room and have something to eat, while my poor boy lies down for a while."

"That's okay, mother," Pres said quickly, wheeling himself ahead of her. "I'm here and I'm starved, and I can rest later. I say, let the party begin!"

Olivia and Duffy decided to explore while the others glommed onto the food. They wandered out of the dining room and down the hall to the formal parlor, replete with two antique horsehair sofas and a chandelier that must have had about a thousand crystal facets. It was the stuffiest room either of them had ever seen.

"Really something, these Tilfords." Duffy chuckled, picking up a tiny porcelain figurine from the mantelpiece. "All this dough, and they can't buy themselves happiness."

"What you mean is, they'd probably chuck it all and go live in a shack if they could have their son up and around again," Olivia said.

"Exactly. Well, we're trying, aren't we? What do you think would do it, Olivia?" he asked. "What about cornering the wolf they've sighted up in the hills and sticking him in Pres's bedroom in the middle of the night. Think the shock might do him good?"

"Sure." Olivia laughed. "But it would kill the wolf."

Duffy grabbed her by the shoulders and gave her a kiss. He looked down at her small, delicate face, the tiny body encased in an oversized blue ski sweater with white stars around the yoke. Just the sight of her made him feel good. "You worry too much," he said affectionately, rubbing one thumb absently over her eyebrow to smooth it.

"So how do you intend to make me stop?" she challenged him, her brown eyes teasing.

"I don't know. How's this to take away trouble and care?" He folded her back into his arms, and this time they just hugged, exchanging warm feelings that went beyond friendship. They spent so much time together these days, they were beginning to feel like one person.

"We better get back," Olivia suggested, "before they send a search party."

"In a house this size, they might have to." Duffy grinned. They linked arms, and together they skipped down the hall and back to the dining room.

Mrs. Tilford and the private nurse were hovering over Pres when they returned. Pres, not one to be easily smothered, had parked himself in front of the huge mahogany table to survey the spread.

"I'll make you a plate, Pres," Tara offered, jumping ahead of the others and heaping a plate with cold cuts, different salads, and a big handful of potato chips.

"Sean, why don't you get me something to eat?" Kate asked him, drawing him to the other side of the table.

"Oh, Pres, dear." Mrs. Tilford walked over to her son. "I only want you eating healthy things now. Lots of protein for my poor baby. You have to get your strength back, you know."

"Right, Mom." Pres was not in the mood to make waves.

But Sean was getting a little hot under the collar. First the car, now putting up with his mother's nonsense. "You want me to fix you a plate?" he said to Kate. "I will. For a price. All I want is just a little information on a certain subject."

"I thought we agreed not to discuss that," Kate growled.

"Well, I just *un*agreed. Time's getting short, Katie." He knew that this line of questioning made Kate mad, but he was upset, too. It wasn't fair that such a great guy should be stuck in a wheelchair.

"Oh, forget it. Just forget it." Kate grabbed a piece of roast beef and stuffed it into her mouth, then stomped over to David Duffy.

Sean sighed and moved closer to Hope and

106

Peter. They were standing with Mrs. Tilford and the private nurse, right near Pres.

"I'm not sure the doctors here know everything," he heard the nurse say. "You and your husband might consider sending Pres to the Mayo Clinic for a while. He'd have the best of care."

"Do you think so?" Mrs. Tilford worried. "I really wanted the boy home until he's fully recuperated, but — "

"Mrs. Tilford," Hope broke in, "Haven Lake Medical Center has some of the best physicians in the country. If they say that your son is coming along fine, then why don't you trust them?"

"Mayo is an internationally renowned facility," the nurse countered. "If Preston is ever to walk again — "

Sean couldn't take any more. He marched purposefully up to Pres, who was deep in conversation with Tara, Jessica, Patrick, and Olivia, and he wheeled him away, out the door, down the hall, and into the study that was just off the dining room. He turned to Pres with an intense expression on his face.

"You've got to get out of this house, man," Sean demanded.

Pres looked puzzled. "What?"

"There's too much weirdness going on here."

Pres gave him a lopsided smile. "I'm sorry. It's the only kind of party my mother knows how to throw."

"C'mon, man, you know what I mean. I am sick and tired of everybody mooning around you. It's rubbing off." Sean walked over to the wheelchair and gave it a kick. "You look lousy."

"Thanks a lot."

"But you don't have to stay that way. Some good times, a few laughs, and you'll be back on your feet again. Literally. Now, I have a plan — see how you like it. First of all, you need something to do with your spare time. Your dad can spare you at the office for a while, right?"

"I guess so." Pres grinned.

"Okay, I'm putting you on mascot duty. We're getting down to the wire on this thing, and we could use all the help we can get. Diana might even behave around you. So consider yourself recruited. Then, next weekend. I think you need to get away, take a trip somewhere. You talk it over with Mary Ellen. Maybe you and Patrick and Peter and I can take off in the van, go ice-fishing. How about it? Then there's a game the following Friday, and after that — "

"Hey, hey! Stop just a second." Pres shook his head. "You seem to be forgetting something, Sean. It's real nice of you to want to include me in all this stuff, but I can't." He looked down at his limp legs. "I just can't."

"Who says? Who told you you couldn't do lots of stuff from that chair? And then, after you've been in therapy for a while — "

"That's enough." Pres abruptly wheeled himself around and started for the door. "I've had everybody on my back about this, and I'm fed up. What I need right now is rest, see? I'm going to lay back, take it easy, and catch up on my TV game shows. And that's about the most strenuous activity I've got planned right now."

Sean walked around in front of him, holding

108

onto the wheelchair so that Pres couldn't advance forward. "Oh, I see. This is the end, right? Is that what you're telling me? I didn't know you'd given up."

"I haven't — "

"I had to hear it from you. You sit around and let nurses and doctors make decisions about your life. What is this? Don't you think *you* deserve to be in charge of your life?"

"Deserve? Yes. Am I able to be? Well, that's anybody's guess."

"You're going to get back on your feet," Sean said between clenched teeth.

Pres looked at Sean curiously. "Yeah, who's gonna make me?"

"I am," Sean said decisively. "I'll be here after practice to pick you up and take you to therapy. Or to the school. Or to a party. I'll come during my lunch hour and drag you out of this house, kicking and screaming — whatever. You're going to walk again whether you like it or not." He stalked out of the room just as Kate and Olivia were coming in to find out where the guys were.

"What's gotten into him?" Kate asked.

Pres looked down the hall after his friend. "The man's got a mission," he said thoughtfully. "And I'm it."

CHAPTER

9

Diana was feeling very pleased with herself. Here she had almost four weeks left before the Rivals Game, and the wolf was really taking shape. It had a wonderful grizzled gray head, with holes cut for two of the biggest, blackest eyes that Tommy Bridgeman could make and motorize; its claws had been painted a brilliant Chinese red, just for dramatic effect; and its body was mean and lean — just like the team it was supposed to represent. The second tail that Hope had put together was even better than the first. Excellent!

They were ready to put it to the test. Four layers of protective basecoat, two of oil-based paint, and two more of polyurethane on top. If that didn't protect the animal from the elements, nothing would. And this afternoon, thanks to the weather, they could send it off on its maiden voyage. If the wolf could withstand the rain and thunder and lightning going on outside the shop window at that very moment, it could take the worst of a snowy Tarenton football game.

It would be nice, Diana thought, to take credit for the whole thing, but it would be hard to get away with that with so many pesky cheerleaders hanging around. Still, she intended to sign her work at the end — maybe a small, delicate *Diana Tucker* scratched in lavender ink in the crook of the wolf's neck. Nobody on the committee would have to know. But she'd know, and she would see to it that a friend of hers on the yearbook committee knew. Posterity would remember Diana as being responsible for one of Tarenton High's greatest achievements.

What would be even better was the story about how she had rescued the poor beast from the jaws of doom. She smiled to herself as she surveyed the work in progress. Alison was putting an additional application of polyurethane lacquer on each joint of the animal; Tara and Mike were coating the bottoms of the paws with a thin chemical solution that dried as hard and waterproof as rubber. Gracie, Olivia, and Hope were over in the corner, weaving numerous cut-up wigs for the pelt that would be glued and sewn on the final, painted product.

She glanced over at the third group — Sean, Peter, Beef, and Jim — in annoyance when she heard the crackle of a radio. Sean was flipping the dials on the boom box he'd brought along, trying to find a good station.

"Would you mind?" Diana asked him. "I'm trying to think."

111

"Well, that does take a lot of effort, I'll admit," Sean grinned.

There was silence in the shop as everyone tried not to laugh. It was always a big mistake to give Diana something to hold a grudge over. Tara stuffed a knuckle into her mouth, but then she saw Sean making faces at her out of the corner of her eye, and she couldn't hold back any longer. A huge guffaw burst out of her. Then another. Finally, she was laughing so uncontrollably, she couldn't stop. She coughed and wheezed, and when she lost her breath and started to choke, she submitted to Sean pounding her on the back.

"She must have swallowed the wrong way or something. She needs a drink of water," Sean explained to the others, dragging Tara out of the shop.

"Well, are we doing the test today or not?" Olivia demanded, to get the attention away from her two unruly squad members. "If we're going to see if the mascot sinks or swims, this is the time. Look at that rain coming down!"

Diana glanced out the window and nodded. "Get the wolf on the dolly, Beef. We'll leave it in the middle of the playing field for an hour. C'mon, everyone, let's get this thing ready to roll!"

As the others threw on their raincoats and hats, Sean got Tara to the water fountain. She had calmed down considerably, but her face was beet red and her breathing sounded like a locomotive engine after a long, arduous trip.

"Well, that's one mark against you in her black book." Sean nodded, crossing his arms over his chest and leaning against the wall.

"What do you mean, *against me*? You've done nothing but provoke her since we started this project," Tara insisted. She leaned down for a drink, then stood up, wiping the tears of mirth from her eyes. Her mascara was smeared, but she couldn't worry about that now. "Maybe you should let the rest of us finish the wolf. You could get out of Diana's hair and concentrate on the big project," Tara suggested.

"Pres," Sean said thoughtfully.

"Right. How many days has he been home now? Mary Ellen says he sleeps till noon, then watches the soaps, reads the paper, and plays Solitaire till dinner. It's all wrong, Sean. I know there has to be something we can do to motivate him, but what? The longer he stays in bed, the less chance he has of getting up again. And I refuse to believe he wants to be a cripple for the rest of his life."

She sat down on the floor beside the water fountain, resting her chin in her cupped hands. "I would have thought that having his friends to spur him on would make a difference, but it hasn't. Even Mary Ellen. He's so in love with her — at least he *was* — and she can't even talk to him now. You look at them when they're together, and they're like strangers." She shuddered slightly, and then whispered, "I can't imagine what I'd do if it were me."

Sean slid down beside her, taking her hand. "I know what you mean. But what you were saying just now, about friends. I wonder — "

They were interrupted by a hulking shadow crossing over them, blocking the fluorescent hallway light. It was Beef. "Ah, Diana wants to know if you're coming back. She has an announcement," he said, almost apologetically.

"Oh, what a bore. Well, all right," Tara grunted, getting up and brushing off the back of her pleated skirt.

Diana had the group back from the playing field, assembled around her in a circle. Olivia gave the two escapees a warning look, and Hope and Peter made room for them on the floor.

"Now, is everyone here?" Diana did a quick head count, coming up one short. "Oh, I forgot," she smirked, flipping her perfectly curled blonde hair over one shoulder. "One of our number is always missing. I guess I don't have to ask where Jessica is today — off on her mission of charity."

"You know, Diana," Peter said testily, "some things are just a little more important than papier-mâché."

"Like cheerleading," she suggested, knowing perfectly well that he was talking about Pres.

"Like human beings," Tara answered back. "But you wouldn't know anything about that."

Diana shrugged. "Everyone's entitled to her opinion, no matter how misguided. You can think whatever you'd like about me. And in turn, I suppose I can think what I want about you." She turned on the five of them, clustered in one corner.

"For instance?" Olivia asked pointedly.

"For instance, I think that some of us in this room — I wouldn't dream of mentioning names — are less than totally loyal and committed to Tarenton High."

None of the cheerleaders bothered to comment. They all knew what Diana was getting at.

"We had hoped, a while back, that one member of our committee might be instrumental in getting a piece of vital information — that is, the nature of the rival team's mascot."

All eyes in the room drifted toward Sean, then backed away.

"But perhaps it was too much to expect." Diana sighed. She sat down on a folding chair, neatly crossing her legs. Then she crossed her hands on her knee. "So we have to take action. Mike and Jim, I'm assigning you to go out into the fray and bring back results. Just what exactly is St. Cloud cooking up, and, more important, how good does it look?"

"Ah, Diana — " Mike began, but she overrode him.

"I don't care what you have to do to procure these facts. Is that clear? Just get them." She raised her voice and looked straight at Sean. "If you try to block me by letting on to your girl friend, I'll deny everything. And if you already know what their mascot is — as I suspect you do — it won't help a bit for you to keep the secret any longer."

Sean rubbed his forehead wearily. "Okay, Diana. So you find out. Big deal. There's not a whole lot you can do about it."

A delighted smile spread across Diana's face. "Oh, really? Well, I just might have a few tricks left up my sleeve that you don't know about."

Olivia stood up, outraged. "If you're contemplating sabotage, you better just forget it. The

115

whole notion of the Rivals Game is honest, above-board competition, Diana. You can't mess up someone else's mascot so you'll win. That's — that's just disgusting."

"What's really disgusting," Diana said pointedly, "is fraternizing with the enemy. It's difficult for me to believe that a Tarenton High student, and a student on the mascot committee, no less!" — she glared at Sean as she said this — "would be dating the committee chairman of the opposition school."

Sean grabbed his practice bag and got to his feet, smiling. "I'm really thankful to you, Diana, to have given me this opportunity. I resign. How about that? I am no longer a member of this committee, which means that I am no longer obligated to keep secrets of either side."

Without a backward glance, he walked out of the shop.

Diana looked after him with an expression of triumph on her face. "Well, boys and girls," she breathed softly, "it's all out in the open now. Everyone for himself. The sky's the limit. Jim, Mike, get busy on that assignment, will you? The rest of you, I think it's about time we put the wolf to bed for the night. You four, get out there and bring him inside."

She had pointed, of course, to the remaining four cheerleaders, who grabbed their rain gear to go back out into the storm.

"Sean was right," Hope grumbled, as she pushed the dolly and Peter and Olivia pulled it across the slick, wet grass. "We should all quit."

"If we do, nobody monitors Diana. And if she

116

does something really despicable, St. Cloud might just win by default," Tara pointed out, her red hair streaming with raindrops. She steered the dolly as the others eased it onto the pavement that led to the shop door. "I guess we stick it out." She sighed.

Peter picked Hope up early the next morning, so they'd have a head start on their way to school. Duffy did the same for Olivia; Patrick did the same for Jessica. They all knew that the traffic was sure to be terrible, given the storm the previous night. The roads were congested, slippery, and generally awful.

Sean and Tara pulled into the Tarenton High lot at about the same time as the others. They had been arguing about Kate, and about Sean's valiant gesture the previous day, and what the best way to handle the situation was, but they stopped as soon as they noticed the crowd around the front steps of the high school.

"What's going on?" Tara demanded, jumping out of the car even before Sean could park.

"Wait for me," he insisted, as he pulled the key from the ignition and ran after her.

Some of the students were laughing, some were shaking their heads. There were teachers in the group, too, including Ardith Engborg, and the principal, Mrs. Oetjen. Diana, standing at the top of the steps, her blonde hair flying every which way in the wind, was white-faced with rage and indignation.

"I can't imagine how this happened, Mrs. Oetjen," Diana was saying as Sean and Tara joined Patrick and Jessica at the base of the steps. Hope, Olivia, and Peter were blocking their view of the object of everyone's attention. "But I promise you, I will find the person who did it and make sure he's punished."

"I thought you said you brought the mascot in after an hour," the principal quizzed her closely.

"We did, of course, and locked it up in the shop the way we always do," Olivia chimed in. As she moved back, Sean caught a glimpse of the valiant wolf who represented their school — or what was left of him. Pieces of papier mâché hung in tatters from his haunches, and his paws were a wreck from having been drenched in the rain all night. There wasn't a trace of Chinese red left on his claws.

"I don't believe this!" Tara exclaimed. "Who would have had the nerve — and the stupidity — to go in there and lug this thing out in the storm?"

Diana's eyes raked the crowd, coming to rest on Sean. "Oh, I think I have a pretty good idea."

"Don't be ridiculous, Diana," Jessica jumped to Sean's rescue, taking his right arm. "He wouldn't do anything to hurt Tarenton."

"I'd like all of you to remember that he resigned from the mascot committee in anger yesterday afternoon," Diana said, raising her voice so that the entire mass of students could hear.

"After you provoked me one time too many," Sean cut in, stalking up to her. "You know, you give me a pain, Diana."

"Come to think of it," Diana continued, as

118

though Sean hadn't spoken, "he was conveniently missing the day the tail vanished."

"Where do you get off blaming him for something that anyone could have done?" Jessica demanded, rushing to Sean's defense. "You don't have any of the facts yet."

Mrs. Oetjen, her hands on her hips, was about to tell them all to come into her office for a discussion, when a tall man with a shock of wavy blond hair and strong features stepped out of the crowd and walked up to the group. Tara instinctively moved away. It was Nick Stewart, the math teacher she had dated for a while. There was an unspoken pact between them that they would avoid one another whenever possible. Today, in the midst of a crisis, it just wasn't possible.

"It seems to me," Nick said, "that the main order of business ought to be salvaging whatever's usable of this poor beast. You kids have a lot of repairs to do before the big day. Why sit around trying to find the culprit? What you need to do is clean up this wolf, get him working again, and make sure he's the best."

"Mr. Stewart is absolutely right," Hope declared. "Let's get him inside."

As they busied themselves with the mascot, Tara took the opportunity to hurry into the school building. Although there was nothing at all between her and Nick anymore, it was just too embarrassing to have to go through the polite routine of making chitchat whenever they ran into each other. But, despite her best efforts to make it to first-period class early, Nick managed to spot her and catch up to her in the hallway.

"Say, hi!" He smiled, perfect white teeth showing as he grinned down at her.

"Hello, Nick," she said softly. No matter what, she would never be able to call him Mr. Stewart. Since their breakup, they had slowly but surely forgiven and forgotten.

"You've been making yourself scarce," he commented.

"Yes, well, I've been really busy. There's this mascot thing, you see," she began. "As well as cheering. And then, our good friend was in an accident — "

"I heard about that." Nick nodded solemnly. "Sounded really grim. How's he doing?"

Tara shrugged. "He's better, I guess. But it'll be a long time."

The bell cut them off and they stood there, not knowing what else to say. "Well," Nick finally broke the silence, "let's not both get tardy slips."

"Right." Tara nodded.

"You take care of that wolf, will you?" he joked. "Poor guy needs all the help he can get." He gave her a silly salute and then, tucking his books under his arm, he walked past her toward his classroom.

Tara wandered into English class and sat down way in the back of the room, where she hoped the teacher would overlook her. She wasn't in the mood for *Jane Eyre* today. She found her thoughts drifting back and forth, from Jane having her first interview with the mysterious Mr. Rochester, to herself standing with Nick in the hall. Then she thought about Pres, and the awful accident. She wished that Pres would trust his friends, and let them help make him well. And then her thoughts returned to Nick again, what a nice guy he was, and what a shame it was that he was a teacher.

"If I had an older sister, I'd fix them up in a minute," she murmured to herself.

"Were you making an observation about *Jane Eyre*, Tara?" the teacher asked. "And would you kindly share it with the class?"

Tara took a breath and was about to say no, but then something wonderful struck her and she said, "I think people have to trust one another. Like Jane trusts Mr. Rochester, blindly, without knowing whether he's good or bad. Because she senses that he may be all she has in the world. And if we were all that trusting, within reason of course, we might do each other a whole lot of good."

"That's quite true," the teacher noted with shock, because Tara was not one of her better students. "I can see you're deeply involved with this book. Why don't you do a special report on it, and bring it in Thursday?"

"Oh, sure, thanks," Tara grunted, wanting to scream instead. When could she possibly make time to do a special report? What in the world was she going to say? And why did she have to open her big mouth in the first place?

Hope and Peter were doing two-person stretches, warming up before practice, and Jessica and Olivia were over in the corner, practicing aerials on the minitramp, when Sean burst into the gym. Tara wandered in glumly after him.

"I've got it! Eureka!" Sean shouted to the others.

"You mean a way to fix the wolf?" Olivia asked.

"The wolf is not a subject I wish to discuss. Ever again," Sean said forcefully. "No, I'm talking about our real challenge. I've been thinking about this all day. It's brilliant, if I do say so myself."

"You mean about Pres." Tara nodded. She pulled up her leg warmers and started to do her side-to-side stretching.

"Sean, we've tried everything. Mary Ellen has tried, and so has Patrick," Jessica pointed out. "It's just not doing any good."

"I refuse to believe that. Go on, Sean," Olivia urged him.

"It kept coming back to me, this business about friends. When was Pres on top of everything? When was his life right in line? Last year, when he was a cheerleader. He was solid with five other people — just like we are now. That's what kept the man flying — that's what made him a star."

"Yes." Hope nodded. "But things have changed a lot since then."

"But his friends haven't changed, don't you see? We've thought that we should be able to make the difference, because we care about him. But what about the group that meant the most to him — last year's cheerleaders? Seeing that bunch of kids again might just be the piece that's missing from the puzzle, might make him want to throw off his chains and get out of that chair and walk!"

Olivia jumped up, clapping her hands in sheer joy. "Fantastic!" she shouted. Then she threw her arms around Sean's neck and hugged him until he demanded, laughing, that she let him go. "That's it. We'll get Walt and Angie and Nancy back from wherever they are."

"That's an incredible thought." Jessica grinned. "With Olivia and Mary Ellen, that's all of last year's squad. He'd go nuts, seeing everybody he hasn't seen in ages. What a reunion!"

"As soon as practice is over," Tara said eagerly, "we'll get hold of Mary Ellen and start making some phone calls. With all the cheerleaders together for the first time, we'd have to have a winning team. And that'd be the impetus to make him want to move again."

In a jubilant mood, the cheerleaders assembled for their practice session. Olivia led them off, as usual, but this afternoon their cartwheels were crisper, their jumps higher, and their spirits livelier than they had been in weeks.

"Who has the finest athletes?
Who's the best around?
Who has the greatest players?
That ever came to town?

Tarenton's incredible!
We are unforgettable!
Our team is out to win!

Win one!
Win two!
How do we do it?

What do we do?

Together we're unbeatable!
We're simply undefeatable!
YAY, Tarenton!
Yay, team!"

Almost as one body, the six cheerleaders leaped joyfully into the air, their arms raised in celebration. They were going to bring their friend back. They knew it.

CHAPTER

Mary Ellen wandered from one display to the next in Marnie's, absently stroking the lush cashmere sweaters, the brilliantly colored silk scarves, the wildly patterned socks that hung from a rack near the cash register. Business was slow that afternoon, and that was a good thing. She couldn't have modeled to save her life.

She couldn't have done much of anything, actually. She was so preoccupied, she didn't know what to do with herself. She had lost weight since the accident, and all her clothes hung on her. She could see in the mirror that she looked gaunt and pale — and older, suddenly, more mature.

The worst part, though, worse even than the constant worry about Pres getting well, was that she felt so left out. Pres was cordial to her, perfectly friendly, but like a stranger. When she came to him to caress his cheek or give him a loving kiss, he seemed, well, almost surprised. She used to love the way he would rush up behind her and plant a big kiss on her neck when she was least expecting it.

She just wasn't needed. Mrs. Tilford had everything under control, and the nurse took care of Pres all day. The cook prepared his favorite foods — which he hardly touched — and the maid kept his room in order. Mary Ellen was grateful to all the cheerleaders for coming around and keeping him company, of course, but when they were there, jabbering about school and games, she just didn't have anything to say. The only one who ever bothered to stop and talk with her was Patrick, but their only topic of conversation seemed to be how to get Pres up and about. They talked until they were blue in the face, but they still hadn't come up with a solution.

Frankly, she was sick of all the people waiting on her husband hand and foot. She had decided, finally, that Pres shouldn't be coddled anymore. And he shouldn't be in his parents' house. They treated him like a child, so he acted like one. She wanted to take care of him — yes, that was part of her reason for wanting him back home with her. But she was also beginning to think that being too nice to him was a mistake. The only way pearls ever grow is when oysters get grit inside them and get irritated, she thought as she hung up another row of costume jewelry beside the new shipment of barrettes and combs. The only way to get Pres moving was to rile him.

"Aren't you almost through for the day? We need you." A breathless voice behind her made her turn around.

"Olivia! Hi! What are you doing here? Don't you have mascot duty this afternoon?"

Olivia grinned and shook her head. "My day off. You and I have something very important to take care of. Where's your address book?"

Briefly, she told Mary Ellen the plan, and watched as her friend's face went from skepticism to curiosity to interest to excitement. Mary Ellen told Mrs. Gunderson she was leaving for the day, grabbed her model's bag and her coat, and walked out into the mall with Olivia.

"It would be wonderful *if.* . . ."

"You mean, if we can get hold of the three of them." Olivia nodded.

"And if they want to come. And if Pres is thrilled to see them. And if they can do what we haven't been able to do so far. And by the way, how do you feel about seeing Walt again?"

Olivia shrugged. When she and Walt were on the team together, they were inseparable, but it had been a first relationship for both of them. When it ended, they were both ready to move on. And Duffy was . . . well . . . he was Duffy. There was no comparison. "It'll be fine," she said truthfully.

"Oh, how great it'd be if they could all come," Mary Ellen enthused. "I've been dying for a good talk with Nancy and Angie for the longest time. And especially now. . . ."

Olivia looked at her friend, seeing the pain in her eyes. Spontaneously, she reached over and put her arms around Mary Ellen. "Especially now. Everybody's been so anxious to take care of Pres, nobody's thought to take care of you. I'm sorry, Mary Ellen. You got hurt in that accident, too."

Mary Ellen was moved by her friend's concern, but somehow she couldn't talk about that. "Hey, we don't have time to wallow in all this mushy stuff," she joked, pulling away. "We have to get to my house and make some phone calls."

Walt Manners was a freshman at Columbia, and loving big city life as well as college. In her modeling days in New York City, Mary Ellen had seen him a couple of times for dinner, and it was clear that Walt was in his element. He had never really been a small-town boy after all — he was much more at home in Manhattan than he'd ever been in Tarenton.

The guy who picked up the phone in Walt's dorm said he didn't know when he'd be back, but he'd leave the message. Olivia gave him Mary Ellen's number and hung up.

Nancy Goldstein's phone at Brown in Providence, Rhode Island, was busy, so Mary Ellen dialed Angie Poletti at Hunterdon Community College at the other end of the state. Angie had just moved to a new dorm, and her old roommate wasn't sure which one. Four wrong numbers later, Mary Ellen finally got hold of Angie.

"Well, at last!" she said triumphantly as she heard the familiar voice.

"Mary Ellen!" Angie yelled. "Is it really you? I can't believe my ears."

"Honest to goodness, it's me. Olivia's sitting right beside me."

"Oh, how neat! Boy, am I glad to hear from you. I've been meaning to get in touch, but you

128

know how it is. How's Pres? How's everybody?"

Mary Ellen took a breath. "Well, actually, that's why I'm calling."

And then, as gently as she could, she told her. It took about fifteen minutes to calm Angie down. She had always been the most emotional one of the group, and to hear that Pres was incapacitated was almost unbearable to her. Especially the part about his not wanting to do anything to help himself. The thought of him in misery made *her* miserable.

Angie was fighting back tears as she began asking a hundred questions, most of which had no answers at all. Then, in midsentence, she stopped. "Look, you have a lot to do, Mary Ellen. We'll talk when I get there. I'm taking the next train. Tell him to hang on, okay?"

As Angie hung up, Mary Ellen hugged the phone to her chest.

Olivia looked at her. "Well?"

"She's pretty fantastic. Angie was always like a sister to Pres. I know it'll do him good to see her."

Mary Ellen was about to pick up the phone again when it rang. Olivia grabbed the receiver before her friend could make a move. "I'll get this one." Olivia grinned. "Hello, Tilford residence," she answered in a formal voice, knowing full well who was on the other end.

"Oh, is it!" Walt chuckled. "And who are you, the butler?"

"Yeah, what's it to you?" Olivia joked.

"Now don't tell me, let me guess. What are you doing at Mary Ellen's house, answering her phone? Your mother has been incredibly awful lately, and you've run away from home. Pres and Mary Ellen have taken you in out of the kindness of their hearts."

"No, Walt. The real reason — "

"How about this? You've been taken hostage by some opposing cheerleading squad who happened to be standing outside Mary Ellen's house when you walked by."

"Walt! Shut up for a second, so I can talk. Pres has been in an accident," she blurted out.

"Great. Sure, that's the best one of all." Walt laughed. "Pres was in an accident, and you've volunteered to nurse him back to health."

"Yes, sort of." She stopped.

"Sounds like fun. So, what's going on? How are the cheerleaders doing? How's their captain managing the squad?"

Olivia shook her head hopelessly at Mary Ellen, then spoke into the receiver slowly and clearly. "Walt, I was telling you the truth. Pres had a car accident, and he's in a wheelchair. What we were thinking was, if we could get the old squad together for him — "

"Olivia, that's a rotten joke, which, by the way, is completely unfunny," Walt barked at her. "I was having a perfectly lovely time in the library, boning up on the fascinating field of organic chemistry, when I got your message. But if all you want to do is tell me some grisly tale of horror, I'm not biting."

"Look, what do I have to do to convince you?" Olivia yelled.

Mary Ellen walked across the room and took

the phone from her. "Walt, it's me. Olivia's telling the truth. We want you to come as soon as possible."

The understanding that they were completely serious suddenly struck him and he let out a moan. "Oh, no. Oh, for crying out loud." Then he cleared his throat. "I'll be on the next plane, Mary Ellen. Oh, would you apologize to Olivia for me? I just couldn't believe it."

"I know," Mary Ellen said with a rueful smile. "Everyday when I wake up, I still have to tell myself that it really did happen."

She was quiet for a while after hanging up with Walt. Memories rushed back to her. The six of them, laughing, happy, winning games, going to the regional competitions. The feeling of Pres's hands on her waist as he lifted her high over his shoulders, then down to a thigh stand. The sight of him, cartwheeling the length of the basketball court. The taste of his lips on hers after a game, when they were all silly and giggling and triumphant.

She shook the thoughts away and dialed Nancy again. This time, a harried voice answered, "Yes, who's this?"

"Nancy? Mary Ellen."

"Mary who?" As the realization hit her, Nancy smiled into the phone. "How *are* you? What's new in Tarenton? Oh, yes, and how's your wonderful, sexy husband?" she asked.

The news was easier to break the third time. And when Nancy didn't respond Mary Ellen rushed right on. "Look, what Olivia and I were thinking was, he needs his buddies back. Could you take off some time and fly out here? I know it's asking a lot, Nancy — "

"Mary Ellen, I'd do anything for Pres, you know that. It's just, well, this is a really awful time for me. I have a dozen papers to write, and I'm on the swim team and in the drama club, too, and we've just started this new production. I've been so busy this semester, I haven't even had time for a date! And I've been acing my courses up till now, but with all the extracurricular things I've taken on, well — " She stopped for breath and gave Mary Ellen the chance to get a word in.

"You could come for a weekend if that's all the time you can spare."

"I just don't think I could." Nancy sighed.

Olivia was making all sorts of gestures from across the room. Mary Ellen covered the receiver with her hand and whispered, "She's being difficult."

"Convince her!" was Olivia's sharp retort.

Mary Ellen sighed and nodded. "Nancy, our plan is only going to work if *all* of us are there. The point is, we were a team together once, and as a group, we could do anything. We got each other going, made up for each other's weaknesses. If one of us is missing, the whole idea falls apart. Don't you see?"

"I do, but. . . ." There was another long pause.

"Oh, well that's just wonderful," Mary Ellen was getting angry. "If all you can think of is your activities and your exciting life, if all you can think of is yourself — "

"Mary Ellen!" Nancy exclaimed. "That's not it at all. I don't see how you could believe that.

The real reason is, well, this may sound sort of lame, but I don't know that I could do anything to get Pres out of a wheelchair. We were friends and all, but I don't think I was ever that influential in making him do anything."

"That's not true. I know it's not. He always cared a lot about you, Nancy. And if you care at all about him — "

"I'll come," she agreed in a rush. "Of course I will. You know me, Mary Ellen. I take on as much stuff as I possibly can, just to prove to myself that I can do it — whether I want to or not! Maybe I've been running around like a chicken without a head because I didn't have anything as good as cheerleading, as *us*. I can't wait to see all of you — and Pres. Tell him I'm on my way."

The girls said good-bye, and Mary Ellen put down the receiver with a triumphant flourish. She gave Olivia the thumbs-up sign. "We've got 'em," she crowed.

"Terrific." Olivia smiled. Then she picked up the phone again to call the others.

"Whooee! Hey, you're here!" Walt yelled as he ran down the airport's arrivals corridor and met Mary Ellen and Olivia on the other side of the metal detector. He grabbed a girl on each arm and whirled them around until they were both dizzy.

"Let me look at you," Mary Ellen demanded, taking him by both shoulders. His round, open face was just the same; his stocky, muscular body gave her a welcome feeling when she hugged him. He was wearing his New York finery: Army/Navy store camouflage pants with a khaki flak jacket and work boots. "You look great," she declared.

Olivia gave him a quick peck on the cheek. "You are a sight for sore eyes," she said, "but naturally, you would have to get a plane that was an hour late. Nancy's must have landed by now."

Nancy was waiting for them at the information booth, her long, dark pageboy pulled back on either side with blue butterfly combs. She was wearing a smooth blue wool shirtdress with a gigantic metallic belt, and holding her reefer coat over one arm. She was positively elegant.

But as she saw them, her serious face lit up and she dropped her coat and bag as she ran, arms open, into their embrace. "Ooh! It's wonderful to be here. Every time I come home I say I'll never leave again." Then she took Mary Ellen's hand and clutched it. "How's Pres doing?"

The reply was a simple shrug that said much more than words. "You'll be the best medicine he's had so far," she finally answered.

"Angie's been in town for hours," Olivia reported. "She's meeting us at Tara's." She glanced down at her watch and yelped. "Hey, are we late! Let's go!"

"When can we see Pres?" Walt demanded, taking his luggage and Nancy's and tossing both bags easily over a shoulder.

"Tomorrow," Mary Ellen said. "It's a surprise."

Angie was sitting on Tara's porch, her cheeks rosy not with cold but with anticipation. When she spotted her friends, she jumped up and ran down the block to greet them. "This is better than — " she gasped as she rushed toward them " — than chocolate cake with three scoops of ice cream, than a bucket of fried chicken, than pizza with everything on it — "

"You still dream in food, huh, Angie." Walt chuckled. "You're lucky it doesn't show."

Angie sucked in her waist. "That's only because I dream about it instead of eating it." She grinned.

Tara came out on her porch, followed by the other cheerleaders and Patrick. "Are you people having your party outside? Ours is in here. What about joining us?"

Holding hands, talking at once, they walked inside and downstairs, to Tara's den. They were still gabbing away an hour later, so thrilled to be together again that they couldn't contain themselves.

The new cheerleaders sat back and let the reunion happen. Hope and Peter stayed by themselves on the sidelines, Tara and Sean rushed around getting everyone sodas and chips, and Jessica insisted that Patrick photograph the whole thing.

"Oh, there, get that shot of Olivia and Walt sitting at the piano together," she whispered.

"Are you kidding? She'd kill me," Patrick laughed, aiming at Sean who was juggling two bottles of Coke and a bucket of ice cubes in one hand. "And what if it fell into the wrong hands and Duffy got hold of it? Say, there's an idea!" he chuckled. "Sell it to Duffy for a good price."

"Rat!" Jessica poked him in the ribs.

Patrick shot a few of Nancy and Angie doing

a two-step together, the brunette and blonde heads close, their hands at graceful angles. Then he turned the camera on Hope, who was showing Peter and Sean how to fold a napkin so it looked like a bird.

He turned the camera again and got Mary Ellen in his sights, but the expression on her face froze his finger on the shutter. She was looking around at the group, half in tears, half in laughter. She seemed so lonely, so lost, that he couldn't photograph the moment. It was too private.

He had considered telling her about the conversation he'd had with Pres, that first night after the accident. He knew, as well as he knew his own name, that Pres would never confide all his feelings about being a physical person to Mary Ellen. It would be too crushing, too humiliating a thing to say. Sure, it was dumb of Pres to feel that Mary Ellen only cared about him because he was strong and healthy, but who can tell anybody how they ought to feel? And this was the reason, of course, that Pres refused to try. If he failed, *that* would be the worst disaster. Worse than any car accident.

Patrick put down his camera and walked over to Mary Ellen, casually putting an arm around her shoulder. "Kind of like old times, huh?" he said.

"But different." She nodded. "I don't feel the same. And I wish I did."

"No, Mary Ellen," he whispered. "Don't ask for the past back again. It's bad luck. I know you're going through a really rough period, but it's going to pass. Believe me."

She bit her lower lip and sat down on the bottom step of the basement stairs. "You're a sweetheart, Patrick." She sighed, fighting back tears.

"What are you guys doing?" Tara raced over with sandwiches, which she pressed into their hands. "You are being Class-A party-poopers, that's what. Now, come on over here and let's talk turkey."

Mary Ellen let the two of them draw her into the circle of joyful faces. Angie draped an arm around her shoulder, and Hope took her other hand.

It was good to have friends — wonderful, in fact. But all she could think of was the fact that the party wasn't complete because her best friend was missing.

Pres.

CHAPTER

"Well, you look comfortable." Mary Ellen opened the French doors and walked out onto the Tilfords' flagstone patio. Pres was in his wheelchair, wrapped in blankets, a baseball cap on his tousled dark blond hair, his head tipped up to the sun.

He smiled and maneuvered the chair around so that he could look at her. "I am. It's nice here. Gives me a chance to think."

She came over and wrapped her arms around his neck, depositing a kiss on his exposed ear. "Not too chilly?"

"No, I like it."

They were quiet together for a moment, and then Mary Ellen pulled up a chair beside him. "What are you thinking about?" she asked.

He shook his head, as if he didn't want to tell her. Then, so softly that she had to move closer to hear him, he said, "How much I'd like to hold you."

"Well, why don't you?" She got up and came to him, standing beside the chair. "I could sit on your lap. The casts would keep my weight off you."

He looked nervously back through the windows. "Someone might see."

"Pres, we're married." She was so happy that the subject had come up — that he had brought it up — because he had stayed so far away from her since the accident. But it was exasperating to have him make excuses.

"But we're on my parents' turf." He wheeled himself away.

She stood there, an anxious feeling growing in the pit of her stomach. "How about coming home, to our turf?" she finally asked.

He frowned and shrugged. "I don't know."

"Pres. Listen to me, the ramp is all built, and I had the carpenter do a few things inside to make the house wheelchair-accessible. It's time that we got on with our lives. Not that your parents don't mean well — they've been great through this whole thing. But you said it yourself, you're comfortable here. Maybe too comfortable."

"Now don't you start, Mary Ellen."

"It's all arranged. All we have to do is tell your parents you're moving. But I think you should do that, don't you?"

He was about to answer when they both heard the sound of a truck coming up the drive.

"Sounds like Patrick's van! Great. I've been meaning to talk to him about a few things," Pres declared, moving himself over to the ramp that led to the porch.

Mary Ellen licked her lips, pulling her jacket collar closer around her neck. She had made virtually no progress on any front. She wasn't helping him at all, and she felt frustrated and annoyed that, as close as they were, he just didn't trust her enough. Well, he was in for a big surprise. And she would feel absolutely no jealousy at all if the visitors could make the difference that she could not.

Patrick and Jessica jumped out of the cab and waved at the couple on the porch, big grins on both their faces.

"How're you doing?" Patrick called.

"Great. C'mon up. Hey, Mary Ellen, could you look in the kitchen and see if we have a couple extra Cokes for these two?"

Patrick shook his head. "I think we're going to need more than a couple. Try fourteen. That's a nice even number." He walked around to the back of the van and unlocked the door.

Pres looked puzzled, then astounded, as people began pouring out from the back of the van. The five other cheerleaders were followed by Duffy and Kate, who were followed by Angie, Walt, and Nancy. They all came running, leaping, and jumping across the lawn toward him. Pres just stared.

"Well, aren't you going to say anything?" Mary Ellen giggled.

"I — I didn't think there was anything wrong with my eyes, but I must be seeing things."

Walt ran around the side of the truck, then

jumped up on the porch and began pumping Pres's hand. "You're seeing the real item. Us!" he declared.

Angie and Nancy came up on either side of Pres and left big lipstick marks on his cheeks, but he didn't need any artificial color — he was glowing.

"I can't believe this! Why didn't you people tell me?" he demanded of Mary Ellen and Patrick.

"Okay, so we've seen the Houdini trick where the guy gets himself stuck in a chair." Walt chuckled, kicking the base of the wheelchair. "Now let's see you get out of it."

There was silence. Pres looked at his old friend and his eyes suddenly grew misty. "I can't."

Nancy sat down on the porch steps and took his hand. "We're here to make sure that you can and will walk again, do you hear? And none of us is going anywhere until you're well on the road to recovery."

"She's telling you the truth," Angie said, close to tears herself.

Pres grinned at them, drawing them closer. "This is great! You're great. You know, I was just sitting here this morning thinking about you, about all of us last year, and everything that's happened since then. So, tell me about yourselves. How does Tarenton look to you? What's going on at college? What's new in your lives?"

"Give them a break, Pres." Sean laughed. "They only just got here."

"He wants the entire last six months in twenty-five words or less." Angie giggled.

"Wait a second," Mary Ellen said. "This calls

141

for something to eat and drink. I'll be right back."

She started to get up, but Nancy pushed her back down in the seat beside Pres. "No, you stay," Nancy said, looking at her old friend with compassion. He needs you with him all the time, she was thinking. "Just remind me where the Tilford kitchen is, and I'll rustle something up."

"I'll show you," Tara offered, leading the way.

The girls wandered down the long hall and turned right, into the deserted pantry. It wasn't difficult to find the "kid food," as Mrs. Tilford insisted on calling it, that she had stockpiled for Pres when he came home from the hospital. There were cases of soda, boxes of chips and pretzels, and plenty of frozen pizzas in the freezer.

"I take it he's not doing so well," Nancy said, as she found a tray and set three six-packs of sodas on it.

"That's the trouble." Tara sighed, getting out some crackers and several bags of chips. "He thinks the status quo is perfect. But between you and me, I think he's getting worse. It's like, I don't know, his personality has changed or . . . vanished."

"What are you talking about?" Nancy looked very worried.

"He's not the same person," Tara told her. "He doesn't have opinions about anything anymore — except about not doing too much. He's very big on that. I've been over here a lot, just to gossip, tell him about school and stuff, try to get him interested in cards or board games or anything, but he's just blank. It's really scary."

"That's awful." Nancy set her tray down.

"We're all really glad you've come. Mary Ellen is going to be a basket case if somebody doesn't get Pres out of that chair soon."

"Well, how could she not be?" Nancy sighed. "If I were married, especially to somebody like Pres, I'd go to pieces if he was hurt."

"Are you, ah, seeing anyone at college?" Tara asked, as if by changing the subject she could lighten the mood between them.

"Nope. No danger of marriage, engagement, or even serious commitment in the near future," Nancy smiled ruefully. "Everybody said I'd be swamped with guys at Brown," she went on, "but I've been too busy to even meet many new people. I guess I'm sort of shy."

"You?" Tara had never talked to Nancy before, but she certainly didn't strike her as shy. With her exotic good looks and her elegant clothes, she looked like the sort of person who would attract boys just by standing around. "Maybe college kids are too immature for you," she suggested.

"Could be," Nancy said. "Or maybe I'm not enough of a fun-seeker for most of them."

They were on their way back outside with the food when Tara thought of something. "Say, how would you like to meet somebody terrific?" she demanded. "Somebody right here in Tarenton?"

"Well, I. . . ." Nancy shook her head. "Tara, we're here to take care of Pres."

"You can't do that day and night."

"No, of course not, but it would be dumb to get mixed up with somebody and then have to leave town," Nancy pointed out.

143

"I'm not suggesting you get 'mixed up.' Just meet him. He's nice! C'mon, can you really afford to pass up meeting a wonderful person?"

Nancy laughed. "No, I guess not. Life's too short and there are too many creeps around. Well, if you say he's wonderful. . . ."

"As a matter of fact," Tara confided, "I'm sure he is because I dated him myself until I found out he was a faculty member. His name is Nick Stewart and he's the only math teacher I ever talked to who doesn't think that logarithms and advanced algebra are the beginning and end of the world. And he's a nice guy — not to mention gorgeous. So what do you say? Let me arrange it all. Oh, this will be fun! And it'll be a good break for you. Believe me, you don't want to play nurse/cheerleader all the time. Especially on this tough case."

Nancy smiled at her incorrigible new friend. "Well, if you want. But I warn you, I'm the worst on blind dates. Guys have been known to run screaming from the premises."

"I don't believe that for a second. I'll call him tonight, and get him to phone you. So you better be home," Tara warned her as they stepped back out onto the patio. "What the — "

The girls stopped and stared in astonishment. The cheerleaders were playing basketball — and Pres had joined them. He was zooming his chair around on the driveway like a pro, chasing the ball whenever Sean or Patrick dropped it.

"This is insane!" Tara exclaimed.

Kate, who was running solidly down the driveway toward the garage where the hoop was set up, dodged Peter, then Sean, and leaped gracefully into the air. A perfect dunk shot. She passed the ball to Pres, who careened around in a circle and made tracks away from Patrick and Olivia. Then Hope ran in from behind and snatched the ball away from him.

"Hey, no fair! I can't turn that fast," he complained, spinning his wheels wildly.

"Then learn how to!" she yelled, running for the basket full tilt.

"How in the world did you ever get him to try that?" Tara asked Duffy, who was standing on the sidelines beside Mary Ellen and Angie.

"It was weird. Patrick just went to the garage and got out the ball and started shooting baskets," Duffy told her. "Then he swiveled around and socked the ball to Pres. For a second, he just sat there holding the thing like he was afraid it was going to bite him. And then he aimed and shot. Got a basket first time out."

"He's a natural." Angie grinned.

The game was going fast and furious. Then Hope lost concentration for a second, and Jessica was able to intercept the ball. Jessica feinted right, away from Pres, then ran swiftly to the left and aimed. Walt knocked the ball away, and was about to make the shot himself when Pres sped in from out of nowhere, grabbing the ball and looping it up into the air. It fell into the basket and back down on the blacktop with a resounding plop.

"Yay, Pres!" Angie yelled.

"Let's give them a cheer," Mary Ellen suggested. She grabbed Nancy, and Angie and Tara

145

followed them into the middle of the driveway. "Wait right here. We need a guy," Mary Ellen said, going back for Duffy.

"Oh, no. This is where I get off!" Duffy shook his head vehemently, but Mary Ellen wouldn't let him go.

"You have to. It's easy. All in the line of a reporter's experience, 3-D. Look, left foot, kick. Right foot, kick. Show him, Tara! That's it! Now, let's hear it."

> "One, two, three, four,
> Who's the man that we adore?
>
> Five, six, seven, eight,
> Who's the guy who's really great?
>
> Eight, seven, six, five,
> He'll skin the competition alive!
>
> Four, three, two, one,
> Pres can always get it done!
>
> YAY, Pres!"

The others joined in immediately. Even Duffy, stumbling over his own feet and Angie's and Tara's, seemed to be getting it toward the end.

Mary Ellen broke away from her impromptu squad and rushed to Pres. She threw her arms around his neck and hugged him joyfully, planting a warm kiss on his lips. "I love you," she whispered.

But Pres couldn't stop moving. As soon as she

146

leaned away, he was off again, angling the chair so that he could shoot, racing away to retrieve the ball, then speeding back to shoot again. He didn't know how he'd been brave enough to start this, but he was going like the wind, and it was wonderful. It was as if, after a long time underground, he had suddenly dug his way to the surface and saw the sun. It was as if he was living again.

"Great, sweetie! Keep it up!" called Mary Ellen as he tried for an over-the-shoulder shot. But he didn't watch where he was going, and suddenly the chair was out of control. It careened backwards into the garage. Pres hit it with a thunk, banging his head on the door.

Mary Ellen felt herself running toward him, although she couldn't have accounted for any of her movements afterward. Her face was white and there was a sick feeling in the bottom of her stomach. Suppose he had jolted something out of place? Suppose he had been on his way to recovery and this caused a setback? Suppose —

The other kids were right behind her, swooping down on Pres, demanding to know if he was all right. They hardly heard the sound of a Honda wagon pulling up in the drive, and weren't aware that someone else was with them, until they heard an unfamiliar voice down the driveway.

"What's going on?" Connie Lapino asked.

"What's *she* doing here?" Pres murmured. "Hey, everybody, it's okay. I just knocked my head a little."

The small figure down the driveway came closer, and Pres instinctively moved his chair away, as though he were trying not to be seen.

"Look, all of you," Pres said, "I'm really okay. I was having a great time. I'm really fine, Connie," he said, speaking to her directly for the first time. "For those of you who haven't been introduced," he said, "this is Ms. Lapino, the physical therapist at the hospital, who, as I understand it, was not invited here today. She just came under her own steam."

Connie was unfazed by Pres's hostility. She walked over to him and picked up the basketball. "Say, this was a neat idea. I guess you've been playing possum with me, huh? You were ready to get out of bed, after all."

"I told you," he said in a low tone. "I'd do it in my own way, in my own time."

"Sure. I can see that. I only came here to wish you the best of luck, Pres. It's evident to me that you don't want my help, or don't feel you need it. You seem to have a lot of support now, so I won't be concerned about you." She twirled the ball in one hand and aimed carelessly for the basket. It didn't even strike the rim, but arched into the net like a dolphin leaping from the water.

Mary Ellen walked over to her. "Pres just hurt himself, Connie. I think you should check him."

She shook her head. "He's not my responsibility now. I'm sorry. If you're worried, you can call his doctor." Connie smiled and started back toward her car. "Well, it's been great. Sorry I didn't get to know you all better."

Pres rubbed his head thoughtfully, watching her go. "I thought people like that hounded you until you gave in."

148

Patrick took the wheelchair by the handles and started to push Pres back to the house. "Hey, man. You asked for it, you got it. You wanted people to leave you alone, so now they are." He looked at Mary Ellen over the top of Pres's head, as if to say, "Don't worry, he'll come around." But he wasn't sure himself. If this was Connie's idea of reverse psychology, it might not work with Pres.

Mary Ellen walked beside her husband, glancing down at him. "How's your head? Shall I call somebody?"

"Is there anything we can do?" Nancy asked, trailing along beside them.

Pres reached over and squeezed her hand. "Everybody, really, nothing happened. I feel better than I have in weeks. When the casts come off, I may just go sign up for the NBA tryouts."

Angie and Walt came up from the rear of the group. "Hey, man, we're in town as long as you need us, you know," Walt told Pres. "But that therapist will be here when we leave. No saying you have to make up your mind now. You can always call her later."

Pres chuckled and shook his head. "This reunion was a real nice idea. I know you have to care about me to fly across the country to see me." He turned toward Mary Ellen. "This is it, sweetie. This is what it's all about. Friends."

"Honestly, Pres, I wish you'd reconsider about Connie. Walt is right. Maybe when the casts are removed — "

"Hey, she's written me off. She as much as said so. So it really doesn't make any difference now."

Mary Ellen was nervous. All this good work was about to dissolve before her very eyes. "That's not true, Pres. She was just trying another ploy to get you to cooperate. She wants you to walk. And I do, too!" She was practically yelling.

"Look, you saw me playing ball, right?" Pres demanded, getting angry himself. "Why are you so hot to get me out of this chair so fast? Maybe I like it here, Mary Ellen — you ever think of that? Maybe I'm really happy here."

Mary Ellen gasped. Olivia was right; maybe he didn't want to walk again. It was unbearable to feel that way, just when she thought things had turned around, had changed for the better. The sight of Nancy, Walt, and Angie had been enough to get him excited, make him participate, and give him the spirit he'd been lacking. If Connie hadn't spoiled the moment, he might have even kissed Mary Ellen back.

It was like being on a desert island, Mary Ellen thought, and seeing a bottle bobbing on the waves, a short distance away. If she could just get hold of it, put a note in it, and send it off, someone might answer.

So close, and yet so far. Right now, it seemed totally out of reach.

CHAPTER

12

The Rivals Game had been postponed two weeks, due to "unforeseen circumstances on both sides," as the official memo put it. Diana claimed to have given an extraordinarily persuasive speech to the judges of the mascot competition, but it was rumored that St. Cloud was having trouble, too, so the two schools were even.

"Okay, I'd like a full report." Diana gave Mike and Jim the cold stare that made her beautiful blue eyes considerably less attractive.

"It's a cloud, Diana," Jim said authoritatively.

"Hey, great! Now we know their secret!" Beef piped up.

Diana looked at him with disgust. "A cloud is obvious, boys," she said in a disparaging voice. "But what I want to know is, what kind of cloud, how big is it, what accessories does it have, and what problems is Kate Harmon's committee running into that bought us the extra time."

"Diana, none of this is going to help us win. Why don't we stop right here and just get busy on our wolf?" Hope suggested. Jessica and Tara seconded the motion, even though Diana didn't bother to call on them. As far as she was concerned, the cheerleaders were a hindrance rather than a help to her.

"I want to know," she said in a quiet, menacing voice. Then she walked over to Jim and took him by one lapel of his plaid shirt. "You find out — and fast."

Jim and Mike exchanged glances. "But Diana," Jim said, trying to calm her, "the last time we snuck over there in the middle of the night, a squad car spotted us and we almost got arrested. Do we really have to go back?" he asked. Diana didn't even deign to answer — the answer was yes.

There was no getting around it. If the wolf was going to be finished in time for the Rivals Game, the cheerleaders were going to have to work overtime. It was tiring, it was thankless, and it was Diana's aim in life to make them miserable, but what could they do? Pretty soon now, it would be over.

They had repaired the damage done to the mascot by the rain, and learned from their mistake.

"When is Tommy Bridgeman coming to fit the mechanical stuff inside the wolf?" Olivia asked one evening in the shop about seven o'clock. Her fingers were so full of grooves and cuts from sewing pieces of wig together for the pelt, she kept a bottle of hand lotion with her at all times.

"Supposed to come over tomorrow afternoon," Peter told her, holding up a paint can for Hope as she stood on a ladder working on the details of the wolf's face.

"He's got this incredible system all ready to go," Hope told them. "I saw it in the physics lab. That guy is incredible. I mean, you can't carry on a conversation with him, because he talks in computerese, but he sure knows what he's doing."

"I wish I did." Jessica groaned, separating pieces of wig for Olivia to sew. "This doesn't look right." She shook her head.

"It's fine. Just tear some bigger lumps for right over here, near the tail," Olivia suggested.

Diana, who was never very far away, wandered over to the group and took Jessica's work out of her hand. "What are you doing? Honestly, I wish you had resigned from this committee instead of Sean. He may have committed sabotage, but at least when he did some work on our mascot, he was competent."

"Well, Diana, it's a toss-up." Jessica, thinking on her feet, was unmoved. There was nothing better than a good comeback. "Either you get Sean, whom you can accuse of something he didn't do, or you get me — whom you can abuse because you don't know what else to do."

"Oh, Jessica." Diana's blue eyes flashed with annoyance. "You really are clever with words, but there are certain drawbacks to having a high SAT score in English. Bo-*ring*," she chanted. "You are one big yawn."

"Thanks," Jessica answered cheerily.

"And speaking of tired subjects, do I hear that Pres is getting out of his casts this week? Poor boy."

"He's okay, Diana," Peter growled.

"I just can't imagine how poor Mary Ellen takes it." She shook her head. "And of course, with the casts off and no improvement at all, he'll be *really* depressed. So sad, too, with his three old friends coming to visit and all."

Hope climbed down from her ladder, paintbrush in hand. "Gee, why don't you go over and talk to him, Diana. A few discouraging words from you might be exactly what he needs to get on his feet again. Just to show you he could."

Diana was off before the words could hit home. She had a talent for getting out of the way of flying objects. "Beef!" she called. "I want the wolf brought up to the science department for Tommy tomorrow. And be careful getting him in the elevator. Oh, everybody, by the way, we've decided this mascot needs a name. So put on your thinking caps!" Her forced cheer floated toward the group as she wandered over to her friends at the other end of the shop. "Quitting time, guys!" she yelled.

"I'm sick and tired and I'm going home." Jessica sighed, throwing a heap of wigs back on the shelf. "Somehow, every time I walk out of this place, I feel contaminated. So I am going straight to my bathroom with a peanut butter and jelly sandwich and soak in a tub full of bubbles." She picked up her parka and started for the shop door.

"Wait for me," Olivia said. "This thing is beginning to give me the creeps. A testimony to Hope's expert painting, but he just looks too real."

"Looks like Diana, if you ask me," Hope said. "Say, there's a name for you. Diana, goddess of the hunt. It works!"

"She's never going to go for it," Peter said. "Hits too close to home. And anyway, I thought old Wolfie was a male critter."

"I guess." Hope turned and took a last look at her masterpiece. The others had left already, so it was their job to close up the shop for the night. She flicked the light switch, leaving only the emergency light burning. In the dim glow, the wolf's face took on an eery, overly realistic cast.

The others all noticed it, too. "Whew, let's get out of here," Peter said. "In another couple of minutes, I'm going to start believing this is one of the pack that came out of the woods."

They all shuddered involuntarily and quickly left the shop. But none of them really thought seriously about his statement until the next day.

Nancy's parents had been so glad to have her home, they took her on a shopping spree for a whole new spring wardrobe, and only when all the stores had closed did they end up at the Manor for dinner. It was one of the fanciest restaurants in Tarenton.

"You look exhausted," Nancy's mother said to her as their green Volvo pulled into the driveway of their house at about nine-thirty.

"I am, kind of. Guess I'll go to bed early tonight, if you and Dad don't mind."

"Of course not, Nancy. See you in the morning. And Nancy," her mother added as she started to climb the stairs to her bedroom, "it's wonderful to have you back."

Nancy had to admit that it was good to be back, to be tucked snugly in the cozy nest of home. College was fine and nice, but it wasn't the adventure she had dreamed it might be. Part of her wanted desperately to transfer to someplace closer to her family; the more prudent, future-oriented part of her told her to stay put. Brown was Brown, after all — a good place for meeting the right people and getting the right job when she graduated.

The trip back to Tarenton had made her nostalgic for all that had passed, for a life she would never have again. It was sort of a vacation, and yet it was hard work. All psychological, which made it even harder. Nancy was a psych major, and she had never encountered anything in any of her textbooks as bizarre as the change in Pres. She supposed you didn't really know people until they were involved in some traumatic situation, when their true colors rose to the surface. It was so weird — sometimes Pres was kind, accommodating and charming; other times he acted like a spoiled toddler.

That day had been the last straw. Getting Pres and Mary Ellen settled back in their own house was something Nancy would never want to tackle again. At first, all Pres did was complain about how his casts itched. Then, when he went to start up the Porsche, he decided that the engine sounded awful and that Mary Ellen had been letting the oil get too low. Nancy left in the middle of *that* conversation.

Being alone together had been wonderful before, but now, after Pres's injury, well, it was anybody's guess how their marriage would stand up. Nancy certainly didn't envy them.

The phone jangled, startling her. Nancy let it ring once more, then picked it up.

"Hello?"

"Hi. Is this Nancy?"

It was an unfamiliar male voice, low and appealing, with a hint of good humor behind the simple greeting. The caller sounded as if he couldn't believe he had actually picked up the receiver and dialed her number.

"Yes. Who's this?"

"Ah, my name is Nick Stewart. I'm a friend of Tara Armstrong's."

"Oh! Yes, of course." Nancy was flabbergasted. It had been almost a week since she'd discussed the blind date with Tara, and when the guy hadn't called, she'd just forgotten the whole thing. "She mentioned you. I mean, she spoke very highly of you. That is — " She kept stopping herself, listening with disbelief to the stupid things she was saying.

But Nick didn't respond the way she expected. He laughed, then said, "It sounds like you're as bad about blind dates as I am. And even worse about talking to strangers on the phone. It only took me a week to get up the nerve to call you."

Nancy felt relief flood through her, and she

eased up on the telephone cord, which she had managed to wind so tightly around her left hand, she had practically cut off circulation. "I'm totally awful," she admitted. "I mean, it's not that *I'm* awful, it's just that I have a lot of trouble with this kind of thing."

"Me, too," Nick confessed. "Look, let's get this over with. I'm six-one and one hundred eighty pounds, I have blue eyes and kind of wavy blond hair, I hate fruit of any kind, and I am a sucker for sci-fi movies and walks in the country. Oh, and I teach math."

Nancy found herself smiling into the telephone. "Well, I'm five-six and one hundred fifteen, I have long, dark hair, and dark eyes. I'm a freshman at Brown, majoring in psych, and I used to be a cheerleader. I'm allergic to cats, and I love sci-fi. I also have a terrific pair of boots for country walks. And I'm not doing so great in calculus right now," she finished in a whisper.

"Phew!" Nick breathed. "We sound like a couple of 'Personals' ads."

"People do seem sort of peculiar when you break them down to their basic elements." Nancy chuckled. "But since everybody seems equally weird, I guess it's all right."

"So, how long are you going to be in town?" Nick asked. "If we're going to get together, I guess we'd better do it soon."

"I don't really know. I'm here because of Pres Tilford's accident, but I suppose Tara told you that. I just can't leave until he's making a little progress. I'm missing a lot of classes, but I know

I can make up the work. I can't always make a good friend — and Pres is one of those."

There was a pause, and then Nick said, "You just told me more about yourself than all those other details put together. I'd love to meet you."

She found herself blushing over the phone. "Same here."

"What about dinner tomorrow night? We can make it early in case you want to get over to the Tilfords' afterward."

"Sounds good. I live at — "

"I know where. I looked you up in the phone book when Tara gave me your number. How's six o'clock?"

"Fine. See you then."

"Good night, Nancy."

" 'Night."

Nancy hung up the receiver and leaned back against her pillow, linking her hands behind her neck. She stared dreamily at the ceiling, trying to imagine this person who had been so understanding, so compassionate in such a potentially awkward situation. Tara was right — he was a good guy, and that was an increasingly difficult thing to find.

But was it wrong to be all excited about a man, when Pres was confined to a wheelchair and Mary Ellen was tearing her hair out? She felt slightly guilty about this extracurricular activity, and yet, she knew that she had her own life to take care of — as well as her friend's. If she were like Angie, simply happy to be home with her mother and brothers, and passionately committed to getting Pres well; or if she were like Walt, a person who tackled one job at a time and worked at it until it was completed. . . .

But she wasn't. Whether it was good or bad, she couldn't say, but she was unable to stay with one thing single-mindedly, to the exclusion of everything else. She had to have a little diversion, and it seemed like Nick could be just that.

As she leaned over to switch off her bedside lamp, it occurred to her that this would probably be nothing at all — one date and then, poof, a pleasant handshake good-bye at the door. But that would be fine. After all, she didn't want to get involved with somebody wonderful for only a week or so and then never see him again.

With a firm resolve in her mind to be extra-nice to Pres the following day, she closed her eyes and promptly fell asleep. But in the morning, she woke with a smile on her face, and for the life of her, she couldn't figure out why.

"Come on in. Yes, that's fine." Dr. Adelman ushered the crowd into his examining room. Mr. and Mrs. Tilford sat uneasily in the large chairs to one side of the table, and Mary Ellen remained standing beside Pres's wheelchair. Nancy, Angie, Walt, and Olivia hung back at the door. Pres had insisted that the old squad be present when the casts came off, and they had all readily agreed to come to the hospital with him, but none of them felt particularly cheery to be here.

"Well, this is the big day," Dr. Adelman said pointedly. "How do you feel, Pres?"

"Itchy," the patient responded vehemently.

"I've been trying to scratch with my mother's knitting needles, but I can't get down far enough. I'm going batty, Doc. Last night I thought I was going to tear these casts off with my bare hands."

The doctor pushed the button on his intercom and spoke into the box. "Ruth, tell Paul Davies to get in here, would you?"

Mary Ellen took Pres's hand and found it as damp and clammy as her own. They had talked about this day for weeks, but now that it had arrived, neither of them could really believe it.

"Well, hop up here, young man," Dr. Adelman joked, patting the examining table. He helped Pres out of the wheelchair and, with the assistance of Walt and Mr. Tilford, lifted him onto the table. He pressed a button on the side of the table, which raised the top half so that Pres could lean his back against it. His legs in the casts were stretched out straight in front of him.

"Comfortable? Fine." The doctor nodded. "Now let's get that buzz saw going." He stepped over to the closet beside the examining table and took out his machinery, which he hooked up by means of a heavy-duty cable to one of the outlets. "Don't worry," he said when he saw Pres's face. "I know how to do this. I chop down my own Christmas tree every year."

"That's good," Pres growled. He was sick and tired of stupid jokes, sick of the whole ridiculous experience. Somewhere, way back in his mind, he had this fantasy of the doctor sawing off the casts and him jumping off the table. The breaks would be healed, the muscles would be in tone, the legs would even have a pretty good tan. The other fantasy, the one where nothing moved and he still didn't feel a pinprick on the bottom of his foot, was one he shoved away whenever it came to his mind.

The doctor picked up the saw and put on a pair of protective glasses. He turned on the motor and Nancy and Angie flinched involuntarily. Everyone else took a breath.

The whine of the saw permeated the room. Pres's eyes were riveted to the leg, and the ever-growing crack in the cast. The doctor flung the cable behind him and started on the second leg. Painstakingly, he made several lateral cuts in the plaster, so that he could remove the casts in pieces. The smell of the hot motor filled the air, then the sound of the casts cracking apart.

When the doctor was through most of the thickness of plaster, he turned off the machine and went to work with a hand saw, cutting the casts down to the gauze. This was the tedious part, and took a good fifteen minutes.

"Is there anything in there?" Walt asked after a while. Olivia gave him a disparaging look.

"Let's hope so," said Dr. Adelman just as the door to the office opened and Dr. Davies walked in. "Good! Just in time. Okay, folks, let's get rid of this debris." He put down the saw and carefully jiggled the first piece off. With a pair of surgical scissors, he snipped off the gauze and bared the leg to view.

It was white, with deep grooves along its side. The thigh was thin. It didn't resemble Pres Tilford's leg in the slightest.

"It looks disgusting," Pres muttered.

"Um-hmm," Dr. Adelman said, looking over at his colleague. "About what we'd expect from being in a box this long. Don't worry about it, son."

He worked on the rest of the pieces of the cast, prying them off and placing them in the trash barrel beside him. Then he went on to the second leg, working more quickly now.

Pres sat propped up on the table, looking at the two white legs in front of him. They were like a marionette's legs, limp and crumpled. He felt tears coming, and he choked them down.

"Pres, my brother Al busted his arm once," Angie offered. "It looked just like this when the cast came off. He was like Popeye on one side, and Olive Oyl on the other." She giggled, but nobody else did.

Walt kept remembering the way Pres's legs used to look. It was impossible that they'd ever get back to the way they'd been. He shuddered a little as he gazed at his friend.

Olivia examined the legs clinically. She knew how long it took to really mend a body, and she wasn't particularly frightened by what she saw on the table. But as she looked into Pres's eyes, she knew he hadn't healed yet. His spirit — that was the key to the whole thing.

Nancy was torn between laughing and crying. It was an odd sensation, as though she were on the verge of a really important thought. She remembered what Tara had said about Pres's personality, and she wondered whether this moment, as the casts came off, might give him back what he had lost. It was a hopeful thought, and it kept her mind off the awful sight of Pres's white legs.

Mary Ellen hadn't taken a breath since the doctor started sawing. She didn't care how the legs looked; she just wanted the doctors to get to the crucial part: the test.

"What do you think, doctor?" Mrs. Tilford asked. It was the question Mary Ellen had been wanting to ask, but not daring to.

"I want some fresh X rays," the doctor said to his nurse, who was standing in the doorway. "Set him up now, would you?" He turned to his colleague. "He's all yours, Paul."

Dr. Davies walked over to the table and slowly, carefully, began to manipulate Pres's legs. "Uh-huh," he nodded. "About right," he murmured. "Yes, that's it," he said.

"What?" Pres was about to explode. "Well, what?"

"You tell me." The doctor put his leg back on the table. "Now, move it. Go on. Give it a try."

Pres stared down at his right foot, willing himself to make the supreme effort. He closed his eyes, trying to imagine himself a cheerleader again on the floor of the basketball court, about to take a leap in the air. How did he do it? What was that incredible combination of muscles, nerves, and tendons that made him shoot up like a rocket into the air?

He pointed his foot.

"Oh, my goodness!" his mother exclaimed. "Oh, Pres!"

"It moved. Sweetheart, I saw it move!" Mary Ellen was weeping suddenly. She kissed Pres

164

again and again, whispering words of encouragement.

"Way to go!" Walt grinned as Angie, Nancy, and Olivia pounded their friend on the back and urged him to do it again, with the left foot.

The doctor watched all this with an inscrutable expression. He didn't say a word until Pres, with streams of perspiration coursing down his face, flexed his left foot. "Very nice," he stated. "We have some lateral as well as diagonal articulation in the metatarsals. No evident ossification," he told the nurse, who wrote it down on his chart.

"I don't really know what all that means, Doc," Pres grinned, "but I say we celebrate."

"Not yet, young man. X rays will tell us something. And I have some neurological tests I'd like to perform this afternoon. Naturally, it's a good sign that you can move your feet and ankles, but there's been vast deterioration over the past weeks, and you have a very long way to come back. If you'd had some therapy, there might have been a better chance. Now whether you ever regain full use of your legs . . . well. . . ." He paused and rubbed the bridge of his nose. "Who knows." And as proof that he knew what he was talking about, he bent Pres's legs at the knee, propping them up so that his feet and thighs could support them in that position. The legs flopped over like those of an infant who isn't even ready to crawl.

"You have to give him time!" Mary Ellen cried. "He's just weak, that's all."

But the joy on Pres's face had vanished. He had failed. That was that. He wouldn't try again.

165

CHAPTER

When they got home to their house that evening, they were still silent. They hadn't said a word since they left their friends and Pres's parents at the car rental firm. Since the Porsche was too small for a wheelchair, even when it was folded up, they had rented a big Buick station wagon until Pres didn't need the chair anymore. The suggestion of Pres's father that he spring for a large, second car had been vetoed immediately. Neither Pres nor Mary Ellen wanted to admit that they might need one permanently.

"What do you feel like having for dinner?" Mary Ellen asked, flipping open the back of the car and pulling out the chair.

"I don't care. Anything." He waited for her to pull him forward in his seat so that he could grip the handles of the chair and swing himself into it.

"Burgers or chicken?" she persisted.

"I told you, it doesn't make any difference."

166

He pushed himself up the new ramp, smelling the fresh wood and varnish, wondering whether he would have complimented the carpenter on his work if the ramp had been put up for some other reason.

He let her unlock the door and open it for him. Then he wheeled inside and pushed himself to the kitchen table. There was a stack of mail sitting there; methodically, Pres began to rip open the letters.

The kitchen was the cheeriest room in the house, but it did nothing for their spirits. They had picked the paper themselves and spent a long weekend putting it up, laughing at one another, embracing every once in a while, their kisses smelling of glue and fresh paint.

Mary Ellen got herself a Coke from the refrigerator, then went over to the bulletin board where she had pinned up a recipe she'd cut out of a magazine for chicken with water chestnuts with pineapple-lemon glaze. It had sounded wonderful to her at the time; now, it sounded like the only thing strange enough to whet her own appetite.

"Don't I get something to drink, too?" he asked, without looking up from his reading.

"If you ask nicely, sure," she said, a little annoyed at his attitude. She whipped around the kitchen, beginning to assemble the ingredients.

"Oh, sorry. I didn't realize I was being difficult. Just ignore me, why don't you, and maybe I'll go away."

Mary Ellen's warm blue eyes flashed a warning, but Pres didn't see it. She knew what he'd been through, and obviously he was in a foul mood, but he didn't have to take it out on her. Being an emotional punching bag was not her goal in life. "You can get your own Coke perfectly well," she said between gritted teeth. "All you have to do is go over to the refrigerator, take out a can, and pop it open. I've put the glasses down at a level with your chair so you can reach them, too."

"How kind," he said sarcastically, starting for the refrigerator.

"Yes, as a matter of fact," she exploded, "it *was* kind. So were a lot of other things I've done around here that you haven't noticed or bothered to mention." She could feel a storm brewing in her, and this time, she didn't try to keep it back. Let the hurricane rage! "Give me a little credit, why don't you?"

She turned away from him so she wouldn't have to look at his face, and hurriedly put the chicken pieces in a pan. She dumped a can of water chestnuts in with them, then squeezed lemon juice into the pan. She shook the salt and pepper furiously, covering the food with black and white specks. This wasn't exactly how the recipe read, but she was too angry to do it properly.

"Hey, I give you credit. Really," he growled. He knew she was approaching her boiling point, but he couldn't stop himself. Something inside him, some demon of sorrow and self-pity, was making him say these things. "You're about the only girl in this town who could stand being around someone like me. I take my hat off to you."

She turned away from the counter, tears streaming down her face. "You can be really awful, do you know that? I don't have to take any of this, understand? Make your own stupid dinner!" She shoved the can of crushed pineapple at him and grabbed her coat.

The words of the vows she'd taken came to her again, just as they had before her wedding, that night of the big party when she was wondering whether Pres was really serious about wanting to marry her. *In sickness and in health,* she'd said — And then, had said it again for real on that glorious day that she bound her heart to her husband's forever.

Then this was the test. He was sick, that was true, but so was she. Sick of trying to help, sick of not being needed, sick of being the one doing all the giving and none of the taking.

Slamming the door behind her, she ran out into the evening. It was a beautiful night, clear and crisp, but she didn't notice that. She raced around the side of the Buick and got into the Porsche, starting it up with a vengeance. She purposely didn't give it time to warm up and zoomed out of the driveway.

She knew he was watching at the window.

"Give me a break, Katie." Sean had one arm around her waist and was waving a grilled ham and cheese sandwich in her face. "It's all going to be over soon anyway — here, have a bite — so

169

you might as well just confess everything."

"Why should I?"

"Because I love you," he said blatantly.

They were sitting in a booth at Benny's, long after most of the crowd had left, and Kate was trying not to laugh. He was so appealing, after all. She knew he knew at least fifty girls prettier than she was, but Sean wanted her. She chomped on the sandwich and chewed thoughtfully, pondering her options.

She could tell all. Actually, it wouldn't be detrimental to St. Cloud's chances. Sean was off the committee, and was angry enough at Diana not to want to help her out in any way. After Jim Lynch and Mike Ferrara had come snooping around, part of the cat was out of the bag anyway — everybody knew it was some kind of thundercloud — so it didn't matter that much.

She could plant a rumor and hope that Sean would spread it. What really interested him was the setback that, in combination with Tarenton's bad luck to have the wolf stranded out in the rain, had caused the judges to rule on a delay of the Rivals Game. She could tell him that the reason St. Cloud needed more time was because they were constructing neon thunderbolts. *That* would have Diana running scared. The real truth was that the computer nerd who was doing this fancy last-minute addition in the storm cloud had left the metallic arms of the mascot on the radiator, and they'd melted overnight.

The whole thing was, though, that Kate was a person of her word. She had promised to say nothing, and she intended to stick to her promise —

no matter what Sean did, or how affectionate he got.

"How about this?" he suggested. "I'll give you one tidbit about ours and you give me one tidbit about yours. We'll be even."

"But I'm not interested in yours." She grinned, her wide eyes innocent. She took another bite of his sandwich.

"You have to be. It's — it's a question of school spirit, of loyalty, of the best man winning," Sean said.

She sighed, leaning back against his chest so that her head of unruly curls was right against his chin. "You mean the best *person* winning."

Sean pounded a fist on the table, making the silverware jump. "You can't tell me you're not curious."

"I can, and I will." She bopped him playfully on the chin.

"All right, then. I'll try another tactic. Do it for me," Sean whispered, gripping her tighter.

"My dear, misguided boy — " she swiveled around so that she could look at him head-on " — what makes you think that *you* are the persuasive argument? I mean, you're a very nice person, and you drive a neat car and all, but. . . ." She was about to tease him unmercifully about the fact that she was not as impressed with him as he was with her, but she stopped as the front door of Benny's opened and a gaunt-looking girl walked into the restaurant.

"Mary Ellen!" Kate breathed. "Wow, she looks positively ghastly. Wasn't today the day — "

Sean didn't give her a chance to finish but

171

raced across the room, grabbing a very shaken Mary Ellen by one arm and hastily ushering her over to their booth.

"Sit down. Have a cup of coffee," he said, waving for the waitress.

"Have a pot," Kate said. "You look awful."

"About the way I feel," Mary Ellen said softly.

"Well, how'd it go?" Sean demanded.

"Horrible. Perfectly awful. The doctor took the casts off," Mary Ellen said with a sigh, "and we all thought everything was terrific, because Pres could move his feet. But as it turns out, that doesn't have anything to do with whether he walks again. If he was depressed before," she finished, "he's totally crazy now. He's just plain mean. I can't. . . ." She paused for a moment. "I know he's been through a lot, but I have, too. I walked out."

Kate whistled through her teeth. "Wow, heavy," she said. "But, Mary Ellen. You've been putting up with so much withdrawal from Pres for weeks, it's a wonder you haven't thrown up your hands before now."

"The guy deserves it," Sean said. He was seething, but he didn't know whether he was angrier at himself or at Pres. He had been so involved when Pres first got out of the hospital — he had a plan to get the guy up and out, and what had he done about it? Absolutely nothing. He'd gotten so wrapped up in the mascot thing and getting back at Diana, he had totally shirked the responsibility he'd decided to shoulder. Mary Ellen's thin face told him all he needed to know about pain. Why don't you grow up, Dubrow? he asked himself.

"He doesn't deserve anything!" Mary Ellen insisted, so loud that people at the next table turned around. "I'm so mad at him, I could spit, but I feel miserable, too. I'll tell you one thing, he certainly doesn't deserve to be sitting there all alone with no one to help him. But I can't go home tonight. I just can't."

"Stay with me," Kate offered. "We can compare notes on rotten guys with ego problems." She smiled across the table.

Mary Ellen's face softened for the first time. "Aw, he's not so bad," she said, looking at Sean.

"He's a sneak and a weaseler of information," Kate told her. "I don't know why I stick with him."

Sean hadn't been listening to any of this banter. He seemed to be lost in thought. Then he threw his red scarf around his neck and thrust his arms into his parka. "Can you two girls get a ride?" he asked. "I have something to do."

Without waiting for an answer, he was up and out the door. He nearly collided with Duffy, Olivia, Walt, and Angie, who were just coming in, but he acted as though he didn't even see them.

"What happened to him?" Duffy asked Kate when he spotted the girls at the table. "Have you people heard the radio or TV lately? Boy, have we got news — "

"Mary Ellen, I'm so sorry," Olivia said, sliding into the booth and taking her friend's hand. "But you have to know this isn't the end. Pres does have a chance."

"It's a chance he doesn't want to take, though," Mary Ellen said matter-of-factly.

"I refuse to believe that, Mary Ellen," Angie said. She pulled up a chair from the next table, and Walt took another one. He was unusually quiet tonight.

"Nobody is listening!" Duffy insisted, waving his arms. "The wolf is much closer. They've sighted him right in town!"

The people at the next booth heard him and came over at once. Several others picked up on the news and started talking about it, and pretty soon, someone asked Benny to turn on the radio behind the counter, just in case there were late-breaking developments in the story.

"It was right behind the old station," Duffy went on animatedly. "They even found a tuft of wolf hair stuck in a doorway. Unmistakable! The rumor is that there could have been more than one," he added in a hushed tone.

Mary Ellen shook her head. "Why would wolves come right down into town? I mean, even if it's true that they're in the woods, why — ?"

"Not enough food," Duffy went on. "Yesterday, a half-eaten deer was found. The sheriff and the wildlife sanctuary people are starting a hunt tomorrow morning. They're going to track the wolves and try to capture them unharmed."

Angie rubbed her arms, although it was warm in the restaurant. "Do wolves attack people? I mean, if you happened to meet one walking down the street, and it was hungry, would it do anything?"

"Not if you invited it home for a hot dog, Angie." Walt grimaced. "Mary Ellen, you look bushed. How about calling it a day? I'll give you a lift."

She smiled gratefully at him. "I think that's a good idea. Good night, everybody. I'll talk to you in the morning." She let Walt lead her outside, into the brisk night air. But when they got to his car, she said in a low voice, "I'm not going home. Take me to my mom's, would you?"

Walt was the best friend in the world. He didn't ask one question. He just helped her into the car, started it up, and drove.

Sean was driving, too. He zoomed around the lake and started up Fable Point, toward the little carriage house. He had no idea what he was going to say, but he was determined not to leave Pres until he'd done what nobody else had been able to do: Get him mad enough to agree to go into therapy.

He pulled into the driveway and sat in the car for a minute, collecting his thoughts. Then, slowly, he got out and walked to the front door. It was partly open.

"Hello!" He walked in and sniffed, then ran toward the acrid burning odor in the kitchen. "Hey, it's cold in here! And what are you trying to do?" he demanded of Pres. "Set the house on fire?"

"It was just a piece of toast," Pres explained

lamely. "It got stuck in the toaster. I was trying to get it out."

"Well, unplug the thing first, you jerk, unless you want to get electrocuted." Sean scowled at his friend. The kitchen was a wreck. There was a pan of raw chicken, with some strange yellow chunks, on the kitchen table beside an open loaf of bread, a jar of peanut butter, and one of marmalade. A collection of dirty knives, spoons, and plates completed the array.

"Thanks for coming over," Pres chuckled. "You might have saved me from a fate worse than burnt toast. I'm a bachelor tonight," he said quickly.

"So I see." Sean took a fresh piece of bread from the loaf and bit into it. He was going to play dumb about Mary Ellen. Then he looked down at his friend. Pres seemed smaller, somehow, with the casts off. "So you got your wings," he commented. "Way to go."

"Big deal," Pres said with disgust. "Look, I don't want to talk about my condition anymore. As a matter of fact, I don't think I want to talk about it ever again."

"Okay by me." Sean shrugged. He sat down at the kitchen table and dipped his finger in the marmalade. "What do you want to talk about?" he asked.

"How about the mascot? When's the Rivals Game, anyway?"

"Two weeks," Sean told him. "You're coming, right?"

"Sure. They can wheel me in after the wolf." Pres smirked.

176

Sean took a breath. "Diana's been hounding us to think up a name for the thing. We finally got it today."

"Yeah?" Pres reached for the bread. "What is it?"

"We're calling him Preston Tilford *IV*," Sean said, smiling, "because his namesake was the biggest wolf in town until he chucked it all and got married."

Pres's eyes changed. Sean caught the look but pretended to ignore it. "Well, those days are over. I mean, chasing girls."

"Sure you don't mean marriage?" Sean asked pointedly. "I saw Mary Ellen walk into Benny's about an hour ago."

"She needed a breath of air," Pres said evenly.

"Uh-huh. Lots of air in Benny's," Sean went on.

Pres wheeled around the side of the table toward him. "What are you getting at, man? Because if you're implying that my wife — "

"Hey, I'm not implying. There are a lot of guys interested, Pres, now that you're down and out. In fact, I'm kind of interested myself."

Pres's whole body stiffened. His face was a white mask of rage. "If I could get up, I'd flatten you," he growled.

Sean moved away from the table so quickly, his chair fell over. "Well, why don't you?" he challenged. "Come on, I'm not that strong."

Pres's eyes were hot; his skin was cold. He felt a fury unlike any he'd ever known before. At a time when he needed so badly to act, he was unable to.

"You know why you don't get up?" Sean hissed, hovering over him. "Because you're just not the hot shot I thought you were. How I used to look up to you. Last year, seeing you on the squad, seeing how you handled yourself — boy, I don't mind telling you that you were my hero. But I was wrong about you. You're a quitter. No wonder Mary Ellen walked out on you."

It all happened so quickly, he could not have said how he did it. Pres grabbed the edge of the table and, by some superhuman force of effort, he used his torso as a fulcrum to pull himself up. In one wild gesture, he threw his hands up and propelled himself at Sean, using his body as a weapon. "You slime!" he yelled. "I'll get you for that!"

He sent the table crashing down on both of them. Everything — the chicken, bread and jam, peanut butter and dishes — landed on top of them and they lay on the floor together, covered with food. Pres rammed his fist into Sean again and again, and Sean let him, because it was the only way. Pres was crying and yelling and finally, after a while, he just lay there, and he let Sean put an arm around his shoulders.

"You're okay now, man," Sean said softly. "You're okay."

"What am I going to do?" Pres asked miserably.

"You're going to learn how to use your legs again. You're going to go to physical therapy. Right?"

There was a long silence, and the only sound in the room was Pres's ragged breathing. At last, he put up an arm and wiped the jam off his forehead. Then he said, "Right. I'll do it if it kills me."

"I'll pick you up Monday after school," Sean offered. And then he stood up, helped Pres back into his chair, and asked where the mop was.

CHAPTER

14

The man at Nancy's door was nothing like what she'd expected. All male math teachers, in her experience, had deep furrows between their brows and tended to stare off into space with a preoccupied sheep-counting look.

The man standing on her porch was truly handsome, in the old-fashioned sense of the word. He was tall and muscular — a very solid presence. He had rugged features with prominent cheekbones and blue eyes the color of the sea on a brilliant day. A lock of his blond hair tended to fall forward onto his forehead. He was only a little older than the college boys she'd met at Brown, but he had an air of confidence about him that belied his young looks.

And he was smiling at her. She didn't remember any guy smiling so warmly the very first time he looked at her. And certainly not a math teacher.

"Hello." Nick Stewart nodded.

"Hi." Nancy had about a million thoughts at once as she stared into his blue eyes, and for some reason she couldn't explain, they all centered on the future. She had this odd image of the two of them in a canoe on a sunny summer day, sailing down one of the lakes close by, then stopping for a picnic in a pretty cove. Then she saw them out on her porch, sitting in the glider swing on a hot evening when the air is so thick, it's like breathing in a chocolate milk shake. Finally, she saw them out walking in the country after a rainstorm early on a Sunday morning, slogging through the mud in their sturdy boots, just to listen to the birds singing.

"But I've just met you!" she exclaimed, not realizing she had spoken her thoughts.

"Pretty amazing." He grinned. "I feel I've known you all my life." He was laughing, but with her — not at her.

"I'm sorry. Would you like to come in? Or should we just go?"

"Well, I did make a reservation for dinner at Pedro's, and they're pretty strict. Bad report cards for too many late appearances."

Her face softened into a smile. "Then we better make tracks. I'll get my coat."

He watched her walk through the foyer to the coat closet and heard her call a good-bye to her parents. He had been dreading this moment, as he did on all blind dates, the second when the door opened and your companion for the evening stepped out. He was always sure he was going to be disappointed — and up to now, he had been.

Then there was his experience with Tara — a

181

relationship built on lies and misunderstandings. He had promised himself, after that ended, to be terribly careful the next time he got involved. And so he would be.

"Nancy Goldstein is elegant, not just classy" Tara had told him on the phone. "And she really wants to meet you. I mean, it's not like she has dates lined up till the fifth of July," she'd added with a tiny hint of condescension in her voice, implying that *she* could have a date any time she wanted.

"Even if you're lying to me," Nick had said, "it's only one night, right? Only four hours, tops. And I guess you know my type," he'd gone on with a smile in his voice. Tara was his type, except that she was too young. She had, however, been unselfish enough to have given him up when she realized how their romance would hurt him professionally.

"Here I am!" Nancy sang out, walking back onto the porch. She was wearing a lavender coat with a matching beret, and it was wonderful on her.

Nick helped her into his tiny MG. He'd always loved that car because it really impressed the girls he took out — but for some reason, it didn't seem so important to look flashy for Nancy.

"How do you like college — ?"
"How do you like teaching in Tarenton — ?"
They both spoke together, then laughed.
"One, two, three," Nancy conducted.
"Fine," they said in unison.
They got to the restaurant and were seated immediately, much to Nick's relief. There was

nothing worse than having to wait in some crowd with a girl you've just met, while people sloshed their drinks over your arm and complained about the service. There never seemed to be anything appropriate to say, because you didn't know your date well enough to tune out the other people and gaze longingly into her eyes. On the other hand, you couldn't very well ignore her until you were seated at your table and had the privacy to start getting acquainted.

As he pulled out the chair for Nancy, he found himself feeling proud to be seen with her. She might be only a year older than Tara, but she seemed a great deal more mature. Why was that? he asked himself, stealing a glance at her lovely, animated face. It wasn't her conversation or the way she moved, but it had something to do with a sense of being at home that went right down inside her and shone on the outside. He felt a kinship with her, a sense that even if they didn't say a word all night, they would feel comfortable together.

"What's good here?" Nancy asked when the waitress brought them menus.

"My favorite is the nachos with guacamole," Nick confided. "But I'm a sucker for anything with melted cheese."

"Really? Me, too." Nancy smiled. "The only way my mother ever got me to eat vegetables was to melt cheese all over them. To this day, I have trouble recognizing naked broccoli."

He grinned and leaned back in his chair. "We'll have some of that for starters, then. And there's a great fruit punch they do here — you'll like it," he told her confidently. "And I recommend the combination platter for the main course, so you can have a little of everything Mexican."

"Great," she agreed.

The waitress appeared, pencil and notepad ready.

"Unless you'd like something else," he said quickly. Suddenly he heard himself being very directive, like an older brother. He certainly didn't want Nancy to think he was pushing her into anything.

"No, that sounds yummy." She stopped when she realized what she'd just said. Only children say "yummy." It was bad enough that he knew she was just a college freshman — she didn't have to make herself seem any younger.

"So, you're majoring in psych." He nodded as the waitress jotted down their order and left. "Does that mean you're a very analytical person, or just a curious one?"

"That's an interesting question. You mean, do I tear people apart or am I just a born gossip? Well" — she let her breath out sharply — "I hope neither." She pulled absently at the buttons on her black jersey high-necked top. "I really think I picked psych because I want to get to know *myself* better. And then, after that, everybody else."

He folded his arms, liking her more each minute.

"What about you?" she asked. "Why math?"

"Because I was good at it," he said, without a trace of false modesty. "I enjoy it — making equations happen, making numbers work for me. I guess it would be more practical to use that knowledge for business or science, but I can't seem to develop any real love for concrete things. My dad used to say I had my head in the clouds."

When she was silent, sipping at the glass of punch that had just been placed in front of her, he thought maybe he'd said something she didn't like. He wondered where the conversation would go next. And he wondered what she thought of him, whether she was glad that she'd agreed to this date.

"You seem like such a down-to-earth person, though," Nancy said at last. "Of course, I've just met you, and first impressions are misleading, but . . . well, maybe your father was wrong about you. Or maybe he was right when he said it, and then you changed."

Nick laughed aloud. He hadn't told her anything about his parents, but she had put her finger right on the truth. His father was a man of strong opinions, which were sometimes based on fact, and sometimes, on nothing at all. And because Nick had five younger siblings, he tended to take the role of Mr. Wise and All-Knowing when he was around the family. His silence was interpreted as dreaminess.

"You know, Nancy, I think you're going to make a great psychologist — or a great anything, actually."

She blushed, and dug into her nachos.

The meal was a great success, and so was the entire evening. After dinner, they went to a new dance club that had just opened in town, and stayed for a couple of hours. The place was done in plastic and formica — very high tech — and the dance floor was a vast expanse of finished wood. They twirled and gyrated under the flashing colored lights until they were so exhausted they both collapsed on one of the built-in benches that flanked the dance floor.

"Maybe I'm too old for this." Nick panted.

"Maybe we're just too pooped." Nancy laughed. Dancing as they had, fast and wild, they hadn't been physically close all evening, but now, as they relaxed together, their breathing slowly calming, they were practically touching. His hand was lying right beside her shoulder, on the back of the bench, but he didn't move it. She found herself wishing that he would.

"What time is it?" she asked, although she didn't really care. It just gave her the excuse to move a little closer and pick up his wrist to look at his watch. "Midnight," she said, looking up into his clear blue eyes.

"Do you turn into a pumpkin?" He grinned. "Should I be getting you home?" He relished the feeling of her hand on his arm. It seemed to belong there.

"I guess so. Not that I want to go, but I want to get to Pres's early tomorrow."

He nodded and stood up, reaching for her. Then his arm slipped easily around her waist and, as though they had been doing this all their life, they walked to the door together, hugging.

Nick parked in front of Nancy's house twenty minutes later and turned off the engine of his car. He walked around to her side and helped her out. Holding hands, they went up onto the porch.

At the front door, they faced each other, smiling.

"Thank you," Nancy said. "This was really great." She wanted so badly for him to kiss her, but somehow, she didn't think he would. He had been very careful with her, as though he had to test the waters.

"Okay," he said. "I don't know if you want this — "

Nancy held her breath.

" — but I have to, because you'll be going away soon." He drew closer, leaning over her, his hand on the doorpost.

She smelled the clean scent of pine as he put a hand on her shoulder, and then his lips were on her cheek. "I had a wonderful time," he whispered.

"Me, too," she said softly.

Then she felt his lips on hers, warm and sweet.

He drew away quickly and walked back down the porch steps, not trusting himself to stay longer. He couldn't get involved with this girl, not when she was going to be a thousand miles away for the next three and a half years. Tara had burned him, and he couldn't take that again so soon. He knew himself well enough to know how badly he could be hurt.

"Good night, Nancy. Take care." He waved from his car.

And then he was gone, down the block. Nancy took her key from her purse and opened the front door. Well, you win a few, you lose a few, she thought. It had been a splendid date, but maybe he didn't feel the way she did. She certainly wasn't going to lie awake nights, wondering whether or not she had lived up to Nick Stewart's expectations.

But if he wasn't lying, and he'd had a wonderful time, just the way she had, then why wouldn't he have asked to see her again? She closed the door behind her and crept softly upstairs, wishing that life could be just a little less complicated.

Tommy Bridgeman was a small boy — almost as tiny as Olivia and Hope. Everything about him was small, from his stature, to his hands, to his eyes that seemed to peek out from behind his giant wire-rimmed glasses.

Everything about Tommy seemed to be in miniature except his brain. Tara liked to say that he was born normal-sized but his brain grew so fast when he was a kid, it used up all the nourishment that would have made him grow.

Tommy sat on a high stool in the science department and stared at the mascot as though he were trying to communicate with the wolf by ESP. Then he took a small box, from which a variety of different-colored wires protruded, and he turned its switch on. The box hummed a little, then a light on the side began to turn on and off at ten-second intervals.

"It works!" Diana crowed. "Oh, Beef, it works!"

Beef gave the box an approving grin.

"Of course it works, Diana," Tommy said gruffly. "It's a ridiculously simple mechanical system. The electrical impulses generated by the rudimentary batteries here — "

"Oh, don't bore me with the details," Diana said, dismissing Tommy. "Just get the wolf going, would you?"

"Relax, Diana," Hope said, crossing her arms on her chest. "We have two more weeks."

"But who knows what can happen in that period of time?" Diana suddenly turned on her with an ominous look on her face. "Once the wolf is wired and ready to go, that *traitor* in our midst — " she looked around at the group behind Tommy " — might think he has even more ammunition. Of course, he isn't going to realize until he starts whatever hanky-panky he has in mind that the wolf is going to have a guard on duty at all times."

"Really, Diana?" Beef spoke up. "Who's that going to be?"

"You," Diana said. "And when you do have to sleep, we'll get Jim and Mike on the job. Since they've failed so miserably at spying on St. Cloud, we might as well give them something they can handle."

"Everybody's on Diana's hit list these days," Peter whispered to Jessica.

"So what else is new?" Jessica demanded. She hadn't been listening to the conversation, so fascinated was she with what Tommy was doing with the wolf's head. He had taken it off and fitted the box inside the cavity. Some of the wires were hooked up to connections on the back of the black eyes, which were actually two light bulbs on top of small battery packs. He ran the wires down the sides of the papier-mâché and out along the neck. The shut-off switch was buried in a tuft of hair beneath the wolf's chin.

"I'm going to give it a try," Tommy announced. "Is everybody ready?"

"Go ahead," Diana said impatiently.

With a flick of his index finger, Tommy set the eyes in motion. They rolled right and left, blinking on and off.

Diana rubbed her hands together. "Perfect! Ooh, I can't wait to see Kate Harmon's face," she said.

"I haven't done the tail yet," Tommy reminded her. "Then it'll really be spectacular. Except that St. Cloud's lightning bolts are great, too. And the guy who did the sculpture of the storm cloud is a regular Michelangelo."

Diana's mouth fell open. Olivia shook her head. "Oh, boy," she said to Peter, expecting the worst.

"Do you mean to tell me," Diana began ominously "that you knew what their mascot was all the time?"

"Sure, I knew it. Saw it the other day. It would have been finished last week except part of it melted." He chuckled. "That was my cousin's fault."

"Your cousin?" Hope asked.

"Yeah, he lives over in St. Cloud, see. A computer nerd, old Bobby. Real bright guy." Coming from Tommy, that was quite a compliment. "So, you know, we're buddies, and we compare notes on science projects that interest us. The mascots turned out to be really fascinating challenges. We're both thinking of entering the equipment we devised in the state science fair in May."

Diana was so angry, she couldn't speak. This was too unbelievable.

"'What's Bobby's invention?" Tara asked, delighting in the look on Diana's face.

"Well, he made up this program with a little terminal in the storm cloud's head — something that would broadcast the score throughout the game. It's real ingenious."

"I'll bet," Jessica agreed.

"But then he had to take the thing apart to get the miniterminal inside, and when he took off these metal arms, he stuck them on the radiator overnight. Boy, was the committee riled over that one!"

"I'll bet." Olivia smiled.

"But," Diana sputtered, "why didn't you tell me all this?"

Tommy shrugged. "You never asked me."

"He's right, Diana," Beef pointed out. "You asked all of *us*. You never asked Tommy."

Jessica decided to play devil's advocate. "Didn't you think you owed it to your school to rat on your cousin to Diana, Tommy?" she asked with a hint of a chuckle in her voice.

Tommy looked puzzled. "Why should I tell anybody? It's just science."

Tara went over to Diana and patted her hand consolingly. "Scientists are above all that, don't you know?" she said. "But there's one thing to be happy about, Diana. Bobby's probably the same kind of guy. He'd never spill the beans about the Tarenton mascot — he'd never think of it."

"Right," Tommy said. He was busy with the tail now, having a little trouble threading his connectors through the heavy fur.

"This is horrible! Absurd!" Diana yelled. "I think St. Cloud should be disqualified. Beef, come on! We're going to the principal's office."

The rest of the cheerleaders stuck around to watch Tommy finish his work, and they cheered when he flicked the second switch on top of the left rear paw and the large, bushy tail swung left and right.

"You're a genius, Tommy," Olivia said, patting the boy on the back.

"I know." He smiled. "But these things come easy to me."

"Not because of the wolf," Jessica told him, "although that's pretty good, too. It's Diana. You got her."

Tommy frowned. "I don't understand."

"It doesn't matter," Tara grinned. "We do."

CHAPTER

15

Monday morning was cloudy, but it felt even bleaker because Pres had to wake up once again without Mary Ellen beside him. She hadn't phoned since she'd walked out, and he hadn't called her. He wanted to surprise her, and told Sean as much.

Sean agreed to keep the secret from everyone but Patrick, and one or the other of them stopped by at the apartment, helping Pres to get up and dressed in the morning, and washed and ready for bed at night.

The only other person who knew was Connie. With his heart pounding so loudly he was sure she could hear it over in Haven Lake Medical Center, Pres had called to apologize and set up an appointment. Her response, clear-cut and without any trace of emotion, was "How about Sunday?" Buying just a little more time, wanting Mary Ellen to have a chance to cool off, he made an appointment for three on Monday instead. Then he got Olivia on the phone and informed her that she, Angie, Nancy, and Walt were responsible for getting Mary Ellen to the medical center at the right time.

He picked up the thriller he'd been reading and started a new chapter, but he found himself going over the same pages again and again. He just couldn't concentrate. At about noon, he had some fruit and cheese to fortify himself. He looked at himself in the mirror a lot, and stared at the weights he had insisted Mary Ellen bury in the closet before he came home from the hospital. He was tempted to pick one up, but he knew better. If he really did want to get well, he was going to have to put himself in the hands of a professional. Three o'clock couldn't come soon enough for him.

Mary Ellen had an art history class that morning, but she might as well not have gone that day. She didn't know whether the topic of discussion was the use of color in Rembrandt or the sociological significance of Jackson Pollock. By the time she got to Marnie's at lunchtime, all she knew was that her own color was green, and the only significant thing on her mind was her marriage and how she was going to make things up with Pres.

She wanted desperately to call him, but she knew she couldn't. She wasn't the sort of person who bent over backward, but she had done so with Pres. She had moved into his place, bought furnishings that he liked, arranged her schedule around his hours. She said yes too much. And this was one instance where she wasn't going to. She would let him come to her.

It was two-thirty when she finished rearranging the racks in the back of the store and started dressing for her circuit around the mall. She and her boss, Mrs. Gunderson, had decided that one of the best ways to sell clothes was for customers in the mall to see them on Mary Ellen, so her afternoons were generally spent wandering around, wearing Marnie's latest clothes, with price tags dangling.

"Where are those new patterned knee socks, Mary Ellen?" Mrs. Gunderson wandered into the dressing room to check her first outfit of the afternoon.

"Oh, sorry. I didn't know if you wanted me to open a new package," she said, pulling on a bulky plum-colored cotton sweater with a mauve and green flower on the bodice. It had a nice jewel neck and slightly puffed sleeves, and Mary Ellen would have bought it herself in an instant if it hadn't cost $68 — before tax.

"Don't be silly. You have to look right, don't you? My present to you for the day. They're not that much of a loss," she added when Mary Ellen started to protest. "I have to do something to cheer you up. What is it, dear? Do you want to talk about it?"

Mary Ellen slipped on the matching gore-pleated plum skirt and zipped it, noticing how loose it was on her. But she always wore a size 8! It was worry, plain and simple. She was fading away from worry.

"I do, but I don't," she said finally. "I think I

better get moving." Without waiting for the sympathy that was sure to come, she took her price list and walked out into the mall.

The place wasn't very busy on weekdays — just a collection of mothers and babies in strollers, or the occasional business person on a late lunch hour. She walked past the video store, noticing that they had the new film she and Pres had wanted to rent for their VCR. She strolled on, over to menswear, spotting a sports jacket in heather tones that would look perfect on Pres. Everywhere she looked, something reminded her of him, of his face or his voice or his very special touch. It was agonizing.

And then she saw something that made her smile. It was Angie, Walt, Olivia, and Nancy, sitting beside one of the potted palms in the center of the mall right near the fountain. The squad always used to hang out there the year before when they had something vital to discuss. Her friends spotted her and immediately began looking very concerned about something. Angie had her hands pressed against her stomach.

"I thought you were at the high school, helping with the mascot," Mary Ellen said.

"We were, but Diana was so impossible. And then, Angie started having these pains," Walt explained.

"Pains! What do you mean?" Mary Ellen took a seat beside them.

Angie, putting on a forced smile, gripped her stomach harder. "I don't know. It's probably something I ate," she said. "Nancy insisted it had to be fumes from the glue in the shop — maybe I'm allergic — but I can't believe that."

"We came here so she could get a breath of fresh air and feel better," Olivia went on. "But nothing seems to help."

"I told her she ought to get over to the medical center and have someone look at her, but she absolutely refuses," Walt declared, throwing up his hands.

"She's really in bad shape," Nancy said. "You do something," she begged Mary Ellen. "She listens to you."

"Angie," Mary Ellen put an arm around her good friend. "They're right. You are going to the medical center right this minute."

"Well, maybe," Angie shrugged. She winced with convincing pain. "But . . . would you come with me?"

Mary Ellen glanced down at her watch. "I have another hour to go here, Angie," she said. "You get over there and I'll meet you guys, how about that?"

"No," Angie said. "I'll only go if Mary Ellen takes me," she said. She, too, was sneaking a glance at the watch. They'd promised Pres three P.M. on the dot.

"Oh, all right. Mrs. Gunderson probably can't wait to get me out of her hair today, anyway," Mary Ellen agreed. "I'll go change into my clothes and meet you in the parking lot." Actually, it felt wonderful to be needed. If Pres had just once said that he would try — for her — she would have abandoned everything else to become his own personal cheerleader.

197

"Thanks, Melon, you're super!" Angie exclaimed, nearly jumping up. Walt nudged her in the ribs so that she said, "Ooh!" and gripped her stomach again.

"We'll meet you at Walt's Jeep in five, Mary Ellen," Nancy told her, quickly hurrying Angie away before she had too quick a recovery.

Mrs. Gunderson didn't ask questions, but let her prize model go at once. She shook her head as she watched Mary Ellen race out of the store. There was something seriously wrong with that girl — she was going to have to do something about it, and soon.

Walt whizzed out of the mall and over to Haven Lake Medical Center, just as the big clock on the front of the building struck three. He bypassed the emergency entrance and went directly into the parking lot, despite Mary Ellen's objections. Nobody said anything to her as they hurried her inside, past the reception desk and over to the elevator.

"I think it's the fifth floor," Olivia said.

"Right. Room 530," Nancy agreed.

"What are you talking about?" Mary Ellen demanded. "What's with all of you? Angie, we need to get you signed in right away."

"Oh, I feel fine now, Mary Ellen." Angie grinned.

"C'mon, we don't want to be late," Walt cautioned them, practically shoving Mary Ellen into the elevator as soon as the door opened.

With Angie and Olivia on one side of her and Walt and Nancy on the other, she couldn't get away. They led her directly to the door of the therapy room.

The sight that greeted her eyes made her gasp, then clap her hands with happiness. It was like a dream, except much better, because even when she pinched herself, it didn't go away.

Pres was on top of a ramp with bars on either side of him and a series of ladder-rung bars on top. Connie Lapino was right behind him. And the wheelchair was all the way on the opposite side of the room.

Pres was standing up, gripping the bars to his left and right. He saw her in the doorway and his blue eyes twinkled. "Hi, sweetheart," he said. "I've missed you."

Mary Ellen, the tears running down her cheeks, was laughing as she came toward him, her arms outstretched. "Pres, darling" she said. "You're doing it. You're going to get well."

"Yes, I am." He nodded. And he meant it.

Pres was nothing if not uncompromising with himself. Although Connie cautioned him not to overdo, he was determined to get himself back into the shape necessary to start learning to walk again. So every morning, he did Connie's waking-up exercises in bed, then had Mary Ellen drive him over to the pool, where Connie met him. They worked for an hour in the shallow water, moving his limp legs, getting the muscles to respond. After that came a massage, and then lunch.

He was supposed to take a nap before beginning his afternoon regime, but he was too impatient. So he read everything he could get his hands on about the body, and its ability to heal itself. When he'd finished the nitty gritty physical stuff, he picked up a book called *Mind over Muscles*, which told him that the most beneficial thing he could do for himself was to adopt a positive attitude. It seemed like kind of weak advice, but he was so eager to try anything that might work, he began saying to himself throughout the day the little slogans the author had cooked up. They were gems like, "Think yourself up tall," and, "Brain power is body fuel." Weird, but catchy.

The afternoon was the hardest part of Pres's day, and yet, it was the part he looked forward to the most because he was certain he was getting the most out of it. It started in the physical therapy room of the medical center. Connie would put him on the ramp and make him move forward and backward as she helped him rotate his hip joints. Because he had been in such extraordinary physical condition before the accident, he was quick to bounce back. His arms and torso could pull him along the top bars while he dragged his legs, making them move as best he could.

From the ramp, he went to the ankle weights. Lying on the floor, he would move his weighted limbs with Connie's instruction. He would gradually work up from the two-pound weights he had started with to five-pounders and then to eight on each leg. When he was sweating profusely, he would move onto the Cybex machine, a kind of Nautilus for the injured.

Pres would yell at the stupid machine, and Connie would yell back.

"I can't," he said on Friday after five days of diligent work. "It's impossible."

"What are you, chicken?" Connie challenged. "You still have four sets to go. And then the whirlpool and the table."

"Connie, listen. I asked you to push me gently back toward the way I used to be, not shove me over the edge of the cliff."

Her sparkling black eyes gleamed at him. "What can I do? I'm a perfectionist. I will have nothing but the best. Four more, Pres!"

After his sets, he went to the warm whirlpool, a delightful break. Patrick and Sean were there, as they had been every day that week. They always hung around with Pres, splashing water all over the room until Connie yelled that the next session was starting and they had better get Pres back on the table on the double.

The table was torture. First, Pres was allowed to regulate the amount of pain for himself. He was supposed to bring his knees into his chest, looping a towel around the leg in question. All those weeks in the casts had practically petrified his knees, so it took time and a great deal of effort to regain flexibility.

Sean and Patrick always left when Connie took over. They knew from the look on Pres's face that he didn't want them to see him reacting to the pain. It was healthful pain, of course, but when she bent his legs back, there was no way not to yell.

"So tell me," Pres grunted, trying not to think

of the pain. "How come you agreed to work with me? You said when you came over to the house that day that I wasn't your responsibility anymore. Ow!"

She put his right leg down and ran her hand along the tibia. It had healed nicely. "That's right. It's when you became your own responsibility that you started to interest me."

"I thought I'd done a pretty good job of ducking you." He squeezed his eyes shut, then held his breath.

"You certainly did. And I'll admit I doubted you'd ever come around. You're a pretty tough cookie." She hadn't doubted it for an instant, but she didn't want to make him think she expected him to capitulate. The thing was, they all did, sooner or later. All the patients who fought her, despite what they said, really wanted to walk again. It was only a matter of how much time she had to wait.

"Okay, looks good. I think that's enough for today," she said at last. Quickly, she gave him a rap on the chest and the air he had been holding in exploded out of him. Connie laughed. "Your whole problem is you never learned to relax," she said. "When you fight me like that, you tense up, so you're giving yourself the pain. I'm not doing anything."

"Sure, lady. And the moon is made of green cheese." Pres swung himself around on the table and let his legs dangle over the edge. "How much longer do you think I can take this?"

"As long as it takes." She wiped her hands, then

draped the towel around her neck. She was sweating as much as he, and her face was just as flushed from effort. "Pres, you're doing brilliantly, don't get me wrong. But remember that it takes at least four months for the body to rehabilitate itself after a major injury such as the one you sustained. You can't rush that. You can work until you're blue in the face, but tissue, bone, and muscle have their own schedule." She walked to the door to let Sean and Patrick back in.

Pres's response was to reach down for the walker and pull himself off the table. "That's fine for most people, Connie, but not for me. I haven't got the four months to spare."

She turned and stared at him quizzically, one eyebrow raised. "Why? You going someplace?"

He grinned. "Okay, then tell me. You've seen me here for a week now. How's it going? What are my chances?"

She shrugged. "Your guess is as good as mine. We won't know anything definite for a month, at least."

Pres felt himself tense up again. "But that's not good enough."

"No," she agreed, "it's not. According to your latest tests, the nerve damage is minimal, I'm happy to say. But Pres, the spinal column is a peculiar thing. Even hurting a little part of it can wreak havoc with the whole thing. You may get to a point where you can move your legs, but have no control over them. And, if that should be the case, we have a variety of other machines at our disposal to help you."

Pres simply couldn't hear what she was saying. "If I do everything you tell me, and I really work at it, then I should — "

"You *should*. But I can't say that you *will*." She opened the door and threw out over her shoulder, "Get some good rest this weekend. See you Monday." She closed the door before he could yell at her.

Sean and Patrick took him down to the dressing room and helped him get his things out of the locker, helped him out of the wheelchair and onto a bench so that he could put his street clothes back on again. He let them — he had no choice — but he felt like a baby, and he couldn't stand that. When Sean handed him his pants, he grabbed them, and struggled to put them on. He had never realized what coordination it took, just to bend the knee at the correct angle, to get the foot in the right hole, to shift his weight so that he could bring the fabric up to his waist and get the button and zipper done. Getting dressed was such an incredible chore, but he had to do it — he couldn't ask for help. It took about twenty minutes, but neither of his friends made a move toward him.

"So," Patrick said as they began to wheel back down the corridor to the elevator. "How did the week go, all in all?"

"I hurt," Pres told him. He was really mad at Connie, and so confused about his own feelings. He thought he was getting better, but she refused to commit herself to anything. He needed answers, and she wasn't talking. She *had* to know more about his chances than she was saying.

"How long does Connie say before you can do a double back flip?" Sean wanted to know.

Pres was silent for a minute. "I wouldn't ask her that."

The two boys looked at each other over the top of Pres's chair.

"Listen, old buddy, about the weekend," Sean began. "We were thinking — "

"My whole two days are tied up," Pres said quickly. "I don't want to see anybody. I am sawing Z's, period. And when I wake up, I'm going back to sleep again."

"I don't think so." Patrick shook his head.

"You already have plans," Sean told him. He wheeled Pres inside the elevator and pressed the down button.

Pres looked at him quizzically. "What am I doing?"

Sean chuckled. "You'll see."

They wheeled him downstairs to the parking lot. Mary Ellen, Angie, and Nancy were waiting in the Buick, which was jammed to the gills with stuff. Walt's Jeep was waiting behind the Buick, as was Peter's car. Jessica was driving Patrick's van. Everybody except Duffy was present and accounted for.

"What's going on?" Pres demanded, scowling.

"You're going to have fun," Sean said, chuckling, "whether you like it or not."

CHAPTER

Jessica's Aunt Madeline owned a working horse farm about twenty miles from Tarenton. At one time, she'd bred and trained riding and jumping horses for most of the north country, but after her younger brother, Jessica's father, died, she said she had come to her senses. She realized that her life was time-limited, and she had other things to do than muck out stalls and rope ornery stallions for the rest of her days. So she sold off most of her stock and kept only the horses she loved. The farm was hers, free and clear, and she now brought in some income by giving riding lessons to the locals and renting out grazing land to other farmers for their sheep and cattle.

When Jessica was little, she had always looked forward to visits to Aunt Madeline's, and when she grew older, the ranch was a respite she really needed. There, in the quiet of the countryside, she was always able to renew her spirits. She was certain that this place would do as much for Pres.

As for Madeline, she was delighted to have company. She was fond of her niece, but didn't get to see much of her, so when Jessica had called with her plan, she'd agreed at once. Madeline told her she was welcome to bring a houseful, as long as they didn't mind sleeping bags in the bunkhouse. All except for her friend in the wheelchair, of course. He got the guest room in the main house, and breakfast in bed — if his wife was willing to cook it and bring it up to him.

They arrived in a caravan near dusk, with Jessica and Patrick leading the way. The main road turned in at a sign that read Double Knot Drive, and then bent again beside a brook. The water ran fast beside the road.

Patrick drove around the next curve and then drew his breath in sharply. The farm was laid out in squares, each divided with split-rail fences. The horizon seemed so close he could have touched it. At the top of a rise was the red farmhouse and several barns, and dotted here and there on the landscape were the most magnificent horses he had ever seen.

"There! Pull in behind the trough," Jessica directed Patrick as they came up the hill. The sun was going down, and the sky was a strange orange gray, as though it were holding back a storm. Wind whipped through the branches of the pines that flanked the long drive. Out in the pasture, ten horses grazed, their manes and tails tossed by the stiff breeze.

"This place is incredible," Sean said as he parked beside Mary Ellen and went over to help Pres out.

Patrick was already busy setting up the wheelchair. "Jessica!" he called across the growing line of cars. "Why didn't you tell us about this before? It's beautiful!"

Jessica was hugging herself, taking in the beauty of the farm. Actually, she had been planning to introduce her friends to her aunt for a while now. She had felt badly, ever since Pres's accident, that she wasn't doing enough to help him get better. She just had trouble being around sick people. But when it came to surprises, she was an expert. The ranch had always cheered her up. Surely it would be the perfect medicine for Pres. "Isn't it neat? You should see it at Christmas time! Aunt Madeline puts sleigh bells on the horses and hitches up the cart, and you can go for miles in the country without seeing a soul."

"Sounds pretty desolate." Hope climbed out of Peter's car and looked around. "It's gorgeous, I agree, but I prefer the city."

"Absolutely," Tara declared, pulling her make-up kit and two suitcases out of Sean's car. She and Kate had ridden next to each other all the way up, and it had been slightly awkward, because the two girls didn't have much to say to each other. It was a relief to have her squad members around her again. "I mean, where do you get a pizza around here?"

"You have such a pedestrian soul, Tara," Pres chided her, climbing out of the car with Mary Ellen's help, and into the chair. "This place is

A-1 in my book. Hey, does Connie know I'm here?" he asked his wife suddenly.

"Yes, and she thinks it's fine." Mary Ellen smiled. "The only thing she told me was not to let you party all night."

Angie, Olivia, and Walt were already unpacking for Pres so that Mary Ellen could take him into the house. Olivia was enthralled with the beauty around her, and her only regret was that Duffy couldn't be with her to share it. He had gone out with the posse hunting the wolf, of all things. And he assured her that he would not come back without a dynamite story to print. "This will be my real debut as a writer," he had insisted.

"As long as it's not your finale," she had quipped.

But if the truth be known, it might have been hard with Walt around. The two guys had met a few times, and they both understood what Olivia was going through — so the best course of action was to remain distant, but friendly. The more distant, the better.

"Let's unpack and get ready for supper," Jessica urged them all, struggling toward the house with her sleeping bag and roll. "Aunt Madeline is a stickler for supper on time."

"Oh, I'm not that bad. Don't make me out to be some kind of ogre, Jessica." A tall, angular woman wearing jeans, a checked shirt, mud-encrusted riding boots, and a red bandana around her neck, strolled out onto the front porch. Her reddish blonde hair, streaked with gray, was tied in a knot at the nape of her neck. She might have been in her fifties, or even older — but she walked with a youthful stride.

"Maddy!" Jessica yelled, throwing herself into her aunt's arms.

"How are you, pumpkin?" Aunt Madeline asked lovingly, tousling her niece's hair.

"I'm great. This is — " Jessica looked around at the group and was about to name them when her aunt put up a restraining hand.

"Don't bother, we'll take care of introductions as they're needed. Nice to meet you, folks. Dinner's sort of catch as catch can. Hope you don't mind."

"We really appreciate your having us, Mrs. Draper," Mary Ellen said. She looked over at Pres, now flanked by Walt and Peter. His eyes were shining like a kid's, as though he couldn't believe his good luck in being here.

"Don't mention it. Just call me Maddy and I'll be happy," Jessica's aunt told her in a brusque voice. Then she moved over to Pres and put out her hand. "I've heard about you, mister," she nodded. "Got to congratulate you," Madeline went on. "You got guts."

"Thanks." Pres smiled. "But I wish I had more than that."

" 'If wishes were horses, then beggars would ride,' " Madeline quoted, then laughed uproariously. "Speaking of horses, there's somebody I want you to meet."

They unpacked the wheelchair and set it up so that Pres could lead the procession over to the nearest corral where three horses — two white mares and a deep chestnut stallion — were enclosed.

"This here's Confidence," Maddy said, indicating the stallion, who whinnied at her approach. "Confidence, meet the gang."

Jessica looked shocked. "This can't be! Well, you're right, it is." She was dumbfounded. "But I thought . . . you told me Confidence was gone."

"I know, pumpkin." Maddy smiled. She reached over the fence and stroked the length of the horse's head, then scratched around his ears. The horse nuzzled her hand, and shook his head in delight when she reached in her pocket and produced a carrot for him. There was an affinity between the woman and animal that was so palpable, Pres thought that the horse smiled at her.

"I was all set to do it," Madeline admitted. "Had the gun to his head and everything, and then, I don't know what — something stopped my hand. Poor devil had broken his hind leg in two places taking that high jump down near the stream, don'tcha know, and the vet told me it was no use. I've put animals down before, but I looked right in this beast's eyes and he told me not to. Said he was going to get well, and if I knew what was good for me I'd let him be. So I did," she finished.

"I didn't know horses could walk again after their legs were broken," Peter commented.

"Sure can't say I've seen another do it," Maddy told him. "He's a fighter, though. I don't let him do as much as he used to — he's relegated to the beginner riding class, doing a little trotting and cantering — but I bet he could gallop apace if he wanted to," she said proudly.

"This must be some horse," Pres said admiringly.

"Uh-huh." Madeline gave the animal a friendly slap on the flank. "And you know the funny thing is I named him Confidence at birth, without knowing how apt it was. Fits him like a glove, that name."

They all stood before the magnificent horse and were quiet for a moment. Then Madeline asked, "Anybody here hungry? I think I smell some biscuits and gravy. We better get you settled. C'mon to the bunkhouse."

She led the way across the rutted ground to a large structure behind the main house. A wall divided it into two halves. The building was well lit and warm, with cots lined up in a row in each half.

"Now, everybody, this place is centrally heated, so you don't have to worry about frostbite, but it's not exactly the Hilton. Remember, guys on one side, girls can stay over here. There's a bathroom down the hall."

"This is great, Maddy." Nancy smiled. It was a lot more rustic than Nancy was used to, but she thought that roughing it might be good for her. She thought of it as another way to toughen herself up — for what she couldn't say. "Who lives here?" she asked, peering around at all the beds.

"Used to employ twelve men to run this place with me, plus a cook and a foreman. It was quite a place, in the old days. Everybody hung out in the main house most of the time, though, so it was like I had the biggest family in the area. Lots of fun," she said regretfully. "But lots of work. Too much for an old lady like me." She chuckled. "Now, you can wash up and then it's time to eat. See you." She waved, marching out of the bunk-house as though she were in a great hurry to get somewhere.

"I like her," Pres declared to no one in partic-ular.

"I thought you would." Jessica grinned.

They ate at a long country table, so loaded with food that it seemed to sag in the middle each time Maddy's housekeeper, Berta, set down a new bowl. They all found that they had ravenous appetites; even those of the group who were gen-erally fussy eaters dug into the pork pie and fried green tomatoes. There wasn't a crust of the home-made zucchini bread left at the end of the meal, and as for the three pies — applesauce, quince, and lemon meringue — they vanished, along with the two gallons of milk, at a miraculous pace.

"I don't know what got into me." Angie sighed, taking a last sip from her glass.

"It's the country air," Jessica assured her. "It just blows down through your lungs and into your stomach, leaving a gaping pit that simply must be filled with Maddy's fabulous cuisine."

"And you haven't even started chores yet," Maddy said from the head of the table. "Wait'll you see how hungry you are for breakfast at six."

"That's a funny time to eat breakfast," Sean commented, eating the last crumbs of his pie.

"I think she means six A.M., pal," Kate in-formed him.

"You're kidding!" Sean exclaimed. "Who could eat at that hour?"

"Oh, you'll eat, all right." Madeline laughed. "You'll be real hungry after all those chores you have to get up to do at five. You have to rake out stalls, put down clean hay, and curry and water the horses. *Afterward* comes breakfast."

"I think I'll leave now," Tara said, only half-joking.

Jessica shook a finger in her aunt's face. "Not very hospitable, Maddy, to make them all work like dogs when they've just arrived."

"Oh, all right. They're excused tomorrow then. But you're not, young lady." Madeline stood up from the table and started to clear the dishes.

"I'll be up," Jessica told her.

"Then I will, too," Patrick said staunchly, but he shivered a little at the idea of the cold, dark morning.

"Oh, I guess it wouldn't kill me," Walt shrugged. "How about it, Angie? Nancy?"

The girls nodded reluctantly, and pretty soon, they had shamed their less-hardy friends into agreeing, too.

"Is there anything I can do?" Pres asked Madeline quietly.

"Of course," she told him, her eyes sparkling. "You can clean and polish bridles and harnesses. I'll set you up right in front of Confidence's stall, and he can tell you what to do."

When they had cleared the table and started a load of dishes in the commercial-sized dishwasher, they scattered to different parts of the giant living room with its huge stone fireplace and wall-to-wall books. Some of them settled in to read, others to play cards, most of them to talk. Tara and Sean were clearly out of their element and would have preferred the action of Benny's, or the noise of a rock club, and Nancy seemed to be in her own world, but everyone else was enjoying the evening immensely.

At about ten, Olivia stood up and stretched. "I'm going to hit the sack," she said. "Good night, everyone."

"Me, too." Mary Ellen yawned. "Are you coming, Pres?" she asked.

"In a sec." He was busy staring into the fire.

"What about it?" Kate asked Sean. "Time for you to put on your jammies."

"How about a walk in the moonlight first?" Sean whispered in her ear.

"Well, okay." Kate shrugged. "If you want."

"Don't go too far," Madeline warned them. "The horses have been really agitated the past few nights. The wolf was sighted a few miles from here, you know. I haven't seen Confidence kick his stall like that since he was a colt."

"We'll be careful, Maddy," Kate assured her. They grabbed their coats and started for the front door.

Tara gave them a look, but she was getting used to being odd girl out. It didn't bother her so much that Sean was nuts about Kate — although she really didn't understand what he saw in her — but it got to her when other people were paired up and she wasn't. She walked outside, onto the porch, and spotted Nancy on her way to the bunkhouse. "Wait up," she called. She ran ahead, and together the two girls walked to their shelter.

They washed quickly and changed into night-clothes, then zipped themselves into adjoining sleeping bags on the low cots. Tara leaned over and spoke softly.

"I've been dying to talk to you alone," she whispered. "So, tell me."

Nancy cleared her throat and rolled over. "What?"

"About Nick. How'd it go? Isn't he a dream?"

Nancy propped herself up on one elbow. "A dream, yes. But not mine, I don't think. The date was great, but he just doesn't want to see me again. So I'm not crying over spilled milk. I'm being terribly grown-up." As she said it, she knew she was lying.

"Well, that's no fun," Tara declared. "Why don't you call him?"

"Oh, come on, Tara," Nancy said. "I'm not going to force myself on the guy. If he wasn't interested, then he wasn't."

Tara narrowed her eyes. "You sound like you might be fonder of him than you let on."

"Well, maybe." Nancy rolled over and turned her back on Tara. "I don't call guys unless they've made it clear that they want me to."

"Okay, that's easy. Wait a second, wait. . . ." Tara sat up and wracked her brain for a minute. "I'll play Cupid. I'll engineer a chance meeting, how about that?"

"Tara!" Nancy rolled back over. "Look, it was really nice of you to set us up in the first place, but it didn't work. And I'll be going back to Brown at the end of next week, anyhow."

"Does he know that?" Tara was determined.

"No, and I'd appreciate it if you wouldn't tell him. Now, if we're going to get up at the crack of dawn — "

"Hey, five A.M. is long before the crack!" Tara exclaimed.

"Right. Well, let's get some sleep."

A voice floated down over them. "Will you two girls stop talking!" Walt demanded.

Tara and Nancy exchanged looks. "I didn't realize they could hear," Nancy whispered.

"Every little thing." It was Patrick's voice.

"Mind your own business," Tara huffed.

"We will if you will," Peter said. "Go to sleep!"

Sean and Kate were far from asleep, or even tired. As they strolled along the side of the front pasture, they held hands and every once in a while, glanced over at one another.

"I want a place like this some day," Kate sighed.

"You would," Sean said disgustedly. "Can't I persuade you to give this all up for the bright lights and excitement of Tarenton?"

She smiled at him. "You'll never be satisfied with Tarenton," she said to him. "You'll be moving out as soon as you finish school. To New York, I bet. Or maybe Chicago. Yes, you look like Chicago to me."

Sean stopped walking and took her around the waist. "I'd go anywhere with you," he said dramatically.

"Oh, come on," she shoved him away playfully. "Be real."

"I am," he said, suddenly serious. "I love you, Kate. I've never said that to a girl before . . . at least and meant it. I know you're going to think this is dumb, but seeing Pres the way he is — you know, maybe never getting up again — well, it's taught me to look around at what I've got and be grateful for it. And what I've got, I'm not giving up."

He drew her close. His lips touched hers and stayed there, molding to the shape of her mouth, savoring the delicious warmth of her.

But eventually, Kate pulled away and tugged at his hand. He was pushing her too fast, too far. "An early morning means an early night. Let's go."

And because he would do anything Kate asked, he went.

Pres didn't want to go to sleep. Not ever. Going to sleep meant waking up to the chair again, to the possibility that, despite his improvement in the past week, he still might be doomed to that chair for the rest of his life.

He wheeled himself down the hall after everyone had gone to the bunkhouse and, throwing his jacket around his shoulders, maneuvered his way outside. The barn was close, and his arms were now powerful enough to steer himself along the rutted road. He pulled open the barn door and heard the horses whinny, and smelled the sharp animal scent.

Only a small uncovered bulb illuminated the barn. Pres bumped along on the hard dirt floor, strewn with hay, until he came to Confidence's stall. He put out his hand, and the horse came closer, placing his big muzzle against Pres's palm.

"If you can do it," he whispered, "then I can, too. Just . . . would you give me a clue as to how I get started?"

Pres stared into Confidence's liquid brown eyes for a long time, then turned around and went back to the house.

CHAPTER

17

The weekend went too quickly for all of them. The chores turned out to be fun because they were different, and Aunt Madeline was the perfect chaperone, because she made herself scarce. Far away from everyday life — the hospital, and parents, and Diana and the mascot, the group seemed to grow closer together. By Sunday afternoon, they just didn't want to go.

"I guess it's time," Olivia said, as the shadows lengthened on the living room wall. She went over to Maddy and threw her arms around her. "It's been wonderful."

"If anyone had ever told me that I would actually enjoy having a bevy of teenagers over for the weekend, I would have told them they were cracked in two." Madeline smiled. "Thank goodness I have an open mind about these things. See, you're never too old to learn."

"We have a little something for you," Angie

said. "It's for you and Pres. Kind of an end-of-weekend treat."

"You're going to love this." Walt grinned.

"Watch carefully, Pres," Angie told him. "You'll be quizzed on this later."

"Oh, boy." Pres chuckled. "More tests. Getting me ready for tomorrow, huh?"

"Wait till you see this, love," Mary Ellen said cheerily. She helped Walt wheel him to the side of the living room while Sean and Patrick moved the furniture out of the way.

"What are you doing to my house?" Maddy demanded with a twinkle in her eye.

"It's for a good cause, Maddy," Jessica assured her, seating her in a big wing chair beside Pres.

They had worked on the cheer one day when he was with Connie, sweating his brains out to move one muscle the way she told him to. It was Olivia's idea, something, she said, for him to work toward. Walt and Angie complained that they weren't in shape, and Nancy claimed she was going to be too charley-horsed the next day, but Mary Ellen wouldn't let them get away with those lame excuses. "Once a cheerleader, always a cheerleader," she said in her best ex-captain's voice. And when they finally got going, they agreed with her that they weren't that rusty, after all.

Now, only three rehearsals later, they were ready. Angie stood beside Hope, Jessica, and Nancy at the front of the room, near the fireplace. Peter, Sean, and Walt faced them. Mary Ellen and Tara lifted Olivia on their shoulders.

"Where are we going?
Why are we here?
Let everyone around,
Come listen to our cheer!

We are the ones,
C'mon, let's hear it!
No team so fine,
With such great spirit!

Reaching the peak,
Scaling the top!
We are the winners
'Cause we just won't stop!

YAY, team! Yay, Tarenton!"

Olivia somersaulted into Walt's waiting arms, and he caught her as if they were still partners, just like the year before. Hope and Nancy did cartwheels that ended in magnificent splits. While Peter did a stag leap in front of Tara's back flip, Jessica was in the air, being handed to Walt and then to Sean. Mary Ellen and Angie did double back walkovers and ended beside the three boys, holding their legs high in the air.

Kate, Patrick, and Maddy were impressed, of course, but Pres was captivated. He sat with his hands gripping the arms of his chair, motionless, taking in each skillful move, hearing the lilt in their voices, almost imagining them in the brilliant red and white uniforms with the big T on the front. It was incredible, the two teams, banded

222

together, as though they were meant to be one. Their movements were fluid, easy, as though the ten of them had been working together for months. If he tried hard, he could even see himself, wearing the Tarenton High colors, leaping high in the air, his body whole and well.

As the group ended the cheer in a semi-circle at his feet, he noticed that they had left a hole in the line. It was his place, beside Mary Ellen. And then he realized that the gaps he had seen throughout the cheer in different places on the floor had been intentional. They had composed the cheer specifically for eleven, not for ten. They had written the piece so that he could take part in it.

"Hey, neat, guys. Is that a new one?" he asked casually, because a thank you seemed too simple and paltry a response.

"The six of us wrote it for the Rivals Game next week, but we adapted it," Olivia said pointedly, "as you can see. It's called 'Cheer for Two Teams,' Pres. We still have one member missing, though."

"Well, it would be nice if you could all stick around long enough for me to join in," he said slowly, "but it's a long shot."

"We'll wait," Angie said quietly.

"Or we'll come back," Nancy added.

"Whenever you're ready," Walt said.

Pres looked at them all and nodded, his heart too full.

"I sure could use a little fresh air," Maddy said, breaking the silence.

"Right. I'm going to start packing up," Walt said, moving the couch back to where it had been before the cheering.

"Pull the cars up next to the bunkhouse," Kate suggested. "Nancy and I will get the stuff and bring it out."

"Thank you for everything, Maddy," Jessica said, hugging her aunt. "I just wish I could take a little ride before we take off."

"Well, why not?" Maddy exclaimed. "These horses are getting soft, not having classes all weekend. I'll saddle a few, if you help me, Jess. Anyone care to join us before you set off for the city?"

"Yes, I would."

Everyone turned to see who had spoken. It was Pres.

"Oh, sweetie," Mary Ellen said.

"I want to ride Confidence," Pres said with stolid insistence. "Let me try."

Mary Ellen looked concerned. "Do you really think — ?"

"Yes, I do," he snapped. "Patrick, you can ride right next to me. Hey, I'm only going to walk the guy around the corral."

They all just stood there. Nobody knew exactly what Pres's body was and was not capable of, but riding a horse seemed plain dumb.

"You know, man, you really are asking for it," Sean said, playfully shadow-boxing around Pres's chair. "I thought you needed a permission slip from Connie for stuff like that."

"Here's the deal, Pres," Angie grinned. "You

can ride him if you cook us all dinner tonight when we get home."

Pres knew they were putting him off. He had been in good spirits until now, but there was no way to get around the fact that they were humoring him.

"Look, I want to go outside," he said, turning his chair.

"Right, good buddy." Walt came over to Pres's wheelchair and started pushing him out of the living room.

"Are you listening to me? I want to ride." Pres jerked the chair out of Walt's hands and continued under his own steam.

Maddy met him at the front door. "I see no reason why you can't," she said. "As long as you let me show you what to do."

She took the handles of the wheelchair and steered him outside, toward the barn.

"I am absolutely opposed to this," Mary Ellen said, as she ran after them.

Jessica put a hand on her arm. "Don't worry. My aunt knows horses. She knows *this* horse. Confidence is as gentle as they come."

"It's not the horse I'm worried about," Mary Ellen said.

But she apparently had no choice, because by the time she and the rest of the group arrived at the barn, Maddy already had the horse saddled and ready to go.

"Two of you boys will have to help me," she stated, placing mounting boxes on either side of Confidence. The horse seemed completely unfazed by this unorthodox procedure.

"Patrick, you're the tallest," Maddy said. "You lift Pres onto the box and put one of his feet in the stirrups. You can push him up so he can grab the reins. Then Sean, you get on the other side, and you can maneuver him across the horse's back.

"That's it," Maddy directed him. "Let's try it, Pres."

His legs were dead weight, but he reached for the side of the horse's stall and pulled himself upright. Patrick gave him a boost and suddenly, he was flat out, lying face down on top of the horse. It was embarrassing and it was difficult, but it was really pretty funny. He found himself smiling as he sat up and took the reins.

Sean helped guide his other leg into the second stirrup, and Jessica opened the door of the stall. Confidence walked out into the fading sunlight. Because he had walked this route a thousand times, the horse knew exactly what to do and where to go. He didn't even need the gentle hints from Maddy, who had mounted a second horse and was following right beside Pres.

"How does it feel?" she asked.

"Great." He grinned. "Would you believe I don't ride very often? Cars are more my speed."

"Speed is right," Sean chuckled, leaning on a side of the fence and staring at his friend in disbelief.

But no one there had to guess whether Pres Tilford was happy. He looked in control — somehow, guiding the horse had given him back the element that had been missing since he was injured.

"Can I go faster?" he asked Maddy.

"You could try a trot," she suggested. "Dig in with your knees. Can you do that?"

He looked down at his legs and thought hard, willing them to move. He thought about the strength he used to have in his thighs, and he summoned it back. Then he pushed that strength down to his knees.

It worked! Because of the past week's exercises, he could exert just enough pressure to begin to post. Confidence took the hint and started to move at a trot.

"That's it, Pres! Keep it up!" Jessica yelled from the sidelines. She threw her arms around Mary Ellen, whose cornflower blue eyes were glued to her husband. "Look at what he's doing, Mary Ellen!" Jessica cried. "He can move his legs. If he can post, he can walk."

The others, who hadn't quite understood the significance of this, were immediately elated. Olivia started the cheer for the Rivals Game all over again, and the others joined in. At the end, they screamed, "Yay, Pres!" at the top of their lungs.

The object of their attention was jubilant. He knew there was something different about his capabilities now. In just this short time, he had proved to himself that he was coming back. It was possible.

Only when Maddy insisted that he slow to a walk and take Confidence back to the barn did he stop grinning. "This is wonderful," he told her when they were near the stall. "Can I come back sometime and ride again?"

"Any time you like," the older woman promised. She was so thrilled for Pres, she didn't see him lift the leg on the far side of Confidence by himself, without waiting for her help. With both feet out of the stirrups, he had no way to catch himself, and he lost his balance. Reaching blindly for the reins, he toppled directly over, falling off the horse with an ungraceful plop onto the hay beneath.

Pres cursed and pounded his fist into the hard-packed earth floor.

"Oh, no!" At the sound of his fall, Madeline came running. "It's my fault. You'd think at my age I'd have gotten some more sense. Well, where do you hurt? What's your doctor's number?" She had an arm around him, but he pushed her away.

"I'm fine," he said. "It was a soft landing."

"Are you sure?" Maddy could see now that only his pride had been hurt — and that, pretty badly.

"I told you. No problem." The sullen tone had come back into his voice. It was just like Connie had said — he could move his legs but he had no control. Great, just great.

"Pres, we really should — " Mary Ellen stood in the door of the barn with the wheelchair, staring at Pres. She didn't seem to realize why he was on the ground until Confidence whinnied and tossed his head. "Did he throw you? Oh, no! Oh, Pres, your legs!"

"No, he was a perfect gentleman," Pres told her. This time, he waited for Maddy to assist him.

"I think Pres is just anxious to get going. And

who can blame him?" Maddy took Mary Ellen's hand. "Good luck. And I mean that."

"Thanks," Pres said. "We'll be seeing you again, Maddy. And listen, I can't tell you what this weekend has meant to me."

"You don't have to." Maddy smiled.

Pres swiveled into the chair and let Mary Ellen steer him to the door. "Wait a sec, sweetie," he said. Then he turned himself around and wheeled his way back to the horse. "Thanks to you, too, pal."

Pres put up his hand, and Confidence nuzzled it softly. "You understand, don't you?" he whispered.

The horse stomped his bad leg as though it had never been broken. It was all the answer Pres needed.

CHAPTER

18

Walt dropped Nancy off at her house about eight-thirty. She was feeling mellow, and very good about herself and the old group. She was sorry she hadn't kept in closer touch since she'd been at Brown. These were people she wanted to have as friends all her life.

Unlike some others she could mention.

Much as she tried to force him from her mind, she was still thinking about Nick. All the way home in the car, she had fantasized about running into him when she was helping out with the mascot in the shop. Or maybe at Benny's. She'd be looking smashing, dressed in something casual but sophisticated, and he would stare at her and regret terribly not calling again. And then she'd pretend to be surprised to see him, maybe even not remember his last name. She'd tell him she was on her way back East and it had been such a treat to visit Tarenton again. She had a real desire to tell him off, but that was childish. After all, she'd only met the guy once. He didn't owe her anything; she didn't have a right to be angry.

But having a right and having feelings were two different things. And she couldn't deny that the feelings she had for Nick Stewart were very strong.

She threw her duffel bag over her shoulder and reluctantly began to climb the porch steps. Her parents were out to dinner with friends, so the house was dark. It looked so uninviting.

She sat down on the porch swing and pushed off with her toes. The night air was chilly, but it felt good on her face. And there was nothing like the smell of that north country air! You just didn't get air like that in Rhode Island.

As she was swinging, she noticed a car down the block. A small car. She couldn't really tell very well in the dark, but it looked like there was someone sitting in the driver's seat. But the lights were out, and as far as she could remember, the car had been there when she walked up onto the porch. That was odd.

She got off the swing and went to the edge of the steps to get a better look. It was definitely a sports car, maybe . . . no, it was *definitely* an MG. And the person in the car was getting out and coming toward her.

He was tall and blond and walked as though he knew just where he was going. Nancy started back toward the front door.

She was fumbling in her purse for her keys when she heard his step right behind her. He took her arm and whirled her around.

"You're home at last!" he exclaimed. "I must have dozed off. It's amazing some cop didn't come along and ask me what in the world I was doing."

"Hi, Nick," she said with studied casualness. "How are you?"

"I've been a mess since Friday," he confessed. Then he dropped his voice to a whisper. "There must be something the matter with me. I can't get you out of my head."

She ignored the words, pretending nonchalance. "Why? What happened on Friday?"

"Well," he said, leading her to the porch swing and sitting her down, "Friday was the day I finally got up the courage to call you. You think it's hard calling a girl the first time for a blind date! But that's a piece of cake compared to the second time, when it counts — and when you might have misread all her signals. And so when I called and your mother said you were away for the weekend, I started worrying."

Nancy frowned and shook her head. "I thought I'd misread *your* signals."

"Oh, Nancy." He took her hands in his and rubbed them together. They were so warm, they seemed to melt the anger she had been carrying with her for a week. "I figured I couldn't handle getting involved with somebody who was living hundreds of miles from me. So I resolved to stay away completely."

"Well, that was probably smart," she said as though she meant it. "I can't take all that meaningless junk about of course we'll write, and the next time you're in town. . . ." She wanted to be cool. "I mean, one date in a situation like this

232

is fine, but following up on it is asking for trouble."

"I guess I'm asking, then," Nick told her. "Because by Friday, I was kicking myself. Life is too short to give up on really good people."

Where had she heard that before? Of course, Tara.

"You, ah . . . you didn't by any chance speak to Tara Armstrong on Friday, did you?"

"No. I was meaning to call her to thank her for introducing us, but you know . . . the telephone, my worst enemy." He shrugged. "Listen, are you hungry? Because I could really use a hamburger," Nick said.

"Ah." A hamburger couldn't hurt. After all, she hadn't had a thing to eat since lunch. "Okay."

"And tomorrow, after my last class, I was thinking there's a neat old movie playing in town we could see. Then Tuesday, it might be kind of fun to take that hike we were discussing, and Wednesday, there's all kinds of excitement at the roller rink. Thursday's free. You get to pick."

She couldn't help but laugh. "And what about Friday?"

"Hey, what planet have you been on? The Rivals Game, did you forget? You're my date. And for the Tarenton celebration party afterward, too."

Nancy cleared her throat. "Saturday I'm flying back to Brown."

"I guessed that. That's why I want to monopolize your time completely while you're here," Nick said simply.

She put her hands to her temples and massaged

them slowly. "This is not a wise idea. This makes zero sense."

"Zero plus zero equals zero. Take it from me — I'm a math teacher."

She had to laugh. "Oh, all right. I'll regret it; but it'll be fun while it lasts."

"More than fun." He bent his head to hers and kissed her, and this time he didn't move away. His arms folded her in, held her firmly, and his mouth molded to hers. She felt warm and very much desired. He put his hands along the sides of her face and she put one of her hands over his. She had dreamed about this, but it was much better in reality.

At last they drew apart, and stared at each other. "How about that?" Nick murmured.

"Pretty nice," Nancy agreed.

It would be less than a week, that was true, but they would make the most of the time they had. They had no other choice now.

"Well, I guess it's finished." Diana grinned. She put her hands on her hips and assessed the mascot. The Boss, as he had been named, had been given his final finishing touch. He was wearing a red and white Tarenton High sweat shirt, which Angie's mother, an accomplished seamstress, had sewn for him at the last minute. Hope, Olivia, and Jessica had stuck on the whiskers the previous day, Tara had given his nails one last coat of Chinese red, and everyone had completed the arduous gluing on of the pelt all over the wolf's body. Tommy Bridgeman had fiddled with the electronic stuff until it was functioning perfectly, and everyone had to agree that this was, without doubt, *the* prize-winning mascot. He was big, he was fierce, and he looked like a true Tarenton hero.

"Now, on Friday evening, just before the game, I want you all here with me, and Beef will already have moved him up to the gym. Beef, you have that ramp we used before, right?"

"Check and double check." Beef gave her the thumbs-up sign.

"Okay, good, and don't forget that — " She stopped as Olivia got up and went to the window again. "Excuse me. I hate to interrupt while you're wandering," Diana said sarcastically.

"I thought I heard a car," Olivia explained brusquely. "Go on." The wolf-hunters still weren't back, and she was more than worried about Duffy. She was frantic.

"Thank you," Diana growled. "Now, as I was saying, you all have to crowd around and rush The Boss into the room as soon as the bleachers are filled and Mrs. Oetjen has introduced St. Cloud. Because they're the opposition, they get to go first," Diana added with a smirk. "Not that it will help them."

"Well, we won't be with you," Jessica explained, "because the cheerleaders always do the pregame warm-up. But as soon as it's time to present the mascots, we'll come join you on the floor."

"Well, that's just great, isn't it?" Diana fixed the five cheerleaders with a scathing look. "You have to do your own thing, and of course, cheerleading is much more important than the once-in-a-lifetime chance to have your mascot win the Rivals Game competition."

Gracie put a hand on Diana's arm. "We can handle it without them, Diana," she assured her.

"Naturally we can. I know that," Diana said. "And where do you think you're going *now*?" she demanded of Olivia, who was walking toward the door. "I'm not through yet."

"That's too bad, Diana," she said over her shoulder. "I know the sound of Duffy's car, and I'm sure that was it."

"How terrible this whole ordeal of waiting has been for you." Diana clucked in phony sympathy. "Of course, if he'd been mauled by a wild animal, or eaten or something, we would have heard about it on the news."

The door was already opening by the time Olivia put her hand on the knob. Angie, Nancy, and Walt walked in, and without bothering to say hello to anyone, Walt took Olivia by the arm and hustled her out of the room.

"Are you people quite finished ruining my speech?" Diana said, but her tone was slightly milder because Angie and Nancy were graduates, and therefore, possibly deserving of some respect. Even if they *had* been cheerleaders and she wasn't.

"We're really sorry," Nancy told her. "But the posse just got back in town. Duffy would have come over here himself, except that he wanted to get over to the paper and log in his story. So we decided to come and take Olivia to him. Everything's okay, by the way. But they didn't find any wolf."

"Well, then," Diana said, smiling, "there's no story, is there? David Duffy should wait around for an exclusive on our baby here." She went over to The Boss and patted him gently, like a proud parent. "Now, unless anyone has questions about Friday, I guess you can go. You've all been great. I couldn't have done it without you," Diana said magnanimously.

Hope cleared her throat. Diana had done zilch — and everybody knew it. "So kind of you to say so." Hope grinned, taking Peter's hand and getting up to leave.

"Diana, your leadership has been inspiring," Tara said overly sweetly. "I've learned so much about how to handle people — I have to thank you." Choking back laughter, she joined Nancy at the door and walked outside with her as the others followed.

"Boy, did I ever mean that," she told Nancy when they got to the parking lot. "Diana Tucker is a lesson in how *not* to be."

"Really?" Nancy was staring dreamily into space, not really listening. Then, suddenly, she looked at her watch. "Oh, no, I didn't realize it was so late. Tara, can you drop me back at my house?"

"Sure." Tara took her car keys from her pocket and led the way across the lot. "You sound like you have some kind of, ah, appointment."

Nancy grinned. "Right. Nick called."

Tara threw back her red hair and laughed delightedly. "I had a feeling. Call it woman's intuition or second sight or something, but I just knew you were made for each other."

"Well, I don't know about that," Nancy said. "But we are booked up every free afternoon or evening this week, until I leave."

Tara hugged her impetuously. "I think that's wonderful."

"I do, too, sort of. I just wish it weren't going to be over as soon as it's begun." Nancy sighed.

"Hey, you," Tara chided her. "Why can't you just enjoy what's going on now, without thinking about the future? He's a nice person; you're a nice person. Just . . . be nice together."

Nancy nodded, her full mouth creasing into a smile. "I wish I could have as much common sense as you," she said.

Tara nudged her in the ribs. "Yeah, sure. I'm Miss Practicality when it's somebody else's problem. Try me sometime on my own!" And throwing up her hands in mock despair, she fastened her seatbelt and took off.

Pres pushed at the Cybex one last time. The machine resisted, and then, seemed to give in.

"Wonderful!" Connie yelled. "That's the way! Gimme another!"

She was a great coach, knowing exactly when to praise and when to ask for just a little more. He willed his legs to lift the bar — and they did.

"At this rate, you're going to be mobile in no time," Connie said. "You know, it's like you're a different person since the weekend. Like you woke up, or something."

"Or something," Pres said enigmatically. He didn't want to talk about it or analyze it. He just wanted to do it.

On Wednesday, for the first time, he was able to move his legs along the ramp by himself. On Thursday, he was able to pick himself up out of the wheelchair and grab the crutches leaning against it. Then, on Friday afternoon, he took his first steps. He was leaning heavily on the crutches, but it was walking nonetheless.

Mary Ellen was in tears when Connie told her, but Pres was laughing. This was it — the breakthrough he needed. He was certain now that it was only a matter of time before he regained all his former abilities.

His life was coming together again. And so was he.

CHAPTER

19

Their coach worked them particularly hard at Thursday night's cheering practice. They'd committed so much of their time to the mascot, it was beginning to show in their work. Pikes that had been sharp and neat were sloppy, and handsprings and walkovers tended to be limp instead of crisp. And, as Mrs. Engborg said, it would look pretty stupid to have Tarenton win the Rivals Game and then have the squad fall on their faces when they led the school in a rousing cheer.

"Jessica, let Sean help you in this 'Around The World,'" Ardith Engborg counseled when it was just about time to call it a day — or, rather, a night. "That back arch is very graceful, but you're doing too much, and not letting him support you. Hope, you try it with Peter."

Their coordination, usually flawless, was a little shaky, but as the two couples practiced the moves again and again, the synchronization returned. It was as if their bodies remembered, and snapped into line when asked to do so. Angie, Walt, and Patrick, sitting and watching up in the bleachers, could see the improvement at once.

Olivia went over the lineup of cheers, and reminded the group that it might be necessary to throw in one or two extras when the judges announced that Tarenton had taken the prize and the entire school went wild with glee. She and the others hadn't a doubt that their wolf would win. And even Sean, who had mixed feelings about Kate's having to be the opposition the next night, was rooting for the Boss.

"All right," Coach Engborg said, "I want to see the new cheer once again. Lots of pep, lots of smiles, and I want each move done so smartly you could cut it with a knife. Olivia, line them up."

This time, it all worked beautifully. It was impossible not to think of Pres as they did the cheer, now scaled down for the six of them. But from what they'd heard from Mary Ellen this week, it might not be too long before "The Cheer For Two Teams" was performed right. So now, with hope in their hearts, they yelled,

"We are the ones,
C'mon, let's hear it!
No team so fine,
With such great spirit

Reaching the peak!
Scaling the top!"

They were sailing now, and when Hope and

Jessica leaped high into the guys' arms, Patrick, Angie, and Walt were inspired to cheer along with them.

> "We are the winners,
> 'Cause we just won't stop!
>
> YAY, Tarenton! YAY, team!"

They were making so much noise, they didn't hear the gate of the newly painted blue pickup truck in the parking lot slam closed. They didn't hear it spin its wheels and screech along the pavement and out into the road. And even if they had, they wouldn't have had any idea where the driver was going in such a hurry.

The session was over, and it was none too soon for the cheerleaders.

"See you tomorrow," Mrs. Engborg said. "Kindly remember that warm-up means just that. One hour before the game, please."

Everyone murmured their assent and started gathering up their things to leave.

"I'll be so glad when tomorrow is over, I just might bake some more brownies in celebration," said Tara, as she wrapped a towel around her neck and picked up her practice bag.

"Oh, please, restrain yourself," Sean implored, chuckling. Olivia had told him about Tara's cooking. "But I know exactly what you mean," he went on. "I think Kate and I have enough strain in our relationship without a wolf and a storm cloud sitting on our respective shoulders."

"Right." Tara walked down the hall beside him,

wondering if Sean would ever give up Kate. She felt pretty lonely right now.

As if he could read her mind, he said suddenly, "Say, didn't I see Nancy hanging out with Nick Stewart the other day?"

"Uh-huh," Tara said with a pleased gleam in her eye.

"Do I take it correctly that you were responsible for that?" Sean sometimes knew her better than she knew herself.

"It's certainly possible," Tara said enigmatically.

"Well, that's awfully nice of you," Sean declared. "First you give him up, then you give him away."

Tara shook her head as she reached the locker room door. "Call me Santa Claus," she quipped.

He grabbed her hand just as she was about to leave him. "Hey, Tara, you're all right," Sean said warmly. "One day soon, in the near future, I bet, somebody's going to come along who really appreciates you. Honest."

She smiled and nodded, but as she walked past him, through the door, she found herself wondering why that person couldn't be Sean. Because he's taken, too, dummy, she told herself harshly. And anyway, he's too much like you. It would never work.

Well, she'd been mature enough to think clearly about Nick, and she was learning to let Sean be a friend and nothing more. Someday, when she was really grown-up, she'd have it all. Or at least, the most important parts. She was sure of that.

* * *

The next morning dawned bright and clear, that special kind of shiny new day that fills everyone's heart with ambition and determination. Pres woke up smiling and threw off the sheets, then looked down at his feet and ankles.

"Okay," he said. "Let's give it a whirl." He flexed his right foot, then rolled it around in a circle. He did the same with his left. He felt like the day he'd seen his Porsche come back from the mechanic's and had admired that wonderful machine in perfect working condition. His body was just like the car, and now *he* was the mechanic.

He swung his legs out of bed and reached for the crutches. The hardest part was transferring his weight, but the more he practiced, the easier it became. Thumping away, he got through the bedroom door, down the hall, and into the kitchen, where Mary Ellen was seated looking over her notes for art history, sipping a cup of coffee while the radio blared their favorite rock station.

"Good morning," he sang out. Then he stood up straight, putting all his weight on his legs. The crutches were just for balance.

She stared up at him in amazement, then stood up, and walked over to him. "Is there anything you can't do?" she asked.

"Nothing at all," he said modestly. "As a matter of fact, remember what we were talking about when we were at my parents' house?"

She thought for a second, but before she could answer, he had leaned one crutch against the counter and taken her around the waist.

"I just wanted to hold you so badly," he said.

She hugged him tightly, so happy to have Pres back again.

"Hey, don't squeeze me to death." He laughed.

Immediately, she backed away. "Sorry."

"No, don't be. After the Rivals Game tonight, we'll practice that a little more." The smile on his face was warm and loving.

"By the way," he said, reaching for the coffee-pot, "I'm driving you to the game tonight. I can do it," he told her confidently, when she looked like she was going to protest. "I've been out in the garage working the pedals every night after you went to bed. Connie approves. Surprise!"

Her response was to kiss him on the cheek and pour him a cup of coffee. Pres, meanwhile, hobbled over to the file box that sat on the counter. "Now where is that?" he muttered, ruffling through the pieces of paper.

"Where's what?" she asked.

"The forms for the car rental company. Connie and I agree that the wheelchair can now be put into permanent storage. Which means the Buick goes back."

"Hooray!" Mary Ellen yelled, doing an impromptu cheer around the kitchen. "I've hated that car since the first day we got it."

"Really," Pres said, reaching for her hand. "I can't imagine why."

"Because it's blue," she teased him. And then she grabbed him around the neck again and gave him a very noisy smack on the lips.

Mary Ellen wanted to yell her joy out the car window as she drove Pres to the medical center that morning for therapy. She wished she could tell every passerby what a wonderful thing had occurred, and how much she loved her husband. Pres was going to be fine, just fine. And their marriage, which had been broken in little pieces after the crash, was mending, too.

Patrick stopped at Jessica's to pick her up and take her to school. He had a big moving job that morning, and a small one in the afternoon, but he'd promised, no matter what, to be at the game that evening to take pictures of the mascot.

They pulled into the parking lot right behind Sean and Tara. Duffy dropped Olivia off at the front door of the school. Just as Jessica was about to climb down from the cab, she spotted Hope and Peter, running toward the other kids.

"She looks really upset about something," Jessica said.

"Want me to stick around?" Patrick asked.

"No, that's okay. See you later." She jumped down and waved good-bye, then made a beeline for the rest of her squad, who had all taken off like rockets toward the back of the school as soon as they'd spoken to Hope.

"What's going on?" she demanded breathlessly as she caught up to them. "Hope, what is it?"

"Hope, you can't be right," Olivia insisted, "I don't believe this."

Hope's face was white. "Peter and I got here real early this morning because I wanted to look over my notes for the French quiz, and we figured we'd sit on the loading dock outside the shop."

She led them up the ramp to the door, which was unlocked.

Peter led them into the darkened shop. "We looked everywhere. We even went up to the science department to see whether Tommy might be working up there."

Jessica peered around, her eyes accustoming themselves to the light. "I know this is a stupid question, but where's The Boss?"

"That's what she's been trying to tell us, you dummy," Sean exploded.

"I didn't know. I didn't hear the beginning of what she said," Jessica protested.

"Hope, you aren't suggesting that the wolf's been stolen or something, are you?" Tara wailed. "It can't be gone. The game's tonight."

"There's a simple explanation, I'm sure," Olivia said. "Diana must have asked Beef to put him in — "

" — the gym?" Peter finished for her. "No such luck. We looked. Believe me."

"We scoured the school," Hope went on. "Cafeteria, classrooms, faculty lounge, you name it."

"This is ridiculous," Sean grunted. "Diana took it."

"How do you know that?" Jessica demanded.

"Oh, don't be such a dodo. She's the one. When you've got a problem, you know she has to be at the bottom of it. And you've got a problem."

"What do you mean, 'you'?" Tara yelled, turning on him. "Just because you walked off the committee doesn't mean you're excluded. I suppose you're happy because you won't have to fight with

247

Kate about who won the competition."

"Come on, you two!" Olivia exploded. "This is no time for one of your knock-down, drag-outs."

"Sean may have a point," Jessica broke in. "Diana's always hated us, and she just might pull something outrageous so she could point the finger at us. The thing is, if she did take it, we have to find out why and how. We've got to find Diana before first period bell," she finished, pushing Sean and Tara in front of her toward the door. But she didn't have to go very far. Diana was standing in the doorway of the shop with Beef and the rest of the mascot committee beside her.

"What's going on in here?" she demanded. The sunlight, streaming in behind her, made her cloud of golden hair look almost white, but her face was in shadow. She looked menacing, and very angry.

"Diana, we smell something fishy here," Olivia said sternly. "There have been too many awful things going on that no one can explain. First, the wolf's tail vanishes, then the mascot's left overnight in the rain, and now" — she paused, hardly able to say it — "now, the mascot is missing."

Diana seemed to grow larger in the doorway. "The what? Is *what?*" She stormed into the place as the others scurried after her.

"Beef, weren't you supposed to move it to the gym?" Peter asked.

"Not till tonight. Hey, this is bad." The huge boy stood with his hands on his hips looking very perplexed. "How are we going to have a competition if there's no Boss?"

"That's the point," Diana fumed at him. Then

she turned on Sean. "Well, we don't have to look very far, do we?" She stalked out of the shop, and he was right behind her.

"C'mon, Diana. You're always blaming me. I'm too easy a target," Sean said. "How about we start looking for a really good target — and then get in some target practice," he said.

"The last time something like this happened," Diana stated, refusing to give him the satisfaction of looking nervous, "you were right there. And you managed to get away with it. But you won't be so lucky this time." She was around the side now, starting for the front steps of the school. "I'm going to have Mrs. Oetjen put you on suspension," she said meanly.

"Diana," Olivia wheeled around in front of her, stopping the tall girl in her tracks, "hold on a minute before you do something you'll regret."

"Oh, Diana won't regret getting Sean in trouble," Beef chuckled.

"This is absurd," Jessica exclaimed. "Why would any of us, including Sean, want to do a stupid thing like stealing the mascot we've been working for weeks to create? There can't be a competition without it."

"Which means Kate's school would win by default," Diana told her. "And as for your reason, that's simple. You guys have been fighting me every step of the way. You're just trying to make the head of the committee — me — look bad. Anyway, despite all your cheering, I know you all too well. I know you don't have any real school spirit. If you did, you wouldn't have sacrificed all the time that should have been spent building the wolf on visiting Pres in the hospital." She pushed Olivia out of the way and ran up the steps, into the school, just as the bell for first period class started to ring.

Hope, bringing up the rear, walked over to her friends. "I'm going to get to the bottom of this," she said. "I'm cutting class. Anyone want to join me?"

The five others turned to stare at her in astonishment. Hope, the A-student, the girl who never defied authority, suggesting that they *not* go to school. Unheard of!

"Yeah, me," Sean agreed readily.

"You can't. You have too many demerits as it is," Tara reminded him.

"So, a few more won't hurt."

"Yes, they will," Olivia assured him. "Listen, it's dumb for us all to get in trouble. Hope, you really want to do this?"

"What do you have in mind?" Peter asked her.

Hope removed a hank of wig from her purse. "Exhibit A," she said.

"That's just some of the leftover pelt that we were gluing on," Tara said, taking it from her.

"No, it came from the wolf himself. It got torn off when he was moved out of the shop. Look at it," she insisted.

As she brushed the pelt back, they could see a distinct line of blue paint along the hairs. No part of the wolf was blue.

Jessica shook her head. "But what does this mean?"

"I don't know," Hope said grimly. "But I'm

going to find out. Meet me after last period right here. I'll have an answer by then," she said.

The rest of them, admiring her bravery, watched her walk away from the school. Then, hurrying so as not to be late, they raced inside to class.

CHAPTER

20

Sean got into trouble anyway. One of the hall monitors stopped him on his way to lunch and told him to get down to the principal's office immediately.

Mrs. Oetjen was confused, puzzled and, needless to say, very upset. "I don't want to cast any aspersions, Sean, but it is necessary for me to question everyone involved very closely. You understand."

"Well, sure but — "

"Diana Tucker has requested that I cancel the game tonight. And I am moving toward that decision, although I really don't wish to make it. Naturally, I will consult with St. Cloud's principal."

"Call the Rivals Game!" Sean blurted out. "You can't do that! I mean — " He corrected himself when she gave him a look. "I really wish you wouldn't. Look, Mrs. Oetjen, there must be a

252

pretty good reason that Diana wants to call it quits, don't you think?"

"It is true, is it not, that you have been . . . friendly with the chairman of St. Cloud's mascot committee," the principal went on.

"Look, Mrs. Oetjen, I'm not a fantastic student, and I mess up sometimes, but I'm not a total jerk. Kate and I have specifically avoided saying anything to each other about the mascots for weeks now. And as for physically getting The Boss off school property, he wouldn't even fit in my car."

It was a lame joke, and the principal did not laugh. Instead, she told him to get to class and stay there. And as soon as school was over, she wanted him back in her office — until game time. She would inform his father where he was. But she wanted to keep an eye on him, if he understood.

Sean understood perfectly. There was no way to get word to Olivia or any of the others, but they'd figure out pretty quickly where he was. All he could do was hope that nobody spotted Hope running around town by herself. *And* that her playing hooky would net some positive results.

By the time the other four got to the shop, it was four-thirty.

"Where is everybody?" Jessica demanded.

"Sean's cooling his heels in Mrs. Oetjen's office. I saw him through the glass at the top of the door," Olivia told her. "And as for Hope — "

But as she spoke, Hope was running up the driveway. Her hair was disheveled, her cheeks were red with cold and exertion, and her parka was flying open. But her eyes were sparkling. "I found him," she yelled in glee. "Quick, let's get in Peter's car. And Jessica, do you have any idea where Patrick is? We're going to need the van."

"Uh, I think he's over on Cutler Avenue, at the Reades'," Jessica ventured.

"We'll try there first. Well, what are we waiting for?"

"But where's the mascot?" Tara demanded. "Where's The Boss?"

"You'll see," Hope said in a particularly close-mouthed fashion.

Patrick didn't want to leave before he'd even started the move, but when the cheerleaders explained the situation to Mrs. Reade, she laughed, said that she was in high school once herself, and let them go. Then they set off for Burd Road.

"Who lives here?" Jessica asked. "And Hope, how did you get all the way out here on foot?"

"It wasn't easy," said the exhausted girl. "And whatever you do, don't tell my parents that I hitched."

Olivia put a hand on Hope's forehead. "Are you feeling all right? First you cut school, then you hitch a ride? Hope, this isn't like you."

"I wouldn't do it with anyone I didn't know, Olivia," Hope assured her. "But, well, Tommy Bridgeman's mother happened to come along at the right time, and she sort of knows me, and she's the type who's always too distracted to ask too many questions. Just like her son!" Hope giggled. "Okay, pull in here. This is it."

She hopped out of the van and ran to the side of a long, low ranch house. There was a newly painted blue truck parked in front, and the garage door was partly open.

"I'd just like to show you Exhibit B," Hope said excitedly. She took the pelt of hair from her purse and brought it over to the truck. "See, this is where the paint came off." There was a distinct smudge on the left rear bumper that matched up perfectly. As though someone had drawn the hair across when the paint was not quite dry on the truck.

"Whose house is this?" Peter asked, looking inside. "Hey, there he is! There's The Boss! And he looks all right."

Patrick lowered the ramp and backed his truck up to the door while the cheerleaders got busy retrieving their mascot. No one even questioned the fact that they were on private property. After all, this was their baby. Someone had stolen him, and they were stealing him back.

"You should have guessed by now," Hope grinned. "This is Beef's house. And that's his truck. I noticed it hadn't been at school for the past few days. Diana was picking Beef up and taking him home so that his wheels wouldn't be too visible. And I also noticed that last week, this truck was gray. He just gave it a new paint job."

"Brilliant, Sherlock!" Tara started pounding her teammate on the back. "You're terrific!"

"Then this was all Diana's idea." Jessica nodded. "I had a feeling."

"Well, what are we waiting for. Let's go!" Hope exclaimed. "We have to get word to Mrs. Oetjen not to call the game. And then we have to warm up." Hope was clearly pleased with herself. And she had every right to be.

They stopped at a pay phone so that Olivia could get hold of the principal and tell her that they had the mascot, but that they wanted it to remain a secret until game time, if that was all right with her. Then, before she could demand any more information, Olivia hung up and they were off to their respective houses to collect their uniforms.

"You're looking beautiful, as usual," Nick told Nancy as he picked her up at her door. She was wearing a creamy white sweater with a high turtleneck and a slim red skirt with matching red tights and ankle-length lace-up white boots.

"I wanted to be as close to the cheerleaders as possible," she told him.

"I want to be as close to you as possible," he whispered, helping her on with her coat. "It's been a perfect week."

"Yes, it has," Nancy agreed, snuggling close to him. She didn't want to think about tomorrow. All she wanted to focus on was the game, the mascot, and the party afterward. And Nick.

Mary Ellen sat beside Pres in the passenger seat, watching in amazement as he steered the car into the Tarenton parking lot beside Walt's Jeep. When Angie emerged from Walt's car and saw who was behind the wheel of the Porsche, she gave a loud whoop of joy. It was nothing short of a miracle. Pres, driving his own car! This deserved more of a celebration than winning the competition that night.

"How does it feel, old buddy?" Walt asked, as they pulled Pres's crutches out and handed them to him.

"Like the best day of my life. Like getting married all over again. Like winning every game we ever played."

Angie couldn't remember her friend ever looking so genuinely handsome. He used to be cocky, self-confident, maybe a little too smug. Tonight, humbled by his experience, he had a glow. She hoped he would keep it forever.

"You will be careful tonight, though, won't you?" Mary Ellen urged him, walking close beside him.

"Are you kidding? I'm counting my steps, just like my blessings, sweetheart."

She took his arm and they walked into the school together.

Kate was around the back with her committee members, their storm cloud wrapped in layers of white dropcloths. She knew nothing about the problems Tarenton had encountered, and she was nervous. Bobby Bridgeman had told her that his cousin had dreamed up something pretty special for Tarenton, and Bobby was not prone to exaggeration. "I just hope you create a real storm in that gym tonight, baby," she said, as she watched two of her teammates push the giant mascot inside.

Diana was dancing. Standing outside the gym,

she had flipped on her portable radio to the best rock station, and she was twirling and leaping the length of the hall. She had tried the impossible and accomplished it. Of course, it had been useful to come up with such a willing and strong — and dumb — helper like Beef, but basically, it was her plan and it had worked. It was too bad the principals wouldn't cancel the game tonight, but this might even be nicer — having the cheerleaders humiliated in front of two schools instead of just one. She couldn't wait for the fun to begin.

"All right, are you ready to take your places?" Mrs. Engborg asked the group. Sean, who had finally been allowed to come down to the lockers and change, was doing a few jumping jacks in the corner. Peter had filled him in on the details, and he was jumping higher than he ever had.

"I think we're set," Olivia told the coach. "How's the crowd?"

"Incredible," Tara told her. "I saw, through the window, busloads of people getting out in the parking lot. They're streaming inside."

"Great. I'll tell Patrick," Jessica said. She squeezed Hope's hand by way of thanks and ran out to the waiting van.

The gym was packed. Everyone, even kids who weren't that interested in basketball and parents who never attended, crammed the bleachers. There were Tarenton and St. Cloud banners waving, and an expectant murmur ran through the crowd when the two principals took their places. Mary Ellen, Pres, Angie, Walt, Nick, and Nancy had found seats on the right, in the midst of the Tarenton spectators. Diana, sitting in the front row with Beef beside her, was like a lizard basking in the sun.

"Ladies and gentlemen," Mrs. Oetjen began, "it is a great pleasure and privilege to welcome you here tonight. Despite a setback in Tarenton's plans, we've decided that the Rivals Game should proceed as scheduled."

Diana smiled when a rousing cheer went up from both sides.

"And first, the two teams! Coaches, name your players."

Coach Cooley for Tarenton and Coach Heath for St. Cloud announced the lineups, and the two teams, brilliant in their colors, ran out onto the floor amidst hollering and screams of encouragement.

The St. Cloud cheerleaders came in next, doing a fast, loud number with megaphones and balloons. And finally, the Tarenton team took the floor. With pride in her voice, Olivia led them in a triumphant rendition of one of their old cheers.

> "We're gonna win it,
> gonna beat 'em, gonna shine
> We're the team that's putting
> all the other guys in line.
> We can go ... (stamp, stamp) hot!
> We can run ... (clap, clap) wild!
> We can WIN! We can WIN!"

Peter swept Hope onto his shoulders as Tara did a thigh stand on Sean, and Jessica and Olivia did a series of straddle jumps, ending in a split in front of the two couples. The crowd went wild.

"And now," Mrs. Oetjen said, "the moment we've all been waiting for. The mascot competition."

For the first time, Diana looked uneasy. She scoured the faces of the cheerleaders, but could read nothing there. Then Kate Harmon led her committee onto the floor, pushing a large wheeled platform. She pulled a string and the storm cloud was revealed, to the amusement and delight of the St. Cloud contingent and the grudging approval of Tarenton.

"This is our entry," Kate announced. "We call it the Weatherperson, because it knows which way the wind is blowing." And then, without missing a beat, she flicked the switch that activated the computer, and a 0–0 score appeared on the screen in the storm cloud's forehead.

The judges began scribbling furiously on their pads as everyone applauded.

Then the back door to the gym opened and Patrick appeared. The cheerleaders ran out and returned, pushing a second platform bearing another huge white-clad shape.

"But. . . ." Diana stood up, sputtering. "But Mrs. Oetjen. . . ." She went over to the principal and began to say something, but no one could hear her. They were too busy yelling and cheering for the wolf, who had just been uncovered.

"This is our mascot, The Boss," Olivia yelled. "He's been through some rough times, but we never doubted for an instant that he'd make it tonight." She activated the tail and eyes, and the sound of hundreds of hands clapping and feet stomping filled the gym. The judges went back to work.

Diana, white-faced, stood up and walked slowly to the cheerleaders. "Where . . . where in the world did you — "

"I think you can answer that one yourself, Diana," Mrs. Oetjen said. While the judges were deliberating and the crowd was making as much noise as possible, she had walked over to the group. She fixed the committee chairman with a steely look. "Would you like to give us an explanation?"

Diana turned frantically. "Beef? Where's Beef?" she called. True to form, her accomplice was already halfway across the gym.

"It wasn't my fault, really, Mrs. Oetjen." Beef was shaking his head and rubbing his hands, his large body fairly jiggling with fear. "She put me up to it."

"We know that, Beef," Jessica said calmly. "Just tell us all about it."

"I mean, I didn't like the idea at the beginning," Beef went on as Diana clenched her fists by her sides and stared at the floor. "I thought it was a terrible thing to mess up the wolf, steal the tail, leave the thing out in the rain, but she said it was for the good of the school. Honest, Mrs. Oetjen, and I believed her."

"I'm sure you did, Beef. Go on."

"Well, she said that when we took it and hid it at my house, that we'd just leave it there for this game. And then Monday, we'd pretend to find it and bring it into school. And everybody would think we were great!" He ended with a smile.

"Didn't it occur to you that we'd get in a lot of hot water over this, Beef?" Sean demanded.

Beef cleared his throat and looked at Diana. "Yeah, sort of. But she said it didn't matter, because when the wolf came back, everybody'd be off the hook. Unless somebody like the cheerleading captain or any of the other cheerleaders got blamed and thrown off the squad in the meantime, and Diana got their place," he finished.

"That's not what I said!" Diana screamed. "Oh, how can any human being be as stupid as you!" She turned away from the group, but Mrs. Oetjen took her arm.

"You'll report to me Monday morning, first thing," the principal said.

Diana nodded. "Well," she said spitefully, turning on the cheerleaders, "we're not going to win anyway, so what difference does it make?"

"Why? Did you fix the judging, too, Diana?" Sean inquired. "My, you've been a busy girl."

But at this point, the judges motioned Mrs. Oetjen over and the room was hushed. Both principals read the piece of paper and smiled at one another. "I probably don't even have to read this," Mrs. Oetjen said to the crowd. "You've all seen for yourselves how good these mascots are. It's a tie."

The cheering was deafening now. Kate ran across the floor to Sean and hugged him, and he lifted her high in the air, swinging her around, until she pounded on his shoulders and told him to stop. "You nut," she screamed in his ear, because that was the only way to be heard.

"No more secrets, okay?" he yelled back.

"It's a deal," she agreed. "Hey, mister," she added as she eased herself out of his arms, "you done good."

"You, too!" He gave her the thumbs-up sign.

The former cheerleaders and the rest of the assembled crowd were making a racket, so that when Olivia led the group in "The Cheer for Two Teams," hardly anyone heard them. They did see the moves of the squad, though: the short scarlet skirts of the girls flashing with the crisp white pleats, the pride with which they all wore the white V-neck sweater with its scarlet bands and the big T on the front, the jubilant leaps and whole-hearted turns of the group, the lifts and the pikes so perfect that even Mrs. Engborg had nothing to complain about.

And then, finally, when the excitement died to a dull roar, it was time to play ball. The basketball game seemed almost secondary to the mascot competition, but once it got going, the crowd was riveted to the floor, as if the very presence of the mascots had really spurred the two teams on to glory.

Unbelievably, at the end of regulation time, Tarenton and St. Cloud were tied, 58–58. They went into overtime and fought fiercely for five long, incredible minutes. The defenses refused to allow the opposition to make one point until, finally, Joe Vogel, the Tarenton center, got an alley-oop from across the court just as the clock was running down again. But St. Cloud quickly put the ball into play and passed it downcourt to one of their forwards, who countered with a reverse lay-up.

Both cheerleading squads, drenched with perspiration, came out for a short display before the game went into double overtime.

"This can't last," Mary Ellen said to Pres. "It just can't."

"We're going to win," Pres said, patting her hand. "Don't worry about it."

Somehow, he knew. When Tarenton got the ball on the tip-off this time, there was no stopping them. In a brilliant series of dodges to foil the opposition's guards, the team kept retrieving the ball, getting it in the basket, and stealing it back. At the end of the final fifteen minutes, Tarenton had won, 69–60. The score was duly registered on St. Cloud's mascot.

The cheerleaders hugged each other, then went over and hugged The Boss. His tail and eyes were twitching so fast, it looked like he understood just what had happened.

As the cheerleaders, soaked but happy, started back to the locker room, they caught a glimpse of Diana, sneaking out the door by herself.

"Who's afraid of the big, bad wolf?" Sean sang, loud enough for her to hear.

She stopped for a minute, straightened up, and turned around to give them all a withering glance. Then she was out the door and gone. She did not appear at the celebration party and, needless to say, nobody missed her at all.

CHAPTER

Pres was too tired to go to the victory party afterward, but Mary Ellen refused to let him drive back alone, so Walt and Angie followed them home and waited for her.

"You sure you don't want me to stay with you?" she asked Pres as she opened the door on the passenger side.

"Naw. You go have a great time," Pres said.

She kissed his cheek. "But a party is never any fun unless we're together. I think I'll tell Walt to drive on."

"Hey. You go," he insisted. "It's not going to be much fun around here. I'm going to sack out, seriously."

She shrugged, then agreed. "Okay, but I won't be long. See you soon, sweetie." She got the crutches out for him, then waited until he had extricated himself from the car and was starting up the path to the house. Then she walked back to Walt's Jeep and got in.

She remembered thinking afterward that it was strange of Pres to urge her to go, because he was never that crazy about being home alone. But the party was terrific, and the dancing fast and furious, and she was really glad she'd come. Sean and Kate had started everyone off, clearing away the furniture and rolling up the rug, and Olivia and Duffy insisted that Mary Ellen join in with them and dance.

When she was too exhausted to move another step, Patrick and Jessica rescued her and dragged her over to the refreshment table. She took two sips of her Coke, then looked at her watch. "You think I should call home?" she asked them.

"You'll just wake him up." Jessica laughed.

"Stop being such a nervous nelly," Patrick said. "Face it, Mary Ellen, he's fine. Tomorrow, or the next day, I bet, he's going to go the distance and walk. You can't treat him like an invalid anymore."

She sighed and plopped down in the nearest chair. "You're right. Absolutely. You know, the two of us adjusted so well to living with problems, we're going to have to adjust to living a nice, normal existence again without them." Then she looked up at the two of them and grinned. "But it does feel great to have him well again."

"So great you could dance?" Patrick asked her.

"Well, maybe one more time. Let's go," she urged Jessica.

And the three of them strolled to the middle of the floor, arm in arm in arm.

The party was getting noisier and better all the time. Ardith Engborg was telling Hope and Peter all about this new cheer she was designing for them, Angie and Walt were catching up on all the news from the kids they hadn't seen in months, and Duffy was going over all the best plays of the game that night with a couple of the members of the basketball team, while Tara and Olivia listened. Over in the corner, Nancy and Nick sat holding hands, just being close. And a little sad, too.

Finally, Nancy stood up. "I hate to play Cinderella," she said, "but I really do I have to get an early start in the morning."

He shook his head. "How come I knew you were going to say that?" He got up and put an arm around her waist. "Can I take you to the airport?"

"My parents are taking me, Nick."

"I'll go with you."

"I don't think so. It would be a little awkward."

"And you'd rather keep our good-bye short and sweet. I see." His voice was harder, and he let go of her quickly.

"Nick, please." Nancy was so confused. She was trying to be terribly practical, trying to live for today and not tomorrow. But he wasn't making it easy.

"Hey, it's all right. Really. We'll say good-bye at your door, and that'll be that." He swept ahead of her into the bedroom where coats were piled in every corner. But he knew exactly where theirs were, and he retrieved them in seconds.

She let him help her into her coat, and they walked in silence to the door as the party raged around them. They didn't bother saying good night to anyone — they certainly didn't feel like part of the celebration that was going on.

He opened the door of the MG and she got in. But when he came around to the driver's side and sat down beside her, she couldn't help herself. "Listen, I'm not as hard-nosed as I make myself out to be," she said quietly. "I don't want to say good-bye at all. This has been a fantastic week. We like the same foods. We have the same sense of humor. We even roller-skate equally badly." She chuckled and looked into his brilliant blue eyes, which were shining with affection for her. "But face it, it's not like we can have a relationship right now."

"You don't like writing letters, I know." He nodded.

"And you hate the telephone."

"I could grow to like it — if you were on the other end."

There was such a note of anguish in his voice that she turned and threw her arms around his neck. "Oh, Nick. You're making this so tough."

He kissed her, but then quickly moved away and started the car. "It's not over till it's over, Nancy. Let's think of it that way. Anything is possible if you want it badly enough, right?"

"Right."

They drove off into the night, their bodies just touching in the small car. And they both felt that something important had happened. Perhaps, even something lasting.

Mary Ellen had Patrick and Jessica take her

home around midnight. She was having fun at the party, but it just wasn't the same without Pres. Of course, the others understood.

They got to the house and noticed immediately that the garage door was open.

"Oh, no." Mary Ellen stared ahead of her in disbelief.

"What is it?" Jessica demanded.

"Look, the Porsche is gone. But why — " She didn't finish her sentence but was out of the car before Patrick had a chance to park it. He jerked the car to a halt and he and Jessica jumped out.

The house was empty, silent, but there was a lamp on in the bedroom. Mary Ellen, her whole body tight as a bow string, raced toward the light.

When Patrick and Jessica walked into the bedroom, they found her holding a piece of paper, her hands shaking as she read the note that Pres had written. Patrick grabbed it from her.

" 'This is something I have to do,' " he read aloud. " 'Don't worry about me. Be back in a couple of days, max. I love you much. Your Pres.' "

"But why wouldn't he have told you where he's going?" Jessica demanded.

"Because he doesn't want me playing nursemaid," Mary Ellen said in a frozen voice. "And I know exactly where he went. "Look." She led them to the closet door, which was ajar. Several pairs of shoes had been tossed aside. Pres's hiking boots were missing.

"He wouldn't try — " Patrick began. "That would be utter lunacy. Of course, Pres sometimes does act like he fell on his head instead of his back," he went on, getting angrier by the minute about his friend's stupidity. "Do you really think he went up into the hills, Mary Ellen?"

"He wants to prove to himself that he can do it," she said slowly. "But he's still in no condition — "

"Let's get back to the party. We can organize a search," Jessica suggested quickly.

They sped back through the darkened streets of Tarenton. The party was still in full swing, the music ringing clearly into the night. Mary Ellen raced inside and rounded up the cheerleaders. Walt and Angie, Sean and Kate, Hope and Peter, Olivia and Duffy, Jessica and Patrick, and Tara gathered around her.

"What is it?" Peter demanded when they were all outside.

"We have to find Pres," she said. "I think he's gone up to the hills."

"Is he nuts? He knows the wolf might be up there," Duffy said at once.

"I think the wolf was the furthest thing from his mind when he started out. He just wanted to climb some rocks — rocks in his head," Patrick muttered glumly as he started for the car with Jessica.

"We'll divide up," Walt suggested. "Take the three separate routes to Grange Valley, see if we can pick him up along the way. If not, we can park down below and continue on foot from there."

"There's this bluff that he and I used to climb over to the north side of the hills," Patrick told them. "I have a feeling that's where he may be headed."

"What are we waiting for?" Olivia demanded impatiently. "Come on!"

The twelve of them took three cars and started off. Mary Ellen, seated between Olivia and Jessica in the backseat of Patrick's car, was purposely not listening to what Duffy was talking about. If she thought about the wolf, she'd positively go mad. She had this awful sinking feeling, as though everything they had worked for and accomplished was about to vanish. They should have told Ardith Engborg, she kept thinking. They should have told the police. What good were a bunch of them going to do if Pres was lost or hurt — or worse? Suppose he fell while he was climbing and couldn't get up? Suppose he was unconscious? Suppose the wolf did find him? How did wild animals react to an injured human?

Sean's was the second car in line, right behind Patrick's. He ignored most of what Kate and Tara were telling him and just thought, What would I do if I were him? Maybe if he could put himself in Pres's shoes, he could find him. After all, he was the one who'd gotten Pres to start trying in the first place. It was just possible that he could get on Pres's screwy wavelength and help him again.

Walt was taking the shortcut to the valley. He, Angie, Peter, and Hope were discussing the pros and cons of flushing Pres out of the woods. Would he be so angry that they had come that he'd just hide out? Or would he be grateful that so many people had cared to make sure he was all right?

They had brought the cheerleader megaphones with them. They'd yell themselves hoarse and hope that he'd respond.

"We're going to spread out in a circle," Patrick told them when they'd all arrived at the site. "We've only got a couple of flashlights — Sean and Walt, you have one each, right? — so we're going to have to stick together. Don't want anyone getting lost. We'll meet by the big pine at the top."

It was so silent, so still. The hills were not particularly treacherous, but at this time of night, with so much at stake, it was slow going. Most of the way was heavily wooded, with only footpaths cut through the thick underbrush. And the group weren't dressed for hiking. The best they could do was to walk carefully and yell for Pres every few yards.

Mary Ellen was so frightened, she didn't think she could make her feet move, but something inside her impelled her to keep going. It was two A.M. now, and the only hopeful sign was the full moon above them. It might help, if only a little. She stayed by Patrick and began to climb.

Sean was with Kate and Tara, and it took the three of them an hour to get to the top of the first plateau of the hilly ledge. He couldn't figure it. On crutches, the guy couldn't get that far. Pres hadn't had that much of a head start to begin with. For some reason, call it a hunch, Sean felt it might work better for him to strike out on his own. When Kate and Tara went left and continued up toward the summit, he veered to the right, through a straight line of pines and on down, to the lowest point before the big boulders started.

"Where are you, Sean?" he heard Tara call. "Stay close."

"I will," he yelled back. But he kept going his way.

The others continued to climb, getting more tired, dirty, and discouraged by the minute. Mary Ellen scraped her face on a branch, but she didn't even feel the pain, she was so worried. By the time her group met up with the other two at the tall pine on top, it was four A.M.

"This is bad," Walt said. "I think some of us should keep looking, but the rest should go for help. It's time to get the police involved."

Jessica put her arms around Mary Ellen and hugged her. "It's going to be fine," she said, although, at this point, she didn't feel fine at all. "We just need some professionals, with some real climbing equipment. What do you say?"

"I guess." Mary Ellen was numb.

"Where's Sean?" Angie said, suddenly realizing that one of their number was missing.

"He went off on his own," Kate explained. "He should join up with us pretty soon, I guess."

Sean was making his way down the hill now, through some of the denser forest. This was it, he was sure. They had misjudged Pres, thought he was going to be a daredevil and try some difficult rock climbing. In reality, all he wanted was to be alone in a beautiful, quiet place. Still a nutty thing to do, but understandable. Sean might try something like that himself.

He pushed back some branches, unveiling a

lovely cove. The darkness was just breaking up, and it was almost sunrise. There, seated on a rock, his crutches by his side, was Pres.

"I thought so!" said Sean triumphantly.

Pres jumped. He had been deep in thought, and certainly never expected to see another human being in this secluded place. "What are you doing here?" he asked calmly. He sounded rather mellow.

"I could ask you the same thing," Sean said pointedly. "Do you have any idea how looney you have gotten everybody? Mary Ellen is just about frantic."

Pres sighed. "I know. I'm sorry I had to do it this way, but I did. I just felt, you know, solitary. And then I got here, and the most incredible thing happened."

"What?" Sean sat beside him, at his feet.

"The wolf showed up. Yeah, really! I met the wolf. Up close and personal. I think he was just as surprised to see me as I was him. He came right through here" — he pointed between two trees — "and then he stopped in his tracks. And I looked into that big guy's eyes, and he looked into mine, and for a second — now this is going to sound pretty weird — we were like brothers. If that animal could talk, he would have been saying, 'Man, you got guts to be here.'

"And then he was gone," Pres continued. "I have a feeling Tarenton's seen the last of him."

"What about the pack theory?" Sean asked. "Duffy seems pretty sure there's more than one around."

"Uh-uh. The guy's a loner. Don't ask me how

— I just know." Then Pres smiled and put a hand on his friend's shoulder, pushing himself into a standing position. "Want to see something?"

Very slowly, as though he were balancing a basket of eggs on his head, he began to walk. All by himself. He almost made it look easy.

"That is incredible! Truly incredible!" Sean started laughing, and Pres laughed with him, and pretty soon the silent forest was alive with sound.

The rest of the group, already on their way back to the cars to get the police, couldn't miss the sound of laughter. They found Sean and Pres almost immediately.

"Oh, Pres!" Mary Ellen burst through the branches, but she stopped dead when she saw Pres take a step toward her. And another, and another. Walt started to clap in time, and the others joined in. A rhythmic sound, very much like the backbeat to a cheer, rang through the woods.

"Don't ever do that to me again," Mary Ellen begged, taking Pres in her arms. "I'm so happy you're all right."

"I had to find out whether I could walk, Mary Ellen. I had to do it this way. See, what I never told you, the reason I was afraid to try in the first place, was that I thought I was only as good as my body. That you wouldn't love me anymore if I didn't get well."

She looked at him in shock. "That's the most outrageous thing I've ever heard in my life. You're totally wrong. Totally."

"I know that now. At least, I think I do. But it

275

took a lot of thinking and feeling on my part. I'm back now. Back for good."

The others gathered around, the old cheerleaders and the new, and made a circle around Pres and Mary Ellen. The sun was just breaking through the trees, and the light was lovely to behold. The pinks and golds touched the faces of the group, and without a word, they began to peel off, starting back toward the town. Peter's arm encircled Hope's waist, Sean hugged Kate close, Duffy held Olivia's hand, Patrick held Jessica's, and Tara, Angie, and Walt, who was carrying the crutches, followed behind them.

Finally, at the end of the procession, came Mary Ellen and Pres. Walking together, one step at a time, walking toward the sunrise.

Is it time for Tara to say no to cheerleading? Read Cheerleaders #33, SAYING NO.

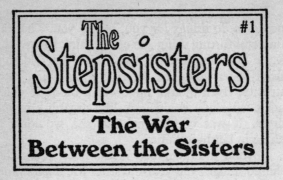

The Stepsisters

#1

The War Between the Sisters

by Tina Oaks

Chapter Excerpt

Paige Whitman unzipped the plastic cover that held the dress she was to wear to her father's wedding. She had put off looking at the dress until the very last minute. When she learned the dress would be pink, she had groaned. There were colors she loved, colors she could take or leave alone, and then there was pink, which hated her as much as she hated it!

And the style was as impossible for her as the color. She didn't even have to try the dress on to know how it would look. At sixteen she was taller than most of her friends, and thinner without being really skinny. But taller meant longer, and she knew her neck was too long to wear a low, rounded neckline like that.

Paige's instinct was to wail. Dresses were supposed to do things *for* you, not *to* you. The only tiny comforting thing she could think of was that Katie Summer Guthrie, her fifteen-year-old stepsister-to-be would be wearing a matching monstrosity. Even though pink was a blonde's color, not even Katie could look like anything in *that* dress. It was comforting that she wouldn't be alone in her humiliation.

Beyond the other bed in the hotel room they shared, Paige's ten-year-old sister Megan hummed happily as she put on her own dress. Megan was a naturally happy-go-lucky girl, but Paige had never seen her as excited as she had been since their father announced his coming marriage to Virginia Mae Guthrie. Her father had tried to control his own excitement and tell them about his bride-to-be in a calm, sensible way. But Paige knew him too well to be fooled, and anyway he gave himself dead away!

He started by telling them how he had met Virginia Mae on a business trip to Atlanta, then how beautiful she was. He went from that to her divorce five years before and how she had been raising her three children alone ever since. Paige almost giggled. Here was William Whitman, whose logic and cool courtroom delivery were legendary in Philadelphia legal circles. Yet he was jumping around from one subject to another as he talked about Virginia Mae.

Paige had driven down to Atlanta with her father and Megan earlier in the summer so the children could meet. Paige had agreed that Virginia Mae Guthrie was as lovely as she was gentle.

Paige had tried to shrug away the twinge of resentment that came when she thought of Katie Summer. The girl had to be putting on an act. *Nobody* could possibly be as lighthearted and happy as she pretended to be. And nobody would be that pretty in a fair world. Seventeen-year-old Tucker seemed like a nice enough guy, although his exaggerated good manners threw Paige off a little. Ten-year-old Mary Emily was cute. But it was awkward to be the only one holding back when her father and Megan were both so obviously deliriously happy.

Her father made the marriage plans sound so simple: "Right after our wedding, Virginia and the children will move up here to Philadelphia. We'll all be one big happy family together."

Paige had said nothing then or since, but concealing her doubts hadn't made them go away. She hated feeling like a sixteen-year-old grouch, but it just didn't make sense that everything would work out that easily. Not only would there be more than twice as many people in the same house as before, but the people themselves would be different.

Even if people from the south didn't think differently than people from the north, they certainly *sounded* different when they talked. And the Guthries were as completely southern as Paige's family was northern. Mrs. Guthrie and her three children had lived in Atlanta all their lives.

Megan giggled and fluffed out her full skirt. "Isn't it great? I can't wait to show this dress back home."

Back home. Philadelphia meant only one person to Paige . . . Jake Carson. She shuddered at the thought of Jake seeing her in that pink dress. She would die, just simply die where she stood, if he ever saw her looking this gross.

She sighed and fiddled with the neck of the pink dress, wishing she hadn't even thought of Jake. Simply running his name through her mind was enough to sweep her with those familiar waves of almost physical pain. It didn't make sense that loving anyone could be so painful. But just the memory of his face, his intense expression, the brooding darkness of his thoughtful eyes was enough to destroy her self-control.

But even when Jake looked at her, he was absolutely blind to who she really was. She knew what he thought: that she was a nice kid, that she was fun to talk to, that she was William Whitman's daughter. Period. He didn't give the slightest indication that he even realized that she was a girl, much less a girl who loved him with such an aching passion that she couldn't meet his eyes for fear he might read her feelings there.

Megan caught Paige around the waist and clung to her. "Sometimes I get scared, thinking about the changes. It *is* going to be wonderful, isn't it, Paige?" Megan's voice held the first tremulous note of doubt Paige had heard from her sister.

"Absolutely wonderful," Paige assured her, wishing she felt as much confidence as she put into her tone.

Even as she spoke, she saw Jake's face again, his dark eyes intent on hers as he had talked to her about the wedding. "Look at your dad," Jake had said. "Anything that makes him that happy has to be a lucky break for all of you."

She had nodded, more conscious of how lucky she was to be with Jake than anything else.

Jake had worked around their house in Philadelphia for about a year and a half. Paige didn't believe in love at first sight, but it had almost been that way with her. From the first day, she found herself waiting breathlessly for the next time he came to work. She found herself remembering every word he said to her, turning them over and over in her mind later. It wasn't that he was mysterious. It was more that she always had the sense of there being so much more in his mind than he was saying. She was curious about him, his life, his friends, how he thought about things. In contrast to a lot of people who smiled easily and laughed or hummed when they worked, he was silent and withdrawn unless he was talking with someone.

Before he came, she hadn't realized how painful it was to love someone the way she did Jake. She hadn't asked to fall in love with him or anybody. She had even tried desperately to convince herself that he wasn't different from other boys, just nicer and older. That didn't work because it wasn't true. Jake really was different from the boys she knew at school. Although he talked enough when he had something to say, he was mostly a little aloof without being awkward and shy. And he wasn't an ordinary kind of handsome. His features were strong, with firm cheekbones; deeply set eyes; and a full, serious mouth.

Maybe one day she would quit loving him as quickly as she had begun. But even thinking about that happening brought a quick thump of panic in her chest. Knowing how it felt to be so much in love, how could she bear to live without it?

Later, when the wedding march began and the doors of the little chapel were opened, Paige was overwhelmed with the strange feeling that she was watching all this from a distance. Even as she walked beside Katie Summer and kept careful time to the music, she didn't feel as if she was a part of what was happening.

Paige felt a touch against her arm and looked over at Katie Summer. Katie flashed her a quick, sly smile that brought a fleeting dimple to her cheek. Paige swallowed hard, ducked her head, and looked away. Later she would have to deal with this girl, but not now, not while her father was repeating the same vows he had made so many years before to her own mother.

But that quick glance had been enough to remind her of how wrong she had been about how Katie Summer would look in her matching pink dress. It made Paige feel leggy and graceless beside her.

All the Guthries were good-looking. Tucker was almost as tall as Paige's father, and comfortingly nice to look at in a different, curly-haired way. Mary Emily, behind with Megan, was button cute. But the girl at Paige's side was just too much! Katie's thick, dark blonde curls spilled in glorious profusion around her glowing face.